FROM
Till Death Do Us Part

The door slowly opened, and the boy from the rec room stood there. "Hi," he said with a sunny grin.

"Do I know you?" she asked.

"Mark Gianni." He held out his hand.

She took it cautiously. His grip was warm, his palm rough. He was tall and had curling dark brown hair and intense deep brown eyes. But Kelli had been right. He was thin, almost gaunt. "And you're here because . . . ?" She allowed the sentence to trail.

"Because I want you to know that you're the most beautiful girl I've ever seen. And I thought I should introduce myself. I mean, we should get to know each other. Since you're the girl I intend to marry."

FROM
For Better, for Worse, Forever

Brandon's request was eloquent and simple and it touched her. April recognized that Brandon wasn't some kid with a hidden agenda. Like her, he was lonely. He also had something buried deep inside his psyche that was painful. She guessed it had to do with the loss of his mother. She wouldn't probe. If he wanted to talk about it, he would.

"I would like that very much," she said. She gazed out to the open sea. A sailboat leaned into the wind against the horizon. "You know, I've watched those boats from the first day I arrived, and I'd love to go sailing on one. Do you think we could do that sometime?"

Lurlene McDaniel

AS LONG AS WE BOTH SHALL LIVE

Two Novels

Published by
Dell Laurel-Leaf
an imprint of
Random House Children's Books
a division of Random House, Inc.
New York

This edition contains the complete and unabridged texts of
the orginal editions. This omnibus was originally published
in separate volumes under the titles:
Till Death Do Us Part copyright © 1997 by Lurlene McDaniel
For Better, for Worse, Forever copyright © 1997
by Lurlene McDaniel

Visit us on the Web! www.randomhouse.com/teens

Educators and librarians, for a variety of teaching tools,
visit us at www.randomhouse.com/teachers

ISBN: 0-553-57108-7

Printed in the United States of America
First Laurel-Leaf Edition October 2003
10 9 8 7 6 5 4 3 2 1
OPM

CONTENTS

Till Death Do Us Part

For Better, for Worse, Forever

Till Death Do Us Part

This book is lovingly dedicated to
Jennifer Dailey,
a victim of cystic fibrosis,
a lovely flower,
plucked up by the angels
after fourteen years on this earth,
March 12, 1997.
*Dear Jennifer, your family and friends
will miss you.*
May your walk in heaven be joyous!

Love is patient, love is kind. It does not envy, it
does not boast, it is not proud. It is not rude, it
is not self-seeking, it is not easily angered, it
keeps no record of wrongs. Love does not
delight in evil but rejoices with the truth. It
always protects, always trusts, always hopes,
always perseveres. Love never fails.

—1 CORINTHIANS 13:4–8
(NIV)

1

"That guy's staring at you again, April."

April Lancaster didn't need Kelli to tell her that the boy on the far side of the hospital's patient rec room was looking at her. She could almost *feel* his gaze. She had been in the hospital for two days and he'd been stealing glances at her every time she ventured out of her room. "Ignore him," April whispered to Kelli. "I do."

"But why? He's cute. Even if he is too skinny for my taste."

"This isn't a social club, Kelli. It's a hospital. I didn't come here to meet guys."

"Well, I say why let a good opportunity slip away?"

April shook her head. "You're impossible."

Her best friend grinned. "I'm only trying to cheer you up. Take your mind off this whole thing. And if you meet a cute guy in the bargain, then what's the harm?"

April pointedly twisted in the lounge chair so that her back was to the boy. She didn't want to be stared at, and she certainly didn't want to meet some guy who was sick. She figured he had to be sick; why else would he be a patient in this huge New York City medical complex?

Kelli interrupted her thoughts. "What is going on with you? Medically, I mean. When can you leave?"

The last thing April wanted to do was dwell on the frightening possibilities as to why she was in the hospital. "I'm only here for testing," she said. "I'm sure I'll be out by the end of the week."

"But by then spring break will be over. We leave tomorrow, and the weatherman said an inch of fresh powder is falling in Vermont as we speak. This might be the last chance for a ski trip this year."

April and her friends had been planning the trip for weeks. It was supposed to be part of her birthday present. And since it was their senior year, it would be their final spring break together as a group. "I can't help it," she said gloomily. "Even if my doctor releases me earlier, my parents won't let me go."

"Why not?"

April didn't want to say. Not while there was so much speculation about the origins of her numbing headaches. The headaches had built in intensity for the past several months, causing her to get dizzy, even sick to her stomach. When she'd passed out from the pain in school two days earlier, her parents had hustled her out of their Long Island community and into a hospital in the city. The headaches could still be nothing.

Or they could be the other thing. The "thing" she had decided *not* to discuss with Kelli. "Oh, you know my parents. They fall to pieces if I have a hangnail. Besides, Dad won't let me drive from New York to Vermont by myself."

Kelli chewed her bottom lip. "I could wait till you're released. Then you and I could drive up together."

"No way." April shook her head. "Kelli, I appreciate it, but you go on with the others."

Kelli slumped in her chair, crossed her arms,

and pouted. "It won't be the same without you there. This is our last spring break together."

April sighed, feeling disappointed too. "Maybe we can do something together our first spring break from college next year."

"Fat chance. We'll all be scattered to the ends of the earth."

"I'm sorry," April said softly, her eyes filling with tears.

Kelli scooted forward and seized April's hands. "Don't cry. I'm such a jerk for making you feel worse than you already do. Tell you what, we'll go to the shore this summer when all this is behind you. You've always liked the beach better than the ski slopes anyway. I'll talk to the others while we're away and devise a plan. What do you say?"

"Okay. Maybe we can go right after graduation, before we have to pack up for college." April did love the beach, the rolling ocean waves, the warm sand and bright sun. "Thanks for thinking of it, Kelli. You're a real friend."

Kelli beamed her a smile. "We'll call you from the ski lodge."

April nodded. "*Don't* break a leg."

Suddenly a male voice burst upon the two girls in the lounge. "There you are, April."

April looked up to see Chris Albright, the senior captain of their high-school soccer team. They'd been dating for a few months, ever since Christmas, but she hadn't expected him to pop into the hospital the day before spring break. She was glad she'd taken the time to put on her sweats and wasn't wearing a hospital gown.

"I couldn't find you in your room," Chris continued. "One of the nurses told me to check in here. You feeling better?"

Chris had caught her when she'd fainted in English class. Literally.

"Nothing to report," she said. He straddled the arm of her chair and took her hand in his. From the corner of her eye, April saw the patient who'd been ogling her lean forward. She turned her full attention to Chris. "I didn't think I'd see you until after the break."

"I can't go off and leave my girlfriend holed up in the hospital."

Kelli, who was out of Chris's line of vision, did an exaggerated swoon that made April giggle. Chris was the catch of their school. April was nuts about him, but she tried not to show it. Clingy girlfriends were a turnoff.

"What's so funny?" Chris asked.

"Nothing. I'm just glad to see you." She laced her fingers through his.

"What's up, Kelli?" Chris asked.

"I came to say goodbye too," Kelli told him. "Actually I was trying to persuade April to sneak away with me and leave her doctor a note about coming back after spring break."

"Makes sense to me," Chris said. "Have they told you anything yet?"

April told Chris what she'd told Kelli. Once again she omitted the information that she didn't want anyone to know. *The headaches can't be related,* she told herself. "So, I guess I'm stuck here until they complete all the tests," she finished aloud.

"What kind of doctor have you got?" Chris wanted to know.

"A neurologist." She leaned forward. "Personally, I think all this is a ploy to find out if I really have a brain."

Kelli rolled her eyes and Chris scoffed. "Right," he said. "You're on the dean's list every reporting period. I don't think brain loss is your problem."

They all laughed and April felt better. More than anything she wanted to be out of the hospital and back in the familiar world of school and friends and graduation plans. Graduation was only nine weeks away. *Stupid headaches!*

"Listen, I'd better run," Kelli said, standing. "I want to catch the train before rush hour."

"Thanks for visiting." April longed to be leaving with her friend.

"I'll call you." Kelli bent and hugged her goodbye. She whispered in April's ear, "I know three's a crowd," and darted out the door.

Chris eased into Kelli's vacated chair. "I miss you, April."

"I miss you too."

"You scared everybody when you blacked out in class."

"Did I ever thank you for catching me before I hit the floor?"

He glanced self-consciously around the room. "Is there any place less public than here?"

"My room."

"Let's go." He helped her to her feet.

The room spun and she clung to him. "It takes me a minute to get my balance whenever I change positions."

He looked concerned and put his arm around her waist. As they walked back to her room, April felt the gaze of the guy on the far side of the lounge area following them. She snuggled closer to Chris.

Once they were in the privacy of her room, Chris took her in his arms and kissed her. "I hate to leave you for a whole week." The soccer team was playing a tournament in Pennsylvania over the break.

"Go have a good time. But not too good a time."

He stayed for another hour before he kissed her goodbye.

Alone, she felt the gloom return. It would be another couple of hours before her parents would arrive. *Stop acting like a baby,* she told herself. *This isn't like before. You're seventeen now, not five.*

She was sitting up in her bed clicking through the TV channels with the remote control when someone rapped on her door. "Come in," she called.

The door slowly opened, and the boy from the rec room stood there. "Hi," he said with a sunny grin.

"Do I know you?" she asked.

"Mark Gianni." He held out his hand.

She took it cautiously. His grip was warm, his palm rough. He was tall and had curling dark brown hair and intense deep brown eyes. But Kelli had been right. He was thin, almost gaunt. "And you're here because . . . ?" She allowed the sentence to trail.

"Because I want you to know that you're the most beautiful girl I've ever seen. And I thought I should introduce myself. I mean, we should get to know each other. Since you're the girl I intend to marry."

2

Although Mark's bold statement shocked April, she refused to let him see her reaction. Without changing her expression, she asked, "And what makes you think I'm not already married?"

Mark looked surprised. But suddenly, an impish grin crossed his face. "No ring," he said, picking up her left hand. "If a guy was married to you, he'd make you wear a ring the size of a baseball. And wouldn't your last name be different from your parents'?"

She tugged her hand out of his. "I don't believe in changing my name." Her eyes narrowed. "And how do you know my last name anyway?"

"I asked the nurses. They said you're April Lancaster and you live on the Island."

She wasn't sure she liked him knowing anything about her without her permission. "Well, they shouldn't have told you anything."

"Don't be mad at them. I've been coming here for years, so I know most of the nurses really well. They like me." He grinned again. "I'll bet you could like me too if you gave me a chance."

His smile was infectious and though she tried to hide it, the corners of her mouth twitched. "Well, I'm not here looking for a husband, thank you."

He shrugged. "Okay, so maybe my proposal was a little premature. I'll ask again once we get to know each other better." Suddenly Mark ducked his head and began coughing deeply into his hand. When the coughing fit finally subsided, he looked up and said in a wheezy voice, "Don't worry. I'm not contagious."

She blushed because that was exactly what she had been thinking. "So what are you here for?"

"CF—cystic fibrosis. I was born with it."

She'd heard of the disease but knew nothing about it. "I'm sorry."

With his coughing spasm over, Mark looked paler, and April saw dark circles under his brown eyes. "Can I sit? I feel a little woozy."

Quickly, she pulled her knees up to allow him room to ease onto her bed. "You all right? Should I call a nurse?"

"I'm all right." His smile was less bold, more wavering, and his sudden vulnerability touched her. "A person learns to live with it. Sometimes CF gets the upper hand and then I have to come here until I get on top of it."

"How often do you get hospitalized?"

"It depends. When I was a kid, I sometimes came three or four times a year. But now that I'm older, I'm doing better. This is only my second time in eighteen months."

"How do you stand it? I hate this place."

"So do I. But I don't have a choice. Randy, my RT—that's respiratory therapist—made me come this time." Mark waved his hand. "But enough of this boring stuff, let's talk about something more interesting—like you, for instance. Why are you here?"

"Testing." Talking to him had made her

forget her problems for the moment, and she hated the reminder.

"Well, they can't be testing for imperfections. You're already perfect."

She rolled her eyes. "Do you ever get results with such lame lines?"

"Ouch! I'm wounded. How could you think I'm feeding you a line?"

"Oh puh-leeze. It's been fun meeting you, but don't I hear the dinner trays?"

Out in the hall there was the unmistakable clatter of the cart carrying the supper trays for the patients. April's door swung open and an orderly carried in a beige plastic tray with plates covered by stainless steel domes. He set it down on her bedside table.

"You got room 423 on that cart still?" Mark asked.

"Yes," the orderly answered.

"Can you bring it in here?" Before April could say anything, Mark turned his beautiful eyes on her. "Would you mind?" he asked shyly. "Eating alone is really a downer."

Instantly, April realized why Mark acted like such a flirt. He was lonely. "Only if you promise not to use any more dumb lines on me."

His grin turned sunny again. "Nothing dumb about them. I work hard to perfect them. After all, it's not easy for me to compete with guys who are healthy."

The orderly plunked Mark's tray on the table in the corner and left. Mark lifted her tray and put it across the table from his. "Dinner is served," he said in a snooty voice.

She joined him, but before she could take a bite, she saw him take a medicine cup full of pills. "What are the pills for?"

"CF is a disease of the pancreas. It affects the lungs and also digestion. I have to take pills before every meal to help me digest food. But why are we talking about me again? I'd rather talk about you."

She made up her mind to ask a nurse more about CF. "I'm a dull subject."

"Not to me. Is that guy who I saw you with earlier your boyfriend?"

"Yes." She wanted Mark to know she was unavailable.

"I'll bet he's a jock."

"He plays soccer."

"When I'm on top of my CF, I play chess." He grinned. "Bet I could take him in chess."

"Maybe." April suppressed a smile. She

hated to admit it, but Mark's charm was getting to her.

"Are you in school?"

"A senior. And you?"

"I graduated three years ago," he said. "I take night classes at NYU and I work in a print shop. My uncle owns it. My father's a cop and Mom . . . well, Mom lives to cook huge family dinners and harass my sisters, who aren't married to nice Italian boys yet. Luckily, my sisters and I each have our own apartments."

"How many sisters do you have?"

His smile lit up his eyes. "Just two—both older. So how about you?" he asked. "Brothers or sisters?"

"I'm an only."

"Makes sense." He nodded slowly. "I mean, how could they follow an act as beautiful as you?"

"You're getting lame again."

"Sorry. I lost my head." He gave himself a slap on the cheek. "I'm better now."

April smiled in spite of herself. "I have terrific parents. My dad's an investment counselor and my mom's part owner of an antique shop in Manhattan."

"Speaking of antiques, do you like cars?" he asked.

"Cars? Sure."

"I rebuild cars—street rods—as a hobby."

"Street rods?"

"Classic cars from the fifties. We've just finished a fifty-seven Chevy. Aqua and white with white leather upholstery." His eyes sparkled. "The most beautiful thing I've ever seen. Before you, that is."

She ignored his flattery. "And what do you do with the cars after they're rebuilt?"

"We show and sometimes race them."

"Like on a racetrack?"

"Out at the speedway. Ever been there?"

"Uh—no."

"If I'd had a choice about my life, I would have been a race car driver."

"I thought you said you *did* race cars."

"I do, but not the way I'd like to. I'd race as a career."

April realized that Mark's CF probably kept him from such a career. Would she be unable to do the things she wanted to do if something really bad was wrong with her?

"Would you come with me to the track

sometime?" Mark's question pulled her away from her dark thoughts.

"I don't think so."

"Why?"

"You know I'm already dating somebody."

Again the quicksilver smile. "Can't blame me for trying."

A rap on April's door caused both of them to start. A nurse entered. "There you are," she said to Mark, her hands on her hips. "We've been looking for you. It's time for therapy."

Mark rose. "I know, but I was hoping you'd forget."

"No way. Not when you're this close to being released."

"Trying to get rid of me?"

The nurse studied him fondly. "Go see your therapist. He's in your room."

He turned back to April, seized her hand, and planted a kiss on it. "Thanks for the company. I'll be back tomorrow."

"But—"

He was out the door before she could finish.

"I see he finally met you," the nurse said with an amused smile.

"What do you mean?"

"He's been maneuvering an introduction ever since you checked in."

"Is he harmless?"

"Very. In fact, Mark's one of the nicest kids to ever come through these doors."

"What kind of therapy is he supposed to have?"

"Respiratory. CF victims don't have the ability to break down mucus, so it turns thick and gummy and clogs the lung tissue so they can't breathe. The mucus is broken up by medications, inhalants, and by thumping the victim's back and chest several times a day."

"*Every* day?" April asked. Cystic fibrosis sounded awful to her. "For how long? Until his breathing gets better and his cough goes away?"

"If only," the nurse said with a sigh. "No, it's a lifelong thing for him."

"Won't he ever get well?"

The nurse shook her head. "There's no cure for CF. It's one hundred percent fatal."

3

Early the next morning April was brought to the hospital's radiology department. She would spend a portion of the day undergoing X-ray procedures, such as CAT scans and an MRI. Her mother had taken the day off from the store to be with her. April had left her floor while most of the patients were still asleep, so she hadn't seen Mark. But she couldn't forget what the nurse had told her about him.

"Do you know anything about cystic fibrosis?" April asked her mother. April lay on a gurney in the hall outside one of the radiology rooms, waiting for her turn.

"Not much. Why do you ask?"

April's mother was a slim, blond-haired

woman in her mid-forties. She was stylishly and expensively dressed, perfectly groomed, and smelled of expensive perfume. The two of them had always been close, probably because Janice Lancaster had endured medical hell in order to conceive a child. April knew that her parents had spent thousands of dollars on four attempts of in vitro fertilization before she'd been conceived.

She knew her parents loved her, but sometimes she felt as if she were being smothered by them. They showered her with material goods and made certain that she had every advantage. She was their princess and they treated her like one.

Kelli once told April that she couldn't believe she was so down-to-earth and not spoiled rotten. April was kind and sensitive, almost mushy, actually. She cried over sad songs, wounded animals, and even TV commercials. When she was little, she'd cried for days after seeing the movie *Bambi,* because Bambi's mother had been killed and the fawn had been orphaned.

Now, looking back, she suspected that what had happened to her when she was five con-

tributed mightily to the person she had become.

"I met this guy on my floor who has CF,"
April explained to her mother. "He's sort of
goofy, but really nice. Lonely too. A nurse
told me that CF is fatal, that it has no cure."

Her mother frowned. "How awful."

"But he doesn't let it get him down. His
hobby is rebuilding old cars and racing."

"Sounds dangerous."

Unable to get her mother interested in discussing Mark, April asked, "Mom, do you
think the same thing's wrong with me now as
when I was five?"

Her mother stiffened and a worried frown
settled over her face. Now that the words were
out, April could see just how much her headaches and blackout had affected her mother.
"That's why we're doing all this testing," her
mother said softly. "To rule it out. I personally don't believe the two things are related.
They told us then they were sure they had
gotten it all." Her mother affectionately
tugged April's long thick red hair. "I think we
should talk about something else and let these
tests tell us what's wrong. No use making up

scenarios. So, are your friends on their way to Vermont yet?"

April was disappointed. She wanted to talk about her fears, but it was clear her mother didn't. Perhaps her mother was right. Why get all worked up before the tests results were in? "They left this morning. I'd give anything to be with them."

"I wish you were, honey."

"Kelli said maybe we could all take off for the shore this summer before we go our separate ways."

"That would be nice."

"I like the beach better anyway."

April's doctor came into the waiting area. "How's it going?"

"Okay," April said, mildly surprised to see him in the middle of the day. He usually visited in the evening.

Dr. Sorenson was a big man with a head of white hair and intelligent blue eyes behind black-rimmed glasses. He was wearing scrub greens. "I'm just out of surgery," he said. "I wanted to check on you. See if that medication is working."

April had been taking special pills for three days for the headaches. "It's doing a good job. I haven't had a headache since I got here."

"Maybe April could just take a prescription of the pills and it would straighten her out," her mother suggested.

"We have to know the cause of the head-aches," Dr. Sorenson said. "Unless we know why her head hurts, the pills will only be a temporary fix. I'll have more information after the results of today's work."

"When can I go home?"

"Not for another few days."

April was frustrated. "I hate this place."

"Food getting to you?" He smiled.

"This entire place is getting to me."

He patted her arm. "Not much longer." He looked at Janice. "I have her old records from when she was five and I've gone over them. Unfortunately, the doctor who treated her then is deceased."

"Dr. Rubin was a good doctor. He oper-ated, drained the tumor, and said he thought she'd be fine." Her mother's voice sounded challenging, as if daring Dr. Sorenson to con-tradict the other doctor's diagnosis.

"Yes, April had a low-grade astrocytoma."

April hated their talking around her, as if

she were still five years old. She remembered the nightmare of that time all too well. She hadn't understood what was happening to her, but she'd never forget the terror from the shots and IVs and being separated from her parents during the X-rays and surgery and recovery in ICU. But she'd recovered fully and up until now had led a perfectly normal life with a perfectly uncomplicated future.

"The headaches aren't the same," she told the doctor and her mother. "Before, when I was little, I mostly got dizzy and fell down a lot."

"She had a seizure," her mother confirmed. "We rushed her to the emergency room. But this time it seems different."

"No use speculating," Dr. Sorenson said. "We'll have some answers soon enough."

He left and April again thought about Mark. It was easier to think about him and his disease than it was to think about her own problems.

Eventually, her session in radiology was complete and she returned to her room. By now it was late afternoon and pale spring sunlight slanted through the window. Her father was waiting when they arrived. "How's my girl?"

She hugged him. "Bored. I didn't expect you here so early."

"I couldn't concentrate at the office, so I came over." He kissed his wife.

April saw the look that passed between them: *"Any news?"* her father's gaze asked. *"Nothing yet,"* her mother's eyes answered.

"Did you bring me these flowers?" April asked, wanting to distract them.

"I brought those." He pointed to a huge spring bouquet of irises, jonquils, and sweetheart roses. "I don't know who sent the other."

The other was a single red rose in a blue bud vase.

"It has a card." Her mother handed her a small envelope.

April opened it and read: *You're beautiful. Mark.*

"A secret admirer?" Her father craned his neck to see the signature. "I'm jealous."

April quickly shoved the card back inside the envelope. "No need to be. I'm still yours."

He laughed and looped his arm around his wife's waist. This was the way April was used to seeing them. None of her friends' parents acted as much in love as hers did. When her friends complained about parents who argued and threatened divorce, April could only listen, glad that her parents' relationship was so totally different.

"When this is over," her father said, "when they release you to go home, why don't we think about going to Spain again? We had such a good time there last summer."

"Oh, Hugh, let's!" her mother said. "Caroline won't miss me at the store. I'll tell her I'll pick up some special pieces. We actually had a customer come in looking for some fifteenth-century Spanish chairs the other day."

"Excuse me," April said, holding up her hand to stop their plan before her father rushed out and bought the tickets. "But I still have this small matter of finishing my senior year."

"You could miss a couple of weeks," her father declared.

April smiled indulgently. "Sorry, I don't want to go. I've spent twelve years slogging through classes so that I could enjoy being a senior. Kelli and I have a big countdown calendar on the inside of my locker where we're marking off each day till graduation. So count me out of your impromptu trip."

"We can't go without you." Her mother looked thoughtful. "Maybe we could think about going right after graduation."

"It could be your graduation present," her father added.

April wanted to spend the summer with her friends and Chris, and plan for their beach trip. But she decided not to make an issue of it just yet. The rattle of the dinner cart coming down the hall interrupted the conversation. "Are you two going down to the cafeteria?" April asked.

Her mother wrinkled her nose and her father shook his head vigorously. "I've made other arrangements."

"Such as?" her mother asked.

He grinned impishly. "How does The Red Dragon sound?" That was their favorite restaurant—and one of New York's most trendy. "Don't worry," he added quickly, "I've gotten special permission from the hospital. Turns out that the chief administrator is one of my clients. What could he say when I asked?

I mean, he still wants his investments to earn for him, doesn't he?"

"Daddy!" April squealed. "That's criminal."

"No . . . what they pass off as food here is criminal."

Within the hour, two waiters rolled a small cart into April's room, complete with a bright red linen tablecloth and napkins, candles, and succulent-smelling platters of Chinese food. April heard the commotion in the hall as the cart neared her room and she wondered what the other patients and the staff must be thinking. And she wondered what Mark might be thinking too.

She put some classical music on her portable CD player. Her mother made a special arrangement of flowers from those she'd received, and her father turned off all the lights. The three of them ate by candlelight. April listened to her mother describe various oddball customers and her father talk about a client who was also a rock star. And she almost forgot where she was and why she was there.

At the end of the meal, they each opened a fortune cookie. Laughing, they read the strips of paper aloud. April's mother was informed that she would be showered with riches; her father that he was wise and admired.

April pulled out the fortune tucked inside her cookie and a small shiver crept through her as she read the words on the paper. It read: *A change is coming. Be prepared.*

4

April was alone in her room the following day when Mark knocked on her door. "You up for a visit?"

"Sure." April closed the book she was reading. "How are you doing?"

"I may get out tomorrow if I pass all my breath tests." She must have looked puzzled because he explained, "There's a machine I have to blow air into and the gauge has to jump into a certain zone. That lets my doctor know how much lung capacity I've regained."

"I hope you pass."

"How about you?" he asked. "Know anything more about your problems?"

"Not yet. I'm not too sure I want to know

either. I mean, as long as I don't know, I can pretend it's nothing really bad."

"Why do you think it might be bad? You look healthy. I'll bet you've never been sick a day in your life."

"You're wrong." April wanted—*needed*—to confide her fears to somebody. On impulse she decided to tell Mark about her childhood brain tumor. "I've got plenty of reason to be worried," she said, and told him her story.

Mark listened intently, nodding and looking grim. "It must have been horrible for you."

"It was. But why am I telling you? You're certainly no stranger to hospitals."

"I honestly can't remember my life without them. CF and I reluctantly share the same body. Unless medical science comes up with a miracle, it's here to stay."

"I don't know how you stand it."

"I consider the alternative," he said with a wry smile.

April sighed. "I guess you're right. The alternative is what you're trying so hard to avoid."

"So let me get this straight," he said, moving back to their original topic. "After years of feeling fine, you suddenly start getting headaches and dizzy spells again."

"I staggered around like I was drunk. And I blacked out too."

"So you're afraid the tumor is back, even though they told you twelve years ago it was gone?"

"Yes, I am."

He looked at her and for a minute nothing existed except the dark brown of his eyes. "I hope you're wrong," he said softly. "I can't imagine anything terrible happening to you."

April suddenly felt self-conscious. She struggled to find something else to talk about. Her gaze fell on the bud vase. "Thank you for the rose. It was nice of you."

"It looks pretty puny next to your other bouquet."

"My dad never does anything halfway."

"You're lucky he can afford to do things first class." He paused. "April, when this is over, when you're out of here, can I call you? Come see you?"

April hesitated. His interest in her was flattering, but she couldn't lead him on. "No, Mark. I told you I have a boyfriend." His expression told her that he didn't think this was a good reason. "I mean it, Mark. Once I get out of here and back to my real life, I don't want any reminders of this place."

"Including me?"

"You've been nice to me and I appreciate it. But this is only a temporary interruption of my life."

"No matter what your tests say?"

She squared her chin. "No matter what the tests say."

Her parents were with her when Dr. Sorenson came in, pulled up a chair, and said, "I believe we have a diagnosis."

April's mouth went dry and her heart began to hammer. Her parents were on either side of her bed. They reminded her of guard dogs jealously surrounding their young. "May I have the envelope, please?" she said, trying hard to keep things light.

"You *are* having a recurrence of your earlier problem," Dr. Sorenson told them matter-of-factly.

"But they told us it was gone," April's mother said fiercely.

"They told you it was a *low-grade* astrocytoma and that the chances were good that it would not return," Dr. Sorenson corrected her. "But it's never been gone; it's only been dormant."

April suddenly felt cold, as if all her blood had turned to ice. She clenched her teeth to keep them from chattering.

"So what is it now?" April's father growled impatiently.

"Now it's a *high-grade* astrocytoma."

"Meaning?"

"It's growing rapidly and consequently it will be harder to treat."

"This is ridiculous," her father snapped. "First it's there, then it's gone, now it's back. Can't you doctors get it right? This is my daughter we're discussing."

"I'm very sorry," Dr. Sorenson said. "I wish I had better news for you."

Her father rocked back on his heels. "What are our options?"

April scarcely heard him. A rushing sound was filling up her ears and their voices seemed to be coming from far away. This couldn't be happening. It had to be some mistake.

Dr. Sorenson attached X rays to a portable light board he'd brought into the room with him. A human skull was outlined perfectly. "This is your skull, April. And here"—he pointed to a dark area at the base of her skull—"is the tumor. You can see it better on the MRI." They peered at the contours of her brain on another piece of film. The tumor looked dense and sinister. "The tumor's entrenched here, and it's growing."

April shuddered. How could something be growing inside her body without her knowledge or permission? "Can't you cut it out, remove it?" she asked.

"Maybe not."

"Why not?" asked her mother.

"It's embedded itself in the cerebellum here, near the brain stem." Dr. Sorenson pointed to the area on the MRI. "This is the part of your brain that's responsible for involuntary reflexes, like breathing and coordination. That explains your dizzy spells. The tumor mass is pressing and intruding into these areas. If we do traditional surgery, you could be maimed for life. No scalpel can untangle it."

"Are you saying there's nothing you can do?" April's mother gasped, her eyes wide with fear.

"No. We're going to try some things. First, a drug to reduce brain swelling. There are some side effects, but I want to get the swelling down so that you won't have so much pain."

"What kind of side effects?" April swallowed hard, feeling slightly detached, as if they were discussing someone else.

"Water retention, puffiness, and an incredible appetite."

April had always been tall and slim and able to eat whatever she wanted, and she didn't like the idea of a forced weight gain. "I'll look like a freak."

"What else?" her father asked the doctor.

"We'll start her on radiation treatments."

April remembered the radiation sessions from before. They had strapped her on a table, alone in a room, with a massive machine aimed at the back of her head. She'd shrieked and screamed, not because it hurt—it hadn't—but because she couldn't move. And because she was all alone. But she was older now and she knew that the technician had to leave the room to avoid the high doses of gamma rays emitted by the machine. Still, just the memory terrified her. "Will I lose my hair?" she asked. "Will I have to cut it off?"

"Just a little spot in the back. You can comb the rest of it over. No one will be able to tell. Radiation has come a long way. You'll have a radiation oncologist, a special doctor who does only these treatments. It's an exacting science and you'll be in good hands."

"But she's already had radiation once," April's mother interjected.

"It's the best treatment for this kind of tumor," the doctor insisted. "We must radiate again."

"And once it's shrunk?" her mother wanted to know.

"Then more MRIs and X rays to see if she's a candidate for gamma knife surgery."

"I thought you said you couldn't cut out the tumor."

"Not with a regular scalpel, but with a gamma knife, a high concentration of gamma rays aimed at the tumor."

"Why can't you just do that right away?" April asked breathlessly. "Why do I have to go through all the other stuff first?"

"Because we can't use the gamma knife on

anything larger than three centimeters." He pulled a ruler from his pocket and held his thumb on a mark. "Right now, your tumor is larger, about five centimeters."

She watched his thumb slide upward on the ruler and wondered how two centimeters could make such a difference. And yet it did. Surgery was out.

"What about chemotherapy?" her mother asked. "I have a friend who had breast cancer and they gave her chemo. She was sick for a while, but it worked. She's been cancer-free for six years."

Dr. Sorenson shook his head. "Chemo is ineffective on this kind of tumor."

April felt as if the doors of her options were being closed. "I don't have a lot of choices, do I?"

"Radiation's your best hope," the doctor answered.

She felt sick to her stomach. "And if radiation doesn't work?" Her voice trembled, but she *had* to ask the question.

"We'll cross that bridge when we come to it," he said.

But she knew instinctively that the bridge was a narrow rope hanging over a precipice that led down to a dark abyss. She turned her face into her mother's shoulder and hid, like a frightened child.

"You're leaving?"

Mark stood in April's doorway, and she turned at the sound of his voice.

"Mom's downstairs finishing up my paperwork now." April continued to pack her small valise.

He came up beside her. "I'm getting out today too."

"Oh, Mark, that's good. I'm glad for you."

"I'm sorry your news wasn't better."

"I guess I'm not destined to be normal and healthy after all."

"When do you start your radiation?"

She should have been surprised that he knew so much about her case, but she knew that the hospital floor was a hotbed of gossip. "Next week. Five days a week for six weeks. So, I guess I can kiss my extracurricular activities goodbye."

"I brought you a present," he said. From behind his back he pulled a large red balloon with a hand-drawn smiley face on it and tied with a long yellow ribbon. "I blew it up myself . . . which is what I used to do when I was a kid to prove I was well enough to get out of the hospital and go home."

The gift touched her. "Thank you."

Their hands brushed as she took the ribbon from him. Her skin tingled from the contact.

"Take care of yourself."

"I will."

"Uh—my phone number is written on a scrap of paper inside the balloon." A wide grin lit up his face. Then, more soberly, he continued, "Just in case you ever want to talk. Sometimes talking helps. And I'm a good listener."

"I told you—"

"I know, you have a boyfriend. But if things change between you two, call me."

She held on to the bright yellow ribbon and watched him walk from the room.

5

"**A** brain tumor! Oh, April, I can't believe it," Kelli gasped.

Seeing her friend so upset made April want to cry. But she quickly took hold of Kelli's hands. "I'll be okay," she said without much conviction. "Some radiation, some pills, and it'll shrink enough so the doctors can operate."

Kelli had come over the afternoon she'd returned from the ski trip. The two of them were sitting on the bedroom floor on plush pale lavender carpet. April's entire room was decorated in rich shades of purple accented with pure white. The down comforter on her four-poster bed was covered in white eyelet, and plum-colored pillows rested against the pristine whiteness. Without the drabness of the hospital surrounding her, April's diagnosis seemed like a bad dream.

"It's not fair!" Kelli blurted out. "You've never done anything mean to anybody. Why should *you* get sick?"

"What's being mean got to do with anything?"

"Well, there are tons of bad people in the world. They're the ones who should get brain tumors." Kelli sounded furious.

"I guess life doesn't work that way. I'm proof that bad things can happen to anybody."

"Have you told Chris?" Kelli asked.

"I'll tell him tonight. We're supposed to go out to dinner." April hugged her knees. "I'm dreading it."

"Why?"

"I'm not sure how he'll handle it."

"He'll be mad about it—like me."

But Chris wasn't like Kelli. Kelli was her best friend. April and Chris had only been together a few months, and they weren't nearly as close as she and Kelli. How *would* Chris react? "I just don't know," she said, chewing on her bottom lip.

Kelli blew her nose. "This is just the worst thing to ever happen."

"Listen, do me a favor."

"Anything."

"I don't want this to get all around school. It's nobody's business but mine."

"But everyone knew you couldn't go on the ski trip because you were in the hospital. They'll want to know what the doctors told you."

"If anyone asks you, tell them I'm being treated for migraine headaches or something. I don't want them to know about the tumor."

"But why?"

"I don't want kids whispering about me in the halls and treating me like I'm contagious or something."

"But that's dumb. Everybody knows you can't catch a brain tumor like you can a cold." Kelli paused. "Can you?"

For a moment, April couldn't tell if Kelli was joking, but then a sly grin broke across Kelli's face. "Just a little humor," she said.

April nodded sheepishly. She was tired of thinking about what was happening to her. Tired of feeling sorry for herself and for her parents, who had been in despair ever since she'd come home from the hospital. She wanted her life back to normal. She wanted to get on with the radiation treatments and get them over with and have her life the way it used to be. "So, let's talk about something else," she said crisply. "How was the ski trip?"

"All right. Not nearly as much fun as if you'd been there."

"That's nice of you to say."

"It's true."

"Well, I *am* going to the shore with everybody this summer. It'll be our last blowout and I'm not about to miss it."

An awkward silence fell between them. The summer seemed so far away. How could they make plans when no one knew if April would be well?

"What's that?" Kelli broke the silence. She pointed to the limp balloon tied to the doorknob of April's bathroom.

April told her about meeting Mark.

"I remember that he was cute, but gee . . . his being sick—it's kind of a turnoff."

" 'A turnoff'?"

"I didn't mean it the way it sounded," Kelli insisted. "You're not him."

"That's exactly why I don't want kids to know about me," April said emphatically. "It's *all* a big turnoff."

Kelli hung her head and then mumbled, "Sorry."

Already April could feel the gap opening between them. Kelli belonged to the world of perfect health, while she belonged . . . ? Where? Suddenly she didn't know either. She thought of Mark and wondered how he managed to straddle the two worlds of sickness and health. How could she find a place for herself in this new world where all the rules had changed?

Chris picked her up that night and took her to the country club where most people in their Long Island community had memberships. Normally, April didn't mind going there, but tonight she didn't want the quiet country club atmosphere. She felt like loud music and pizza and having to shout above the noise. Maybe because that way Chris might not really hear her when she told him about her tumor. In the quiet elegance of the country club, there would be no mistaking her words.

"You look great," Chris said, taking her hand across the table. "And I missed you like crazy."

"I'll bet you didn't even have time to think about me. What with the tournament and all. How did your team do?"

His face clouded. "We came in second. We should have won, but Andy got a red card and we had to play a man down the whole second half of the final game."

"Bummer."

He grinned and April couldn't help noticing how different his smile was from Mark's. Chris's eyes didn't light up in the same way as Mark's. "But I want to hear about you. What did those doctors say?"

Her heart began to hammer so loudly she was afraid that he might hear it on his side of the table. "Well . . . the news wasn't great."

"What do you mean?"

She forced a smile and said flippantly, "I have some wild and crazy cells growing in my brain. They've set up housekeeping and my doctor has to radiate them out of existence. Actually, it's a recurrence of a tumor that I had when I was five."

He stared at her, as if sorting out her answer. "You've got some kind of tumor? Inside your head?"

"So it seems."

He sagged back in his chair and stared at her. "Is this some kind of joke?"

Her face felt frozen. "No joke."

"I don't believe it."

"I wouldn't make it up."

"I don't know what to say."

Say anything, she thought.

"You had a tumor before?"

"When I was five."

"Why didn't you ever tell me?"

His question made her hesitate. She wasn't sure what she'd expected from him, but she recalled how Kelli had taken the news. And Mark. In so many words they both had said, "I'm here for you." Chris seemed almost angry at her.

She told Chris, "I thought it wouldn't ever be a problem for me again. My doctors told me it wouldn't, so I didn't see any reason to talk about it."

"You shouldn't hide things from people you care about." He sounded upset, accusatory.

"Would it have mattered?" April was feeling light-headed, but it had nothing to do with her medical condition.

"Of course not," he said a little too quickly. "It's just that you should have told me. I would have liked to know."

"I was only five. It wouldn't have made any difference." But the expression on Chris's face told her otherwise. "Would it?"

He quickly reached across the table and took her hand. "No. I—I just can't stand the thought of you being sick. I don't want you to be sick." He was picking through his words like a soldier inching through a field of land mines.

Chris was an athlete. In prime physical condition. Strong, muscular, and fit. To him, being sick must be a horror. "I hate what's happening to me, Chris." Tears swam in her eyes. She didn't want to cry, but she couldn't help herself.

He sprang from his chair, knelt beside her, and pulled her against his chest. "I'm sorry, April. Really sorry."

Everyone was sorry. She wept while he rocked her. As her tears slowed, she noticed other diners staring at her and Chris. Self-consciously, she pulled back and wiped her tears on the linen table napkin. "I didn't mean to lose it like that," she said hoarsely.

"You all better now?" Chris asked.

She wasn't all right. She never would be again. "Sure," she lied. "But I've lost my appetite."

"You want me to take you home?"

"Yes."

They left and Chris was silent during the ride home. It was just as well. April wasn't sure what else to say to him. At her front door, he took her in his arms again, but his touch was tentative, as if she'd suddenly been turned to glass and he had to be extra careful in handling her. "I wish this wasn't happening," he breathed into her hair.

"So do I."

He kissed her and she wanted to cling to him and not let go.

He cleared his throat. "I have a game Monday after school. Will you come cheer for me?"

"I can't. I have a consultation with the doctor who's doing my radiation. Then the treatments start." She explained the schedule.

"Every day!" He protested. "You'll miss my whole soccer season."

"I don't have a choice."

"So will you glow in the dark?"

He was attempting to be funny, but April wasn't in the mood to laugh. "No," she said. "But if I'm lucky, the tumor will shrink."

"Of course it will shrink."

She asked, "Do you want to come in? I could make you a sandwich since I made you miss dinner."

He shook his head. "I'm not hungry."

Chris quickly said goodnight. And as she watched him climb into his sports car, maneuver it around the wide brick circular driveway, and drive away, she felt cold and empty. She wrapped her coat closer around her and hurried inside the house.

6

Dr. Sorenson arranged for April to receive her radiation treatments at a Long Island hospital. She would still have to make the trek into the city to see Dr. Sorenson throughout her treatments, but at least she could be treated each day closer to home.

She tried to go to the hospital by herself Monday afternoon, but Janice Lancaster wouldn't hear of it. "I won't tag along for all your treatments," her mother assured her, "but I want to be there for the preliminaries."

April's radiation oncologist was Dr. Edith Hamilton, a short plump woman with graying hair who wore no makeup. She explained about the treatments thoroughly and then carefully shaved away a hank of April's thick red hair at the base of her skull. While studying April's X rays, she took a pen and mapped out the area that was to be bombarded with the gamma rays. Next, Dr. Hamilton used a small needle to make permanent dots in the skin at the base of April's skull. It didn't really hurt; it felt like tiny pinpricks. "Little tattoos," the doctor called the dots, "so that the technician can always align the machine precisely." Her hands were quick and felt like the fluttering wings of small birds in April's hair.

April's mother watched intently. "I thought this was all behind us," she said. "I feel as though we were lulled into a false sense of security."

"April's case is unusual," Dr. Hamilton answered. "This is rare—one in a thousand."

Why do I have to be the one? April thought. It was a question no one could answer. April straightened her hair, combing it over the bald spot at the back of her head. She still felt as if everyone could see the blue marks through the veil of hair. Her mother assured her that nothing showed.

"Be careful when you wash your hair," Dr. Hamilton said. "We'll re-mark the area from

time to time, but don't get soap on the skin."
April couldn't imagine how she was going to
wash her hair and not get soap on her skin.
The doctor continued. "You will lose some of
your hair, but because the treatment is so lo-
calized, I hope it won't be much. You may
experience dry mouth and food may lose some
of its taste, but don't let it keep you from
eating. Your skin will get red at the site, but
don't use any creams. Creams interfere with
the rays. Toward the end of treatment you
may experience fatigue. All these symptoms
will vanish once the treatment is completed."

"Can't I start today?" April asked.

"Tomorrow," Dr. Hamilton said. "But let
me show you the equipment we'll be using.
It's state of the art."

They went into a large room with a huge
machine. It sprouted a thick mechanical arm
with a cone-shaped device at one end. "We'll
point this at your skull, aim it at the tumor,
and zap the growth," Dr. Hamilton explained
as she touched the cone. "We'll take more
X-ray pictures periodically to track the tumor's
shrinkage."

April felt her hands growing clammy. Memories from when she was five years old and terrified flooded her mind. She told herself that her fear was irrational. "I'll be back tomorrow," she said, turning on her heel, eager to get away from the room and the machine.

School let out at three, so they set her appointments at four o'clock, the last time slot of the day. April went to bed that night and lay in the dark with her eyes open, trying not to cry, trying to grasp the monumental change that was occurring in her life. Just before she finally fell asleep, she realized that Chris hadn't called since their almost dinner date. She knew if it had been Chris going through this ordeal, she would have called.

The next day, at school, she could scarcely keep her mind on her classes. She saw Chris in the lunchroom and he came straight over to her. "How's it going?" he asked.

"I start treatments today at four," she said.

"You're okay with it, aren't you?"

"As okay as a person can be, I guess." She looked up at him. "Why didn't you call me last night?"

He looked away. "The game went into overtime. By the time I got home, showered, and ate, it was late. Then I had to work on a history paper. I tried to call once, but your line was busy."

She would never know if he was telling her the truth.

"I miss you cheering for me," he said.

And I miss you cheering for me, she thought, but she said, "See you in English class."

After school, she went to the hospital, signed in, and fidgeted in the waiting area until her name was called. With her heart pounding, she entered the treatment room, fighting a stomach filled with butterflies. A cheerful technician didn't make her feel any better, and when she lay on the table and heard the machine whirl into gear, she tensed. "Lie perfectly still," the tech said. "You'll hear a buzzing sound, then I'll reposition the machine via remote control, and you'll hear another buzzing sound. I'll be out of the room until it clicks off."

April heard the heavy metal door of the room close as the tech left, and she knew she was all alone. She was shaking. She bit her lip and held her breath, hoping it would stop the trembling.

The treatment was over in a few minutes and the tech returned with a smile. "You did fine." Then he added, "You look pale. Feel all right?"

"I'm okay," she said breathlessly.

"There's free juice in the waiting room. Why don't you grab some on your way out and get your blood sugar up a bit. You'll feel better."

She didn't want juice. She just wanted to leave. Out in the parking lot, she blinked against the brilliant spring sunlight. The air was cool and she slowly began to feel better. She glanced around, trying to remember where she'd parked her car, when she heard a horn honk and turned to see an aqua and white car with gleaming chrome coming toward her. Her mouth dropped as the car stopped in front of her and Mark Gianni grinned at her through the open window. "Want a ride? Hop in."

"I—I have my car . . . ," she sputtered.

"Not so," he said with his million-watt smile. "You have transportation. *This* is a car."

"What are you doing here?"

"When you didn't call me, I decided to come see you."

She'd tossed out the balloon he'd given her

days before, without ever retrieving the slip of paper containing his phone number from it. Now she felt guilty about it. "I had my first treatment," she said.

"I know." He leaned over and popped the passenger door handle. "Come on. Let's go get a soda."

She climbed into the car. The white leather seat felt smooth against the backs of her legs. Mark put the car in gear and drove out of the parking lot toward the small strip mall across the street. "I saw a coffee shop while I waited for you to come out. Is it okay?"

She nodded, still stunned at seeing him. She knew it was a long commute from the city and couldn't figure how he'd managed to track her down.

Inside the coffee shop they ordered cappuccino, and when it was served, she sipped it, waiting for him to explain himself.

"You look beautiful," he said.

"You came all this way to tell me that?"

"I came because I wanted to see you again. Because I *had* to see you again."

"But how—?"

"I can't reveal my sources. But I *did* find

out that your treatments began today and I *am* here to give you moral support. Plus," he added with a grin, "I wanted to be with you again. And since it seemed like you weren't ever going to call me, I decided to make the first move. Or, actually, the second move. So, here I am."

His forwardness made April a little uncomfortable, but she couldn't pretend that his presence didn't mean something to her. "You ever have radiation?" she asked, changing the subject.

"No. But I've had more than my share of medical treatments."

She knew it was true. And while her friends were sympathetic, Mark was *empathetic*—he knew firsthand what she was experiencing. "I thought I'd be able to handle it better than I did," she said. She told him of her fears, and once the words started coming, she couldn't stop them. She told him how she felt alienated from friends and smothered by her parents. She told him things she hadn't even realized she'd been feeling until they spilled out of her. He listened intently, never taking his gaze off her face, and when she was finished, and her eyes had filled with tears, he took a paper napkin and dabbed her cheeks tenderly.

"That's sure a lot of baggage you've been carrying around."

She blew her nose and nodded. "Thanks for letting me dump it on you."

"No thanks necessary. We're comrades in medical misery."

"How have you done it all these years?"

"I keep hoping there will be some big breakthrough, some kind of medical miracle. There's been some progress lately. A new medication. Lung transplants. But nothing that's right for me just yet. So I keep on waiting. And I try to live as normal a life as possible. Because while you have to respect your disease, you can't let it control you. If you do, it robs you of what's good about life." He reached across the table and took her hand. "And there's a lot of good in life."

She felt her heart skip a beat. "Are you flirting with me again?"

"Absolutely."

She smiled, and this time she didn't push him away. "I still have that boyfriend."

"How is Mr. Lucky anyway?"

"Mr. Lucky? You mean Chris?"

"Is that the guy I saw you with at the hospital?"

"Yes." She pulled her hand away. "He's struggling with all this. I understand. But still . . ."

"His loss," Mark said, his smile lighting up his eyes. "My gain."

"But we haven't broken up," she told Mark.

"No problem. All I want is a chance with you. All I want is for you to go out with me, just once, and get to know me. After that, if you tell me to get lost, I'll do it."

"That would be pretty cold."

"Believe me, it's happened."

For a moment she saw through his cheerful smile and into the hurt of rejection beneath it. Ashamed, she recalled that avoiding him had been her first reaction also. "Well, whoever told you to get lost wasn't much of a catch," she said. Then she took a deep breath and added, "If you want to call me, it's all right. If you ask me out, I'll go. Once."

He raised his fist in the air and said, "Yes!"

She laughed. "I'm not that big a deal."

"Yes you are," he said with a grin. "To me, you're a really big deal."

April smiled. For the first time in days, she was looking forward to something.

7

"You told Mark you'd go out with him?" Kelli sounded incredulous.

April sorted through her locker. "What's wrong with that?"

"Well, what about Chris?"

"I don't think I'm at the top of Chris's list anymore."

"Why do you think that?"

"Ever since he found out about my tumor, he's backed off. He hasn't called once since I broke the news to him."

"Maybe he's just going through an adjustment period."

April rolled her eyes. "*You* didn't go through one." She found her literature book and heaved it into her backpack.

"But I'm your best friend."

"And what was Chris? Wasn't he supposed to be my 'best' guy?"

Kelli shrugged. "What makes Mark so special? You weren't interested in him at all before now."

"Mark accepts me." April slammed her locker door. "The way I am."

"You mean he isn't put off by your tumor."

Kelli was right. But April knew it was more than that. There was something special about Mark she couldn't explain. "The next six weeks aren't going to be a picnic," she said, feeling overwhelmed by what lay ahead of her. "Mark seems to understand, without any explanation. He knows because he's been through it too."

"Except that there's one big difference," Kelli said before April could rush off.

"And what's that?"

"You're going to get well. Mark isn't."

April walked away without answering.

By the end of the first week of radiation treatments, April was ready for a change. She was tired of her life revolving around cancer, so when Mark came to pick her up Saturday morning, she was eager to go. Her parents weren't thrilled—they thought he was too old for her—but Mark was charming and pleasant. By the time she and Mark left the house, April thought her parents were somewhat pacified.

Sunshine gleamed through the windshield of Mark's car as they drove toward the city. Blooming wildflowers grew along the sides of the road like bright punctuation marks of color. "So what are we doing today?" April asked.

"I'm introducing you to my world. I've seen yours—lifestyles of the rich and famous—so I thought I'd show you mine."

"You exaggerate."

"I've just been inside your family mansion, so I think I know what I'm talking about."

His tone was friendly, but it hadn't really occurred to April that their material worlds were so very different. "So what part of your world do you want me to see?"

"All of it. Where I work, where I live. Oh, and did I mention, my mother is expecting us for dinner?"

"No, you didn't mention it." She wasn't sure how she felt about being thrust into his family life so soon. She'd barely gotten to know him.

He must have sensed her reluctance because he hastily added, "I told you . . . we're a close family. Mom's a great cook. Her dinners could feed a small country."

"I'll meet your family, but I don't know what they're expecting."

"An angel," he said.

"Then they're in for a rude awakening," she countered.

Mark drove to Brooklyn and he parked his car inside a building that was both a garage and a workshop. It was littered with auto parts and the partial shells of car bodies. "We're restoring a fifty-six Thunderbird now," he said proudly, showing April around. He patted a car that needed a paint job. "And this old Dodge may not look like much, but it has a muscle engine. It's our best racing ma chine."

She thought the place felt cold and looked dingy. It smelled of motor oil and grease, but Mark was obviously proud of it. She stopped beside the Thunderbird. "Will you sell it or race it when you're finished?"

"Sell it. Maybe I'll build one for you some-day. Any preferences?"

She didn't want to admit she didn't know one car from another, so she said, "Surprise me."

Out on the sidewalk he said, "We don't have to be at my parents' place until five."

"All right," she told him. "I glimpsed your world, now I want you to come do something with me in mine."

"Such as?"

"How about lunch at Trump Plaza?"

They took a cab because it was easier than driving through the city. Once inside the op-ulent glass and marble plaza, April felt more comfortable. She chose a quiet restaurant with booths and crisp linen tablecloths, a place where she'd often eaten with her mother.

Mark studied the menu, which was in French. "You know French?"

"Oui." She giggled because he looked im-pressed.

"You've been to France?"

"We went when I was thirteen."

"I've never been out of New York."

"I won't hold it against you."

He put down the menu. "How do you order bread and water?"

"How about onion soup and a salad?" He agreed and when the waiter came, she ordered—in English.

"Cute," he told her, but he smiled because she'd so smoothly taken him in.

Afterward, she dragged him through a few of the trendier stores in the plaza. Mark kept doing double takes at the price tags. He made her laugh, and much later she realized he had made her forget what was really happening in her life.

Late in the afternoon they caught a cab downtown to Little Italy. "My folks have lived here all their lives," Mark told her. When the cab pulled up in front of an old brownstone, Mark paid the driver and, taking April's hand, led her up the front steps. "Pop brought Mom here right after they got married."

Once inside, April smelled rich tomato sauce, garlic, and onions. In a room off the front hallway, a giant-screen television was blaring a basketball game and a man was yelling at the televised image. He sprang to his feet when Mark and April entered the room. "Dad, this is April," Mark said.

He held out his hand and April clasped it. "Been looking forward to this." He pumped her arm vigorously. "Hey, ladies," he yelled. "They're here."

From another room three women emerged, one older with graying hair, wiping her hands on an apron. They hovered around Mark and April, all talking at once, all hugging one another. April learned that the older woman was Rosa, Mark's mother. The others were his sisters, Marnie and Jill. Mark's mother took both of April's hands and beamed her a smile. "Let me get a good look at you. Oh, Mark, you didn't lie. She's beautiful."

April felt her cheeks flame and cast Mark a sidelong look. "Don't smother her," he said with a laugh. "And don't scare her off." He slid his arm around April's waist. "She's not used to being pounced on, you know."

April joined in the laughter with the others, although she felt a bit overwhelmed by his family. "What exactly did you tell them about me?" she whispered to him as Mark's mother led them all to the dining room table.

"Nothing," he insisted innocently.

She sat beside Mark and watched him take

his medication. Her mouth felt parched and she took a sip of water. She wondered if this was a side effect of her radiation.

Platters of food were passed and conversation flowed like water. It was different from meals at her house, but it was fun listening to them talk and joke with one another. She answered questions politely and wondered how much they knew about her, how much Mark might have told them.

"So, Mark," Marnie asked. "You racing next weekend?"

Instantly, April felt tension close around the table like a fist.

"Yeah," he said nonchalantly. "I'm running the Dodge."

"Why?" his mother asked bluntly. "You know it's not good for you."

"Ma, please." He gave her a look and then cut his eyes toward April. "I have a guest. Let's not argue."

"It makes me crazy," his mother insisted, ignoring Mark's plea. "You shouldn't be breathing in all those fumes."

"Ma, please—"

"Leave the kid alone, Rosa," Mark's father said.

"You know you don't approve," Rosa told him. "Why pretend in front of company?"

"Who's pretending? All I'm saying is now isn't the time to bring this up."

"And when should I? When he's in the hospital?"

April felt caught in the cross fire.

Mark pushed back from the table. "Ma, we got to go."

"I just want you to think about the consequences," his mother declared. "Please, Mark, you're barely out of the hospital. Why tempt fate?"

But Mark ignored her and headed for the front door. "I'm out of here," he called over his shoulder.

April hastily wadded her napkin and stood. "Um-m-m . . . thanks for the dinner. It was delicious."

"And thank you for coming," Mark's father said, standing. "Sorry things kind of deteriorated."

"Yes, sorry," Rosa said. "You're a lovely girl. You take good care of my Mark. And try and talk some sense into him. Maybe he'll listen to you."

April bolted from the room, through the front door, and down the steps. She saw Mark halfway up the street. "Wait!" she called.

He stopped and when she caught up with him, she was angry. "What do you think you're doing? Were you going to leave me there?"

He looked miserable. "I just had to get away. I go nuts when they start in on me about my racing."

"Well, they have a point, you know. You have a disease that seriously affects your breathing. Not to mention that speeding cars can be hazardous to your health in general." She was mad. Mad at the way a perfectly fine day had soured. Mad at the way Mark was acting. Mad at herself for caring about what happened to him.

He grabbed her by the shoulders, his eyes fierce with determination. "But it's *my* life!" he exclaimed. "It belongs to *me,* Mark Gianni. You of all people should understand that."

And suddenly, she did understand it. Racing cars was something he could control. Cystic fibrosis was something he couldn't. And neither was brain cancer. Tears filled her eyes.

Mark pulled her to him, crushing her against his chest. He put his finger beneath her chin and tilted her face upward. Their lips met and he kissed her longingly. "I'm sorry, April. I'm sorry. Please give me another chance."

8

The feel of Mark's lips against hers left April breathless. His impassioned plea shocked her. She hadn't anticipated feeling such a strong emotional reaction to him, and she stepped away. "I'm not going to desert you just because you ran off and left me stranded with your parents."

He looked shaken but relieved. "I didn't mean to leave you alone in there, but I had no idea Mom was going to get on her soapbox in front of you. I thought she knew better than to embarrass me like that."

"Parents don't need excuses," April told him. "I think hospitals give out instruction books on 'how to embarrass your kid' when they send parents home with their babies.

Then, no matter what your age, they open the book and drag out some gem, use it in front of your friends, and make you wish you could fade into the floor."

He grinned. "Your parents have done this to you too?"

"I could write a book, but why bother? They'd only embarrass me with it."

His grin broadened. "Thanks for understanding. Sorry if your dinner got ruined."

"It's okay. Who needs the calories?"

He brushed his hand along her cheek, causing a tingle to shoot up her spine. "I've never had a girl like you in my life before. I don't want you to go away."

They started walking along the sidewalk, and he led her into a small café. They sat at a table in the back and ordered two cappuccinos. They didn't speak right away, but stared out the window at the gathering gloom of the evening and at the lights coming on across the street. When the cappuccinos came, he stirred his, stopped, and reached across the table to take her hand. He held it lightly, rubbing his thumb across her knuckles. "If you're right about parents getting 'embarrassment' handbooks, then girls must get 'cruelty' ones."

"How can you say that? It isn't true." She attempted to pull her hand away, but he wouldn't let go.

"Hear me out. Please."

She nodded. "I'm listening."

"I've always been sick, April. I was born with CF, I grew up with CF. I will die with CF." She shuddered but didn't interrupt. "When a person's sick, especially with a disease that's never going to go away, he learns some tough lessons. He learns that other kids always treat him differently. Sometimes they even call him names, make fun of him."

"You were teased because you had CF?" She couldn't imagine it.

"Yeah. Kids can be that way, you know. If they don't understand, if they're afraid, they shun you. Not everybody . . . but most. Grade school was really rough. I was in and out of the hospital so much and I coughed and smelled like medicine. I couldn't play sports, and I was skinny, and nobody wanted to be my friend."

She wondered if she'd ever treated anybody that way, then remembered her first reaction to Mark. She hadn't even wanted to get to know him because *if he was in the hospital, he must be sick.* She sat very still, hoping she wouldn't have to confess she'd felt that way.

"Do you know what the cruelest thing is about being different?" he asked.

She shook her head.

"While your body is all tied up with sickness, your mind and feelings aren't. You still want all the same things that 'regular' people have. You still want to be liked. You still want friends and to be invited to places and, when you're older, to ask a girl out and not have her act all embarrassed . . . or worse, horrified. All through high school I wanted to date. I wanted to kiss a girl. I wanted to have a girlfriend. Look at me: I'm twenty-one years old and I've never heard a girl tell me 'I love you.' "

She didn't know what to say. His pain was real.

"There were times when I realized that I could *live* with my CF—if only I didn't have to *live* with my feelings. Why couldn't CF have taken my emotions away, instead of my breath?"

"I'm sorry for every mean word that was said to you," April told him. "I'm sorry for every girl who hurt you and rejected you."

He shrugged sheepishly. "This isn't a pity party. Honest. The *last* thing I want is for you to feel sorry for me, April. I can't help the way I feel about you. I wanted to date you the first time I laid eyes on you. But I also knew that getting a girl like you to date me was a long-shot. So everything we've done together so far is beyond my expectations."

She felt her face grow warm. She hadn't encouraged him, and now she felt bad about it.

"I knew I was taking a chance at your blowing me off, but I had to try. I wanted to see you as much as you'd let me. Being with you today has been terrific."

His honesty unnerved her. She'd dated Chris for four months and he'd never once been so open with her about his thoughts and feelings. Looking at Mark, seeing his vulnerability in his eyes, twisted her insides. How could anyone have treated him cruelly? How could *she*?

"I do know what it's like to be sick, Mark. I didn't have to live with it like you did, but I have to live with it now. Believe me, it isn't any easier when it happens to you after you've grown up some and had a 'normal' life. I've been afraid of my friends finding out. Only a couple know." Her gaze fell to the coffee in her cup, which looked cold and unappetizing. She felt Mark squeeze her hand and she lifted her gaze and saw his face, compassionate and tender. A lump lodged in her throat. She didn't want to bawl. "My boyfriend," she said, "can't deal with what's happening to me. He's backed off so far, I'd have to fax him to get a message to him."

Mark chuckled. "His loss."

"But it's my problem." She toyed with the ends of her long red hair. "The doctor marked me up with a blue pen and every day I go into this room and they shut the door and shoot me full of radiation. Not very romantic, is it?"

"They only zap the tumor," he said.

"So what? I'm . . . different now. And as you know, different isn't always appreciated."

Mark's grip on her hand tightened. "If you will let me, I'll do everything possible to make you happy again."

"Happy." She said the word without emotion. "It's been so long since I've felt happy, I don't remember what it feels like."

"Let me try. All I want is a chance, April. Is that too much to ask?"

She didn't answer him, because she couldn't. His health was even more fragile than hers. How could she tell him she was frightened of taking a chance?

She resumed radiation treatments on Monday, resigning herself to another week of balancing her life between her regular high-school grind and medical necessity. She had stopped all her after-school activities and, except for Kelli, steered clear of most of her friends. She knew they knew about her problem. There was no way it could be kept a secret, but at least no one bugged her about it, or asked stupid questions like "How are you feeling?" or "Does it hurt?" She was positive that it was Kelli who kept everyone off her back, and she was grateful to her friend.

Mark called her nightly and they talked for hours. One night he told her, "I'm racing this Saturday night. Will you come watch?"

She was hesitant but curious about his passion for racing cars.

"My dad will be there," Mark said. "He's always been my biggest fan. You can sit with him and I'll get you a pass so you can come onto the infield."

April knew that saying yes would mean a shift in their relationship. "If I come, will you win?"

"If you come, I've already won."

She took a deep breath and agreed to go.

On Friday afternoon, as she was leaving school, she ran into Chris in the parking lot. He had his arm around a pretty junior named Hallie, but lowered it when he saw April. She turned on her brightest smile. "How's it going?"

"Fine," he said. "How are things with you?"

Hallie shifted awkwardly, looking as if she'd been caught doing something naughty.

"Couldn't be better."

"That's good."

"I hear you're leading the soccer team to all kinds of wins."

"I'm having a good season."

"And the rumor about you getting an athletic scholarship to Virginia, is that true?"

"It's been offered. I'll probably take it. It's a full ride."

April felt a twinge of jealousy that he was able to make college plans. "I know you'll do well wherever you go."

"And you? You pick a college yet?"

"Not yet," she said smoothly. "Sometimes a person's plans are forced to change."

For an instant, sadness filled his eyes, and . . . hurt? "I'm sorry."

And she saw that he meant it. "Don't worry about it. I'm going to make it through this, and my friends will help me."

His cheeks colored and she knew she'd made her point—he hadn't been much of a friend to her. But there was no way to let him know that in the long run, his abandonment had been the best thing for her. Otherwise she would not have made room for Mark. She slipped the key into the lock of her car door, knowing that if she didn't hurry, she'd be late for radiation. "Got to run," she called, pulling open the door. "Have a good life, Chris."

As she drove off, she saw Chris and Hallie in her rearview mirror. Their arms were linked around each other's waist. April wanted to feel something—remorse, anger, sadness. She and Chris were history. And she felt nothing at all.

9

"Is it always so loud?" April shouted, not certain Mark could hear her over the roar of engine noise from cars warming up around the speedway track. Nighttime blanketed the sky, and artificial lights obscured the stars.

"It's beautiful music," Mark shouted back with a grin. "Come on." He led her around the exterior of the half-mile track and inside the inner field where cars were parked, surrounded by men in jeans and overalls, most smudged with grease and oil. "The crews are car fanatics," he said. "Each pit has a few people who help out. Drivers are usually the cars' owners. No one gets paid."

"You do this for free?"

"For bragging rights and some prize

money. We're pretty small-time, just a group of local car lovers. Of course, the really big races are driven by professionals on two- or three-mile tracks. I'll take you to one sometime."

April smiled. Mark seemed so excited by the whole business. His brown eyes fairly danced and he looked animated and energized. "How long do you race? Is it year-round?"

"Our season is from May until the snow flies. Tonight's for running cars in my car's class. Other nights, other kinds of cars run: dragsters, which are supermodified cars—the 'funny' ones, are over there on the straight track and the late-model stocks here on the oval. This is my first race this year, but I've got a good car and I expect to kick some butt tonight."

April met several of Mark's racing friends. She could barely hear their names above the din of the motors. Mark's car was a Chevelle, unpainted except for a coat of rust-colored primer. The hood was up and she saw a massive engine laced with wires and hoses. The smell of gasoline and exhaust made her eyes water and she wondered how Mark was able to breathe when even she was having trouble.

"How do you manage not to go deaf?" she shouted.

"These will help." He handed her a set of ear protectors that looked like the kind airplane mechanics wore. Putting them on muffled the noise considerably.

His father materialized from the side of the field. "You can sit with me," he yelled.

"I need a token," Mark told her as she started off with his dad.

"A token?"

"Something of yours to bring me luck."

"Gee, I don't know what I've got." She fumbled for some item and settled on the scarf she was wearing. It was an expensive one, given to her by her parents. "Is this okay?"

He grinned and wrapped it around his upper arm into a band, letting the tails flutter. He took her by the shoulders and planted a kiss on her mouth, shouting, "For *better* luck! See you in the winner's circle."

The noise wasn't as loud in the grandstands, which were already crowded with onlookers. "I didn't think so many people were into racing," she told Mark's father.

"It's a whole subculture. A lot of people love hot rods."

"Your wife didn't come?"

"Rosa's still mad because he's racing. It takes her half a season to get over it. Once she does, she comes. I like to come because it's good to see Mark doing something he loves and doing it well."

"Does he win a lot?"

"He's got bookcases full of trophies at his place. Didn't he show them to you?"

"Not yet."

"Well, he was never one to brag. And once a race is over, he forgets about it. He's looking ahead to the next one."

She could tell that Mark's father was proud of him but at the same time worried about him. "His mom's right, isn't she? Racing is hard on his CF."

"It isn't good for it. One whole season he wore a special mask around the track. But Rosa doesn't understand that the kid's got to have something to call his own. That his whole life can't revolve around CF—even though it does."

"I'm happy you support him," April said. "I know it means a lot to him."

He shrugged. "He's my son. I love him."

The racing began, and Mark's father explained that it was done in heats—the top finishers from each heat became the competitors in the final race of the night. The winner of the final heat would take home the prize money and trophy. Mark would race in the third of seven heats, and if he won that, he'd run in the last. The cars were beginning to accelerate around the track in anticipation of the green go-ahead flag dropping and starting their heat. April realized she was growing used to the roar, so she slipped the hearing protectors partway off.

"This is it," she shouted when the cars rolled out for the start of Mark's race. Mark's primer-coated Chevelle looked intimidating on the asphalt oval. She dug her nails into her palms when the starter flag dropped and the cars shot out of their slots, jockeying for position. It didn't take Mark long to push his car to the front of the pack. April let out a whoop when he crossed under the checkered flag in first place. "He made *that* look easy!" she exclaimed.

His father grinned proudly. "He usually does."

For the rest of the evening, she fidgeted in her seat, watching with keen interest the winners of the following heats. By the final race she was squirming. "This is it," she declared as the winners of all the heats took to the track.

"Guess you're becoming a racing fan," Mark's father said with a wink.

"It's loud and smelly, but it's fun."

"True," he said. "And Mark loves it."

April held her breath as the green flag dropped and the cars roared forward. This time, Mark maneuvered quickly behind the lead car, hugging its back bumper. "What's he doing? Why doesn't he go around him?" she yelled.

"He's drafting," Mark's father explained above the whine of the engines. "He's letting the other car slice through the air to pull him along. It cuts down on his car's wind drag. Then, if it's timed just right and he can maneuver past him, the other driver can't do anything but eat his exhaust."

She watched, wide-eyed, as the cars rounded the final turn and roared down the stretch. At seemingly the last moment before the checkered flag dropped, Mark gunned his accelerator and flung his car around his opponent, crossing the finish line just a bumper ahead. The fans went wild. "He won!" April screamed, jumping up and down.

"Let's get to the winner's circle." Mark's father took her arm and pulled her down the steps and through an infield gate, where he showed his badge once more. In the winner's area, Mark's car stopped rolling. He switched off the motor and climbed out. Everyone applauded and she heard shouts of "Good driving!" and "Way to go!"

Mark tugged off his helmet, his smile brighter than the artificial lights over the field, and waved. But his gaze found April in the crowd instantly. She threw herself into his arms and kissed him wildly. "You were wonderful! I'm totally impressed."

He handed her the trophy. "This one's yours."

"I can't keep your trophy!"

"Sure you can." He unwrapped her scarf from his arm, looped it around the back of her neck, and pulled her against him. "You brought me luck."

"You didn't need me or my token tonight," she insisted.

He looked into her eyes, and for a moment the noise of the crowd faded. "You're wrong, April," he said. Her heart hammered crazily. "I need you more than you'll ever know."

10

After her first month of radiation, April returned to the city to meet with Dr. Sorenson. Her mother went with her and, after the routine exam, took her out for lunch and shopping. "I wish he'd told us something," her mother said as they settled into velvet-covered chairs at the restaurant.

"He did," April replied, nibbling on a bread stick. "He said there wasn't anything to tell us yet." Until her radiation therapy was completed, the tumor couldn't be measured, nor could she be given a prognosis report. To April's way of thinking, the visit had been a colossal waste of time. And with only three weeks until graduation, she'd have rather been spending the time at school.

Her mother studied the menu. "Nothing looks good to me. How about you?"

"I don't have much of an appetite. I think the treatments are affecting my taste buds. Everything tastes funny. Sort of dull."

"You should have said something to the doctor."

"It's normal, Mother," April said, although she didn't really think anything about cancer radiation was *normal*.

"You'll get through this, honey," her mother said sympathetically. She lowered her menu. "Oh, by the way, the Stevenses are having a dinner party Saturday evening and they've invited all of us."

The Stevenses were her parents' oldest and best friends, and April usually enjoyed attending their parties. "I can't. Mark's racing this Saturday and I'm going to cheer for him."

"You're certainly spending a lot of time with him."

April felt her radar go up. "And so what if I am?"

"You aren't dating the boys you used to date anymore."

"The boys I used to date are pretty juvenile, Mom."

"They were fine before."

"You mean before I got a brain tumor. They really can't relate to me anymore. High-school guys were fine until I got sick. Now they seem immature."

"But they're teenagers, April. Mark is a young man. What does he see in a girl your age?"

"Oh, thanks, Mother," April said sarcastically. "Maybe he actually *likes* me."

"You know what I mean." Her mother looked flustered, and bright spots of color appeared in her cheeks. "It merely seems odd that he's interested in dating someone four years younger than he is."

"Four years is nothing."

"Maybe you should give the boys from school another chance. Maybe you simply haven't found the right one."

Irritated, April declared, "Maybe I *have* found the right one. I care about Mark. And I'm not going to stop seeing him." Mark had come to mean a lot to her.

"Don't put words in my mouth. I didn't ask you to stop seeing him. I only questioned his motives."

"His motives?"

"Well, I wasn't born yesterday," her mother said in exasperation. "I know that young men don't always have pure and noble intentions."

"Are you saying you don't trust him? Or worse, that you don't trust me?"

"Of course I trust you. I've always trusted you. But you're . . . well . . . vulnerable now. You just said so."

April slumped back into her chair. "I can't believe we're having this conversation. I can't believe you're prying into my life."

"I'm not prying. I'm only making an observation."

"It hurts my feelings that you think Mark's an opportunist. He isn't after anything. He cares about me, and I don't think you should look for ulterior motives. It isn't fair."

April's mother sighed. "I don't want to fight with you, honey. I know what you're going through isn't easy. It isn't easy for your father and me either. You're our only child. A child we'd once given up hope of ever having. I think what's happened to you is one of life's cruelest tricks."

"You feel tricked? How?"

"I'm no stranger to problems, April. I'm

not naive enough to think that anybody goes through life without bumps and lumps. But after all we went through to conceive you, I thought the worst was over." Her mother shook her head. "Your father and I wanted you so badly and when we got you, we believed that you were a gift from heaven."

"Do you wish you never had me?"

"How can you even ask such a thing? You mean everything to us and we're so proud of you. I hate seeing you suffer. I'd give anything if it were me instead of you."

"But it *is* happening to me. I hate radiation. I hate knowing that something horrible is growing inside my head. It scares me."

"I'm scared too," her mother said quietly.

"And that's where Mark comes in," April added. "He makes me happy. He makes me feel less afraid. He makes me feel—" she started to say "loved" but stopped herself. *Love* was such a strong word. She wasn't sure that was how she felt about him yet. "He just makes me feel good about myself," she finished lamely.

"Then I won't hassle you about him. Because I want to see you happy."

Looking into her mother's eyes, April reconnected with the strong bond that had always existed between them. It had always been just the three of them, tightly knit with one another—Hugh and Janice and April—sometimes not knowing where one left off and the other began. Certainly she'd felt smothered by them occasionally. And she'd gone through phases of feeling awkward and embarrassed around them with her friends. But she had never defied them, or resented them, or wished she'd had other parents.

But something was happening between her and Mark. Something she couldn't explain but could only feel. Like a ship drifting away from a dock, her parents were diminishing in importance in her life. Her parents couldn't go with her. It was a journey she had to make without them.

"Don't these things look dorky?"

Kelli stood with April in April's bedroom, staring into a full-length mirror. They were both dressed in their caps and gowns. Graduation was only a week away.

"Pretty dorky," April agreed.

"So where are Armani and Chanel when you need them? Why haven't they tackled this fashion-design problem? I mean, anybody can create a dress or a suit, but a fashionable cap and gown—now, *that's* a challenge."

April chuckled. "These do make us look like cows, don't they?" She lifted the hem of her gown.

"And these hats! Why don't we just wear waffles on our heads? Then at least we could eat them after the ceremony."

April unzipped the navy blue gown and tossed it aside. "You know we have to go through with it. My father's already got the camcorder battery charged and reservations for dinner in the city."

"You aren't coming to Blair's party?" Kelli sounded disappointed.

"No."

"But why? It's going to be a blast."

"I don't mean to be a drag, Kelli, but I'm still not up to speed yet." April had completed radiation and it had left her feeling drained and tired. Now she wanted to rest and reorganize her life. And be with Mark. But she hesitated to say that to Kelli. "I feel as if I've missed out on the last six weeks of my life.

And trying to fit back in at a party isn't going to help."

"But everybody's missed you. I thought that once you were finished with your radiation you'd be right back into the swing of things."

"It's not that easy, Kelli." She did feel bad about isolating herself from her old friends, but it had been necessary. Unlike Mark, who'd desperately wanted to belong when he was growing up, April *had* belonged, but now wanted to be apart. She couldn't explain it. She hardly understood it herself. "High school's over. Nothing's going to be the same again anyway, so why should I try and recapture the past?"

"What about the plans we made for this summer? Do you want to chuck them too?"

"What plans?"

Kelli looked hurt. "The beach plans. When you missed the ski trip, you said you'd like to take a beach trip with the gang."

April thought about the beach, the warm sand and lapping waves. She *did* want to go. "I want to hit the beach."

Kelli's face broke into a grin. "I'll plan everything. I'll get the group together and we'll pick a week and find a place down the coast. I hear the beaches in North Carolina are fabulous. Why don't I check it out?"

"Go right ahead," April said with a smile. Her parents wouldn't object to her going. They knew her school friends and how much she enjoyed the ocean. And she figured that Mark wouldn't mind either. After all, it was only for a week.

But with a start she realized that there was one more person who had to okay her plans. Her doctor would have to give his permission too. Radiation might be over, but she still wasn't free to take charge of her future. It troubled her. The tiny blob at the base of her skull controlled her choices. And that was the most disturbing thing of all.

11

"Happy graduation, honey. Here's a little something from your mom and me." April's father opened a manila envelope and spread a handful of colorful travel brochures across the restaurant tablecloth.

"You're giving me brochures?" she teased. "How original, Daddy." The graduation ceremony was over. April had been one of three students in her class who received top academic honors. She had sent her college applications late, so she didn't know yet where she'd gotten in. But her academic honors, along with her high SAT scores, would improve her chances for entry into several elite schools.

"Not brochures," her father declared, "but a gateway to the world."

She studied the assortment. Greece, Hawaii, Italy, Japan, and China made an exotic fan on the tablecloth. He was offering her a trip to anywhere in the world she wanted to go. "I don't know what to say."

"Just pick your spot. I mean it, sweetheart. I'll take a month off and away we'll go," her father urged.

"How about a cruise to the Greek isles?" April's mother joined in.

"Or the Galápagos Islands," her father suggested. "Wouldn't you like to see the place that inspired Darwin to formulate his theory of evolution?"

"Hold it. We can't all just take off for a month. What about your job, Dad? And Mom, what about the store? What would Caroline say?"

"She's perfectly capable of running the store without me. And any place we go can be a potential treasure trove for the antique store. Why, a month hardly seems long enough. Why not longer?"

April shook her head. "Stop. Please. I appreciate the offer, but I don't want to go away right now. If I go anywhere, it'll be to the beach with my friends."

"But, honey, this is such a wonderful opportunity," said her mother. "You can do both."

"No, I can't."

"But we've always had such a good time on trips," her father interjected. "I thought it would be our last big vacation before you pack off to college."

But it wasn't college that April was thinking about. It was leaving Mark for a month. When they'd spoken on the phone the night before, he had sounded hoarse and wheezy. "Just a cold," he'd said, but she knew that for him a cold could turn into pneumonia. How could she leave him when the slightest complication could land him in the hospital? How could she expect to have a good time when she didn't know if he'd be well from day to day? The beach trip was local. She could return quickly if he had problems. If she was halfway around the world, it wouldn't be so easy.

"Can't we save the trip?"

"But why? You've always liked traveling with us before." Her mother sounded hurt.

"And I still do. Just not right now. It's my

final summer before college. I'd like to hang around, get reacquainted with my friends. The last few months haven't exactly been the most normal time of my life, you know."

Her parents exchanged glances; then her father said, "We don't want to pressure you into anything, April. We only thought an extended vacation would be a good way for you to put those months behind you."

"And," her mother added, "a way for us all to spend time together without the distractions of everyday life."

April couldn't help wondering how much her affection for Mark was entering into their decision. "I don't want to go." She shook her head stubbornly. "Not now. Maybe some other time."

"But—" her mother started.

Hugh Lancaster put a restraining hand on his wife's arm. "We can talk about it later. Tonight is supposed to be a celebration. Let's just have fun." He raised a glass of champagne in a toast. "To you, April. We're very proud of you."

"Yes, darling," her mother said. *"Very* proud."

April smiled at them, happy that the question of traveling with them could be set aside for the time being. Tomorrow night she'd be with Mark. *Mark.* The person who became more important to her with each passing day. The one person she wanted to be with more than any other.

Mark took her to the tiny Italian restaurant in his neighborhood that April had come to think of as their place. It wasn't fancy, but the food was delicious and the booths were encircled by red curtains, so they could be together in privacy. "Are you sure you feel up to eating out?" April asked.

"I'm doing better," Mark told her. "I'm on antibiotics and my respiratory therapist has been keeping a close watch on me. I'm going to be fine." He grinned, but she wasn't convinced.

"I'm not sure I believe you."

"Do you want me to prove it?"

"Right here in the restaurant?"

"The curtains are closed. We're alone."

"How can you?"

He reached into his coat pocket and pulled

out a red balloon. "Want to watch me blow this up?"

She stared. "Are you kidding?"

"Do I look like I'm kidding?" He took the balloon and gave a few puffs. It swelled, but April could see the effort it was costing him. She wanted to tell him to stop. It was painful watching him huff and puff to fill the balloon with his precious breath. But she knew she couldn't stop him. He was proving something to both of them, and she knew she must wait and watch and keep her mouth shut. At last, he tied the balloon and handed it over. "Told you I could do it."

Gold lettering on the balloon spelled out HAPPY GRADUATION, APRIL. A lump rose in her throat. "You couldn't have just bought me a card?"

He smiled, his face still flushed. "I made it in my uncle's print shop. Are you impressed?"

"Totally." She tied the balloon to the strap of her purse.

He reached for her hand. "After dinner, I have something else for you. It's a surprise."

April begged him to tell her what he was planning, but he wouldn't. She ate quickly, and when the meal was over they walked to his apartment, several blocks away. The summer city night felt steamy, and lights shone brightly from store windows. April had never been to Mark's apartment, and she was curious to see where he lived.

"My roommate's out," Mark said, unlocking the door. "I told him to make a night of it."

April's heart began to beat faster as he led her inside. The place was small and stuffy; an aging air conditioner struggled against the New York summer night. "Where's your room?"

He gestured toward a closed door.

"Can I see it?"

"It's a mess."

"But you're still going to let me see it."

"Maybe later. We've got a date up on the roof right now."

"We can go up there in a minute. I want to see your room first." He didn't budge. Slowly she said, "Come on, Mark. What's the big deal about me seeing your room?"

"My room . . . I told you, it's a mess."

"So what? My room's a mess too."

"Because it may scare you off."

"Is there a dead body in it?"

He laughed without humor. "Hardly."

"Then show me."

He led her to the door and opened it, and she stepped into his private world. At first glance, the room was ordinary. There were a bed, a dresser, a desk, and posters of beautiful racing cars on the walls. But she also saw that the top of his dresser was lined with medicine bottles. And there was a portable oxygen tank tucked into a corner near his bed. The odor of medicine hung in the air. "Welcome to my world," he said. "Just like everybody else's. Except for the CF."

She walked around it slowly. The number of medicine bottles stunned her, but she tried not to show it. She stopped in front of his desk, where a computer sat beside a pile of books, most of them about medicine. "I didn't know you were planning on going to medical school," she said.

"I'm not. But I study everything I can about my condition. I surf the Net looking for information too. I have friends in cyberspace. You know what's really nice about cyberspace?" April shook her head. "No one can see you. So everybody's equal. People only know you by your signon name."

"What's yours?"

"Speedman."

She chuckled. "Sounds like a superhero."

He stepped closer to her. "I'm no superhero. If I were, I'd be free of CF. You might say it's my personal form of kryptonite." He took her hand. "All this medicine just keeps me going."

"I'm glad you showed it to me."

"I had to."

"But why? You could have hidden the bottles."

"My mother cornered me last time I went to dinner. She said that if I cared about you—really cared—I should give you the total picture. Not just the fun stuff."

"We met in the hospital, remember? I already know you've got medical problems."

"More than problems, April. A lifelong condition. Barring some medical miracle, I'll never be well."

"Have you forgotten that I have a medical problem of my own?"

"I don't think of you as sick. It's possible for you to get well. Not me."

April swallowed hard. She knew it was true. "Why did you pick tonight to tell me all this? You must have a reason."

Mark's gaze never left her face. "Because I'm in love with you, April. And before we go any further, I need to know how you feel about me."

12

April's heart pounded and her mouth went dry. Mark loved her. Other boys had whispered those words to her, but always in the heat of passion, when they wanted to go further physically than she'd allow them. But Mark had said "I love you" in the cool light of reason. "I—I don't know what to say."

"Tell me how you feel."

"I feel like I need to sit down."

He searched her face. "Come to the roof with me. I've got something special up there for you."

They rode an elevator to the top floor, then trudged up a stairwell, their footfalls echoing behind them. April's head spun with the bombshell Mark had delivered. He loved her.

How did she feel? She knew she cared about him. But love? She wasn't sure.

He led her out onto the flat blacktopped roof above the city. Up there the air was cooler and the sound of the streets muffled. In the center of the roof, resting on a remnant of carpet, stood a table and two chairs. The table was draped with a cloth, and on top sat two candles, which Mark quickly lit. A small package wrapped in foil caught the candlelight and sparkled. Mark pulled out a chair for her.

A vase filled with roses scented the night air and stars twinkled overhead in a black velvet sky, like tiny jewels. A bouquet of balloons, all imprinted with the same message as the one Mark had given her earlier, was tied to her chair.

"You did all this for me?"

He just smiled.

She pointed to the balloons. "You didn't blow up all those, did you?"

"My uncle has a helium tank." Mark's grin was quick. "But thanks for thinking I could."

"Everything's perfect, Mark. Thank you."

"How can you say that? You haven't even opened your gift yet."

She fingered the small box. "You went to so much trouble."

"You're worth it."

With trembling fingers, she tore off the paper and lifted the lid of the box. Inside, on soft white cotton, lay a gold chain and a heart-shaped pendant—or rather half of a heart. The edges were jagged, as if the goldsmith had snapped it in two. Her name was engraved on the broken piece, the *i* in *April* dotted with a diamond chip.

Pulling his chair next to hers, Mark fished his key chain from his pocket. "Here's the other half," he said. On the chain, along with keys to his car, apartment, and garage, she saw the second half of the pendant, engraved with his name. Slowly he slid the two pieces together so that they fit neatly to form a complete golden heart. "Now it's perfect," he said. "Two halves equal one heart. That's how I feel about us. I was just half a person until you came along."

Too moved to speak, afraid her voice would break, April stared at the glittering jewelry. She had no words to tell Mark how much his gesture meant. He'd made her feel more special than any person had ever made her feel. Mark took the chain, drew it around her neck, and clasped it firmly in place.

He turned April to face him. "It looks just right on you."

She put her arms around his neck and buried her face in the hollow of his throat. The beat of her heart accelerated, and she knew that her next words would forever shape the course of their relationship. She knew that if she said them, she must *mean* them with all her heart. She pulled back and peered up at him. Candlelight played across the planes of his face, twinkling in his beautiful brown eyes. "Downstairs, you asked me how I felt about you. I can tell you now. Not because you've given me the sweetest, nicest gift I've ever received, but because I've been thinking about it for a long time."

She took a deep breath. "I love you, Mark. I never expected to, I never even wanted to. But I do."

His arms tightened around her, and she felt his warm breath on her neck. "I don't want you to think that telling me this makes me expect anything more from you."

"What do you mean?"

He held her at arm's length. "Just knowing you love me is its own reward. It's more than I ever hoped for."

She was confused. What was he trying to tell her? "Are you saying that hearing me say 'I love you' is all you want from me?"

"If I had my way, tonight would be the beginning for us. But I know you have plans, April. I know that you want to go to college and do other things with your life. It isn't fair for me to expect more."

That was true. She *did* want to go to college. She *did* want to pursue a career. And she still had a tumor growing inside her head. "How can telling you 'I love you' change my plans? Can't I still go to college and love you? Can't I still have a career and love you?"

"Once you get out in the world, your feelings for me may change."

"That can go both ways. What about your feelings for me?"

"My feelings for you are set in stone. They could never change. I'm just trying to let you know that I love you without strings attached."

"What kind of strings?"

He studied her for a long moment, and she

realized that he was struggling with what he wanted to say. From the street, she heard the wail of an ambulance pierce the night, and suddenly she knew what he wanted to tell her. "You don't want me to feel any obligation to you if you get really sick," she said slowly. "You want me to feel free to walk away."

He nodded. "That's exactly right. I have no right to ask anything from you. Not when I'm facing my particular future."

She never took her gaze from his face. "Don't you know, Mark? Love is a free gift. I can give it to you *if* I want to, *when* I want to, under *any* circumstances I want to." He stared at her, as if she might evaporate and float away. "Don't you believe me?" she asked.

He answered her by sweeping her into his arms and kissing her with an intensity that left her breathless.

"Your necklace is beautiful. Mark must be crazy about you," Kelli remarked.

April fingered the pendant around her neck. They were sunning themselves by the pool in April's yard. She'd already told Kelli about the romantic way Mark had given her his gift, without going into detail about his pledge of love for her. And now, days later, she still felt astounded. "He certainly surprised me with it."

"I'm glad it's him instead of Chris. I never thought Chris was the right one for you."

April rose on her elbows. "You never told me that before."

"You broke up with him, so I was never forced to tell you." Kelli dipped her hand into the water and swirled her fingers lazily. "I got an acceptance letter from the University of Oregon yesterday. It's my dad's alma mater, so it looks like that's where I'll be going."

"That's a long way off."

Kelli sighed. "I know. I won't get home except for Christmas and summer, but going so far away might be the best thing for me. At least I won't have to listen to my parents arguing all the time." Kelli had been unhappy at home for years. "It seems funny to be making plans that don't include each other."

"Yeah, I know. I mean, we've been in school together since the sixth grade. And now . . ." April let her sentence trail.

"How about you? You pick a college yet?"

April had received acceptance letters from

three colleges that week. "I've pretty much decided on Northwestern—it's outside of Chicago. They have top-notch journalism and broadcast schools."

"Chicago's where I'll have to change planes when I'm going to or coming from Oregon. Maybe you can meet me at the airport some-time."

"Maybe." April concentrated on the lap-ping sound of the water, suddenly saddened over the idea of her and Kelli's being so far apart. She slathered on more sunscreen, and the coconut scent reminded her of the beach. "By the way, how are things shaping up for our beach trip?"

"Not too good." Kelli sighed. "Cindy and Beth Ann took off for the summer. And Ashleigh is leaving this Friday to stay with her father and stepmother in Dallas."

"You're kidding! Except for you and me, there's no one left to go."

"They couldn't change their plans."

The news disappointed April, but what had she expected? "I guess when I became a her-mit they wrote me off. I guess I can't blame them."

"We can still go," Kelli offered. "But if we

do, it has to be soon. Dad's decided he wants to drive me and my stuff cross-country and visit some of his old friends on the way." Kelli rolled her eyes. "The university wants freshmen there early for orientation. We're leaving New York August first."

"But that's only six weeks away!" April cried in dismay.

"I know, but what can I do? Hey, how about this weekend? We could drive up the coast and find a comfy hotel on the water for a couple of days."

I have to go for outpatient testing with Dr. Sorenson on Friday, April thought, then asked, "How about during the week? The beaches would be less crowded then anyway."

"Sorry, I can't. Mom's dragging me shopping for clothes and dorm stuff."

April had to do the same things herself. She was excited about going, but also apprehensive. Chicago seemed very far from everything she knew and loved. And if the truth were known, she really didn't want to leave Mark. "So I guess the beach is out."

"How about July fourth weekend?"

"I can't. Mark is driving in a special race."

"Oh," Kelli said, sounding disappointed.

So the long-anticipated beach trip with her friends was out. April told herself not to act disappointed. She stretched out, resumed listening to the gently slapping water, and thought about the few weeks she had left with Mark. It wasn't going to be easy to leave him, but she was certain of her feelings for him. She loved him. And he loved her. Nothing else really mattered.

13

"**D**ad, you didn't have to come today. Mom and I can handle a visit to the doctor by ourselves." April and her parents were in Dr. Sorenson's waiting room at the hospital.

"No way," her father said, balancing his laptop computer on his knees. "I only have to answer some e-mail and do a spreadsheet for one client, so there's not much work to do. Besides I want to take my two favorite women out to dinner when this is over."

April's mother reached over and squeezed his hand, and April realized that he'd really come to lend moral support to his wife, which only made April feel more apprehensive. Did they suspect that the doctor was going to give them bad news? "It's going to be a long, boring day," April said.

"Hey, it's better than being cooped up in the office all day," he said brightly.

Mark had wanted to come also, but she'd told him not to. Her parents still weren't enthusiastic about her relationship with Mark. And to be honest, she had enough on her mind at the moment without dealing with any tension between Mark and her parents.

A nurse ushered them into an examination room. Dr. Sorenson said hello and began to write orders for her day of testing—blood work, X rays, CAT scan. "Will you be able to tell us anything today?" April asked.

He shook his head. "I'll have to evaluate the results and confer with my colleagues. Then we'll set up an appointment and go over everything with you."

"But how do you *think* I'm doing?" she pressed. "You must have some idea."

"I think you look terrific," he said with one of his professional smiles. "And you aren't having any more headaches, are you?"

"No, but—"

"Then let's wait until the results come in."

After a long day of tedious testing, her father took them to a Thai restaurant. April ate without tasting her food and pretended to be having a better time than she was. She didn't want to disappoint her parents, who kept saying, "No news is good news," and "I'm sure this is all behind us." She was glad when the evening was over and she was home again. She phoned Mark immediately.

"How long do you have to wait for the results?" he asked.

"Who knows? Maybe a week."

"Then stop thinking about it. Think about my big race. Think about you and me in the winner's circle. Think about all those new clothes you're going to buy for college. Think about how much fun we're going to have when I come visit you at Northwestern."

"All right, all right, enough," she said with a laugh. "I get the point: Think happy thoughts."

"It works for me. No matter how lousy I feel, I think of you and my whole day improves."

"You say the nicest things."

"Just the truth, and nothing but the truth."

On Monday April and her mother went into

the city and toured the big department stores, buying clothes for college. They also shopped for dorm-room accessories—comforter, sheets, towels, study lamp—everything the "Welcome Freshman" letter she'd received from the registrar suggested. With every purchase, she felt a mounting excitement. In two months she'd be settling into a brand-new life, and except for missing Mark, she was looking forward to it.

She had her mother drop her off at Mark's afterward. "He'll bring me home," she said.

Her mother peered up at the aging apartment building. "Are you sure this place is safe?"

"Of course it's safe. Everybody can't live in Woodmere," April said, naming their exclusive Long Island suburb.

Her mother insisted on coming up with her. They took the elevator to Mark's floor and rang the bell. When the door opened, Mark stood there in his bare feet. He looked flushed and his breath sounded raspy. "You're early," he said, clearing his throat.

Feeling her mother eyeing him, April asked, "Is it okay? We can come back later."

"Come in. Randy was just finishing up my therapy."

Randy sauntered out of Mark's bedroom and gave April a cheerful smile. "I'm out of here." He turned to Mark. "See you later, man."

"What therapy?" April's mother asked once the three of them were alone.

"Respiratory," Mark said. "To break up . . . well . . . to help me breathe better. My lungs get clogged. Want some iced tea?"

"No, thank you." She gazed around the apartment, and April could tell she wasn't overly impressed. "How long have you been living here?"

"Two years. It's not permanent. I have plans to move to a better place."

April's mother walked to the makeshift bookshelves across the room. She stood examining Mark's racing trophies. "It looks as if you've won a lot of races."

"Well . . . a few."

April stepped in front of her mother before she could go back to giving Mark the third degree. "Aren't you supposed to meet Dad for supper?"

"What about your supper?"

"I'm cooking," Mark said with a disarming grin. "I'm not a bad cook. My Mom's Italian and I learned from her."

April could see that her mother was hesitant. April promised to be home before midnight and nearly pushed her mother out the door.

"I don't think she was happy about leaving you here," Mark said when he and April were alone.

"She knows I come here a lot. Today shouldn't make any difference."

"But this is the first time she's seen my place. I don't think she likes it. I can't blame her. You deserve better."

"Get real! Mom's just being Mom. Frowning and disapproving is her natural state." April tried to joke about it.

Mark didn't seem to believe her. "I wish things were different. I wish I had more to offer you."

"What do you mean? What would you offer me?"

He shrugged. "Forget it. You'll be out of here soon and I'll be just a memory."

"Please don't say that."

"Look, I'm sorry. I don't mean to be such a downer. Let's get into the kitchen and see what I can put together. I promised your mother I'd feed you, and I will. I really am a good cook."

She caught his arm. "I'd rather do something else instead."

"What?"

She took a deep breath. "I've been thinking about it for a while, and now seems like the best time to bring it up. You've shut me out of your CF world, Mark."

"What do you mean?"

"I want to learn how to do your thumps. Just like Randy does."

Mark shook his head. "No."

"Why not? I want to learn. I want to help. I hate having to end our evenings early because Randy has to pound your back. Or get a late start because he has to work on you first. I can learn, Mark. I can do it for you and—"

"No!" His tone was firm and sharp. "That's not what I want from you, April. I don't want you to be my nurse."

"You tell me you love me, but you won't let me share this with you. That's not fair." She heard her voice rising. "If we love each other, then you should let me into this part of you. It's a big part, Mark."

He looked away from her. "The answer is no. I don't want you to see me that way."

"But I saw you in the hospital."

"Not the same thing."

"But—"

He took her by her shoulders, pulled her against his chest, wrapped his arms around her, and held her so tightly she could scarcely breathe. "Please, April. Please understand. I love you too much to fight with you. Just don't ask this of me. My therapy is not something I want you to do for me. I want you to love me, not nurse me."

She didn't want to be shut out of any part of his life but decided against arguing with him about it just now. He wanted to spare her, shield her from his fragility. But his stubbornness was driving a wedge between them, and she couldn't make him see it. "I love you, Mark," she whispered. "And nothing's going to change that. Nothing."

Three days later, Dr. Sorenson called April and her parents into his office for a conference. He shuffled papers, steepled his fingers, and studied them across the expanse of his cluttered desk. April knew right away the news wasn't good.

"We aren't seeing the kind of progress that we'd hoped to see in reducing the tumor," he said. A fluorescent bulb buzzed noisily overhead, reminding April of a fly trapped on window glass.

"What does that mean?" Her father asked cautiously. Her mother sat tense and white-lipped.

"It hasn't shrunk appreciably."

"You mean I went through all those weeks of radiation and it didn't help?" April felt numb and detached, as if she were discussing some other person.

"That is correct."

"So I still can't have the gamma knife surgery?"

"Very few neurosurgeons would attempt such a surgery. It's not just the size of the tumor. It's the placement—its growth around the brain stem and cerebellum."

"But I want it out! I want it gone!"

Her mother gripped her hand until April's fingers ached. "What if you did the surgery anyway?" her mother asked.

"We could paralyze her. Or even kill her."

Her father cleared his throat. "All right, you've made your point. So, tell us, where do we go from here? More radiation?"

"Radiation didn't work, and because she also had radiation as a child, we can't put her through that protocol again."

"Then what?" April had to clench her teeth to talk, afraid they would chatter because she was shaking all over.

"The tumor is dormant right now, and it could remain so."

"For how long?"

Dr. Sorenson shook his head. "I don't know. I wish I had better news for you."

He was being purposely evasive and it frightened April. "I'm supposed to go away to college. I've been accepted to Northwestern."

"You don't have to change your plans. Chicago has fine neurologists, and I can get you the name of someone to take over your case."

"No." April stood. *"You* just want to be rid of me because *you* can't fix me."

Dr. Sorenson's face reddened. "That's not true, April."

She turned to her parents, who looked ashen. "I don't have anything left to say to this man. Except, thanks for nothing!" She spun on her heel and stalked from the room.

14

April ran out of the hospital, hailed a cab, and gave the driver Mark's address. She knew his schedule by heart now and was sure he'd be at home. She needed to see him. *Had* to see him. Tears blurred her eyes, and she felt as if a hundred-pound weight were pressing on her chest.

At his apartment, she rang the doorbell. She fidgeted on his doorstep until he opened the door. "April!"

"Mark . . ." April's voice quivered as she tried to tell him what had happened at the doctor's office.

"Come in, honey. Tell me what's going on." Inside, he settled beside her on the couch. "Your doctor didn't give you good news, did he?"

Too choked with emotion to speak, April shook her head. Mark held her close while she cried and sputtered out her story bit by bit. "I'm no better, Mark. No better at all," she finished. "Nothing they did for me has helped."

"Maybe you didn't hang around long enough to hear everything your doctor had to say."

"The expression on his face said it all. He didn't give me any hope because there isn't any."

She watched Mark's eyes fill with tears. "I won't accept that. I won't lose you."

"Aren't we the perfect couple?" she whispered. "You think you have no future, but I don't seem to have one either."

He grabbed her shoulders. "Stop that kind of talk! You don't know your future. The radiation could have damaged the tumor and stopped its growth. It may never flare up again. You may live to be ninety."

April's thoughts were reeling. Deep down, she'd assumed that modern medicine would fix her as it had the first time. That the radiation would have shrunk the tumor enough for surgical removal. She hadn't been prepared to hear that it hadn't worked. "What am I going to do?"

"You don't have to make plans for the rest of your life right this minute. You just have to get through the next minute and then the one after that. That's how I do it."

April realized that every time Mark got sick, he stood at the very crossroads where she now stood. He wondered if he would ever have a tomorrow, ever make plans for a future. Yet he never seemed depressed. He'd shown her that life could be good in spite of bleak medical problems. Mark was strong in a way that April saw she too must be. She couldn't give up. She wouldn't. She took a deep breath. "I feel like I'm going to explode."

"That feeling I can help you with," he said, smoothing her hair. "When things look really bad for me, I drive fast."

"Aren't there laws about speeding?"

"Only if they catch you."

He drove her in his aqua and white Chevy onto the interstate and out into the countryside, turning off onto side roads and finally stopping on what looked like a deserted airstrip. Weeds grew out of the cracked concrete. Mark shut off the engine and turned to her. "This is where I learned to drive. The surface is still decent."

"What do you want me to do?"

"Take the wheel."

"Me? You want me to drive your car?"

"Drive her fast."

"But I can't—"

"Sure you can."

He got out of the car. "Come on, switch places with me." April slid over into the driver's seat, and Mark got into the passenger's seat. She switched on the engine. It rumbled, low and velvety. She let the clutch out slowly and the car eased forward. It felt like a racehorse coiled and waiting to sprint. She pressed on the gas pedal, felt the car lurch, and glanced at Mark. He grinned.

She pulled out onto what had once been a runway. She shifted gears and felt the car gather speed. She shifted again and pushed the pedal lower. Forty, sixty, seventy—the speedometer's needle climbed. She gripped the wheel with both hands, braking as she came to the end of one runway and turning onto another.

Eighty, ninety . . . the speedometer inched higher. The field on either side of the strip became a streaking blur. Her fear faded. She thought of nothing except pushing the car faster. It was pure exhilaration. The engine roared. The needle hit 100, but then a curve forced her to brake and send the needle downward into the 70s.

As she pushed the car along the crisscrossing surfaces of long, deserted runways, her mind emptied of her troubles. Nothing else mattered but the speeding car. Every nerve ending was focused on keeping the car going fast. The tires hit breaks in the concrete, making the car vibrate and making her hold on tighter. And push harder. Finally, exhausted, she slowed, downshifted, and braked.

Her knuckles were white. She'd been gripping the wheel so hard that she'd lost all sensation in her hands. Perspiration poured off her face and neck. Breathing hard, she leaned back against the leather upholstery. The roar in her ears went quiet, so quiet she thought she'd gone deaf. During the drive, she'd forgotten everything. The brain tumor. The doctor's bleak report. Her plans for college. Her family, her friends, even Mark. It all had melted into the white blur of speed and heat and the sound of a racing engine and the smell of gasoline. She turned toward Mark.

His face was awash in afternoon sunlight. He was smiling, and his dark brown eyes danced. "Now you know why I do it."

Later, as he drove her home, April's fear returned. Where had she gotten the nerve to drive so fast? What if she'd crashed? Wrecked his car? She might have killed both herself and Mark! Yet she had tempted fate. And she'd won. She was still alive. She smiled and caught sight of her reflection in the glass window. She looked disheveled but glowing. Mark had given this to her. He had understood exactly what she'd needed to once again feel in control of her life.

It was almost dark when she made him drop her off at the top of her driveway. "Go on home," she said. "I have to face my parents by myself."

"I'll go with you."

She stroked his arm. "This is my battle. I'll call you later."

When she walked through the door, her parents threw themselves at her. "Where have you been? We've been worried sick about you!"

"I went to see Mark."

"Mark! You left us sitting there in the doctor's office. We didn't know where you'd gone, what had happened to you."

"Don't ever do that to us again, April," her father growled.

"I'm sorry I worried you," April said, feeling guilty. "I guess I just figured you'd realize where I'd gone."

"No," her mother said, shrilly. "We didn't realize."

"I said I was sorry." She glanced at them, seeing their anxiety but feeling annoyed. "I'm not a child, you know. I'm almost eighteen."

"You're *our* child." Her father's voice rose. "And I don't care how old you get, we'll always be concerned about you. We all heard some pretty jolting news today. Don't you think we were affected by it too?"

"Yes." She felt tears stinging her eyes, but she didn't want to break down and cry. The exhilaration of the drive was evaporating, and she couldn't hold on to it when her parents kept jerking her back into their reality. "I said I was sorry."

Her father's scowl lessened, and he took her into his arms. "We love you, April. And I don't want you to think for a minute that what the doctor said today is the final word. There are other doctors, other treatment centers. I've placed some calls to European facilities. They don't have to deal with the FDA, so sometimes their treatment techniques and medical protocols aren't as rigid as ours over here."

No! April thought. She didn't want to spend months trekking all over the globe looking for some elusive cure when all that she loved and cared about was right here. "Well, Dr. Sorenson did say that the tumor was dormant now. I think that's a good sign . . . don't you?"

"I do," her mother said. "I think we have to concentrate on the positive aspects."

Her father stepped away, raked his hands

through his graying hair, and said, "Of course we will. I just don't want April to feel as if she's been robbed of hope."

"I still have hope," she assured him. "I see how Mark makes it through a day at a time. And that inspires me. I'll make it through that way too."

"And about college—"

"Not now." April interrupted her mother. "I can't think about that now."

Her father left the room, and her mother sat with her on the sofa. They sat quietly, with only the ticking of the grandfather clock across the room breaking the silence. The tension of the day overcame April, and suddenly she felt exhausted. She put her head back and closed her eyes.

"You really like this boy, don't you?"

April tensed. "I thought we already talked about Mark and me."

"But your feelings for him have deepened, haven't they?"

April heard a melancholy note in her mother's words, and April wondered what she was expected to say. "I like him." She took a deep breath, knowing it was time to be completely truthful. "Actually, I love him."

"*Love*'s a serious word. I've never heard you use it with anybody except family."

"I've never felt this way about anybody else before."

"April, don't—"

"No, Mom, *you* don't." April struggled to her feet. "You don't know what I'm feeling. But I do, so please don't lecture me about my emotions. My whole life changed today. I don't know what it means yet, but I just know things aren't going to move along the way you, Dad, and I had planned them. I need time to think. I need space. And right now, Mark's the only person in the world who understands me."

Without waiting for her mother to reply, April darted from the room and ran up the stairs and into her bedroom, where she threw herself across her bed and wept bitterly.

15

It took April three weeks to decide that she wasn't going to go away to college. Dr. Sorenson's analysis of her case had dashed many of her dreams and ambitions. She knew her parents were relieved because they hadn't wanted her to be far away, but they were also upset because college had been in their plans for her ever since she was born. "We'll find someplace local," her father said. "Good heavens, we live in New York, there are plenty of choices."

"Sure," April said, forcing herself to sound cheery. "Maybe I'll take a few courses—you know, the things every freshman has to take, and then transfer somewhere in January."

Ever since April's argument with her

mother, her parents had been walking on eggshells around her. They had nothing more to say about Mark, which helped her feel less boxed in and defensive, but she knew they'd discussed it between themselves many times. Just as long as they left her alone, she didn't care what they talked about.

On the morning when Kelli was leaving with her father to drive out to Oregon, April showed up in her friend's driveway. They stood beside the trailer hooked to the back of Kelli's father's car, waiting for him to finish up details inside the house. April eyed the trailer solemnly. "I'll bet it's full."

"To the brim. I didn't realize how much of my stuff I wanted to take with me."

"You are planning on coming back, aren't you?"

Kelli cast a furtive glance toward her house. "If I have a place to come back to."

"Are things that bad?"

"I think Dad's using this trip as an excuse to check out his options." April didn't know what to say, but Kelli changed the subject. "I'm going to miss you."

"Same here."

"You are going to be all right, aren't you?"

"As all right as I can be under the circumstances." When she'd first told Kelli about her visit to Dr. Sorenson, her friend had burst into tears, and it had been April who'd ended up comforting Kelli instead of the other way around.

"At least you have Mark," Kelli said. "I'm glad you do."

"Me too. At least some part of my life is perfect."

The front door opened and Kelli's father came out, juggling a Thermos of coffee and a set of road maps. Kelli's mother was right behind him. April waited while Kelli hugged her mother goodbye. Then she hugged her friend. "You write me," Kelli said. Tears brimmed in her eyes.

"I will. You write too." April sniffed. Saying goodbye was harder than she'd imagined.

Kelli climbed into the car, and April called, "See you at Christmas." A lump rose in April's throat. She was supposed to be going away too, and for the first time it struck her how completely her life had changed. She stepped back and stood shoulder to shoulder with Kelli's mother, watching the car and trailer pull slowly out of the driveway and out of her life.

Over the next several weeks, April said goodbye to many of her friends and watched them head off to college, while she enrolled in only two classes at NYU. Freshman orientation was a bewildering maze that left her tired and short-tempered, but Mark picked her up afterward and took her to their favorite little restaurant, where he soothed her with a plate of linguine and a chocolate torte. "Feel better?" he asked as she finished the meal.

"Much. But if I continue to eat like this, you'll have to get a tow truck to drive me around."

He smiled. "I'd love you even if you grew another head."

"I'll keep it in mind." He'd been unusually quiet. "Want to tell me what's bothering you?"

"What makes you think something's bothering me?"

"Isn't something?"

He shrugged, looked sheepish, and said, "I guess I've been thinking about you starting classes. And about all the new guys you'll be meeting."

"Oh, sure. Right. I'm having to beat them off with a stick already."

"I'm serious, April. You're beautiful, and it won't be long before some guy notices and asks you out."

Half exasperated, she said, "So what's your point? Do you want me to say yes?"

"Of course not. But I don't want you to feel obligated to me either."

Completely exasperated now, she snapped, "Is that what you think of me? That I date you because I feel obligated? That's idiotic, Mark! And insulting. Especially after all we've been through together."

"Don't be mad."

"I don't know what else to be. You're really upsetting me."

He rested his elbows on the table and leaned toward her. "That is the last thing I ever wanted to do. I don't know why I'm acting like such a jerk. Forgive me. Okay?"

She couldn't stay angry with him, but she didn't want to let him off too easily either. "So, will you please get over your problem already? I don't know how else to show you I care about you. About us. I don't know what else I can say."

He studied her intently. "All right. Fair enough. I won't question your feelings again." He paused, stared at her thoughtfully, then asked, "Do you believe in love at first sight? I do. And the first time I looked up and saw you across that hospital waiting room, I was dazzled. I know that must sound stupid, but it's the truth. When my grandmother was alive, she used to tell me that every time God creates a soul in heaven, he creates another to be its special mate. And that once we're born, we begin our search for our soul mate, the one person who's the perfect fit for our mind and body. The lucky ones find each other."

Moved, she reached across the table and took his hand. "Mark, I know that we have a place in each other's lives. And no matter what happens, I will never forget you. And I will never feel quite the same way about anybody else again. You are my first—no—you are my *only* love."

His eyes filled with tears and, embarrassed, he glanced away. When he spoke, his voice was gruff. "Come on, let's get out of here. I want to hold you and kiss you and if I do it here—well, we may have to find another restaurant to call ours."

She stood with him, and arm in arm they walked to the cashier, paid, and walked out into the moonlight.

On September fourth Mark turned twenty-two, and his parents threw a family birthday party. Their small house was filled with aunts, uncles, and cousins. Mark's mother cooked platters of food along with several desserts, including an enormous cake that sat in the center of the dining room table. Balloons, trailing long ribbons, floated against the ceiling, and a birthday banner stretched from one side of the dining room to the other. "Having a good time?" Mark yelled to April above the noise of the celebration.

"Terrific!" she answered. When it came time to open presents, she sat on the floor by his feet handing him gifts from a large pile on a nearby table. She held her gift back, waiting until most of the others were opened. Finally she pushed the giant, beautifully wrapped box toward him.

"Open it," April urged, anxious for Mark to see her present.

He ripped off the wrapping paper, reached into the box, and pulled out a complete racing suit made of a flame-retardant fabric. The silvery white material of the coveralls, helmet, and gloves caught the light as he held them up. His jaw dropped. "This is awesome." He stared down at her. "These things cost a fortune!"

"You're worth it," she said, satisfied with his reaction and knowing she'd caught him totally off-guard.

Mark jumped up and held the outfit for all to see. "Look at this! It's the best stuff made for racing today."

She grinned, but stopped grinning when she saw the expression on Mark's mother's face. She was not smiling. She was not one bit impressed with April's gift. April realized that she had only been thinking of what Mark would like when she'd chosen the gift. She'd forgotten how his mother might react.

Later, when April was helping to stack dishes in the kitchen, Rosa said to her, "I know what you gave Mark cost a great deal of money."

"The money isn't important. I picked something that I knew he'd like. I know you don't approve of his racing, but the suit will make it safer. I mean, I worry about him too. I'm sorry if it upset you."

Rosa studied April. "I realize Mark's a grown man. And I know how much his racing means to him. I'm not trying to be an over-protective mother, but put yourself in my place. When he was diagnosed with CF as a little boy, his doctor told us that he probably wouldn't live beyond his sixteenth birthday."

April sucked in her breath. "Really?"

"I never dreamed he'd see twenty-two. Every year now is a special gift from God. What upsets me about the racing is that every time he goes out on that track, he's flirting with death."

"He's a good driver."

"I know he is. But why court disaster? It scares me to watch him drive. That's why I stopped going to the track to watch him. When he began dating you, I thought he might give up the racing."

"I don't think that's going to happen," April replied. "I think the racing sort of balances out the CF in his mind. He can't change his medical condition, but he can affect how fast he pushes his car. Pushing the car to its limit makes him feel in control."

"You're right. But I can't . . ." Mark's mother's voice trailed off, and April could see that the conversation was making Mrs. Gianni very emotional.

"I understand," April told her. "But for him, it's worth the risk. And neither of us really has the right to rob him of that sense of power."

Rosa slipped a pile of dishes into a sinkful of water. "Life never balances out, April. At best, it simply lets you coast along with the illusion of control. At worst, it wrenches control from you totally and then you have to decide how you're going to deal with it."

"Well, I think Mark deals with it by not giving up. And by making plans and acting on them."

"And you?" Rosa asked. "How do you deal with it?"

April knew that Mark's family was aware of her medical problems. She replied, "One day at a time. Mark taught me that."

"You're a lovely girl, April, but you've lived a very privileged life. Mark hasn't."

April was taken aback. "Privilege doesn't make a difference when you get sick, Mrs. Gianni. Or when you get diagnosed with a brain tumor. And all the money in the world can't make either thing go away. So Mark and I are more alike than we are different."

Rosa was about to reply, but the kitchen door swung open and a group of relatives entered, chattering and carrying plates and leftover food. April never knew what Mark's mother might have said, but she did get the impression that it wouldn't have been approving. And she wondered why, after all these months, his mother seemed against April being with her only son.

16

"What were you and my mother talking about in the kitchen?" Mark fumbled with the key to his apartment, his arms heaped with birthday gifts. "I stuck my head into the kitchen and saw that she had you cornered."

April unlocked the door for him. "Girl talk. Nothing important."

"That's hard to believe. She was trying to make you pressure me to give up racing, wasn't she?" He switched on a table lamp, and soft light filled the room.

"It's no secret that she'd rather you didn't race. What's that?" She pointed to an enormous box perched in the middle of the sofa.

"Why don't you check it out?"

She read the tag. "It's for me. And it's from

you." He grinned mischievously. "Why would I get a present? It's *your* birthday."

"Haven't you heard? It's better to give than to receive."

"What are you up to, Mark Gianni?"

"Guess you'll have to open it to find out."

She bounced onto the sofa and studied the box. "Your box for me is bigger than my box for you. Did you get me a racing suit too?" She tore off the outer wrapping, opened the flaps of the box, and discovered—another wrapped box. "What's this?"

He shrugged. "I guess you'll have to keep unwrapping."

Intrigued, she tore off the next box's layer of paper. Inside she found another box. "You're driving me crazy! Is that what you want? A crazy girl on your hands?"

He laughed. "Boy, you get cranky over the smallest details."

She tossed a wad of wrapping paper at him and ripped open the next box. Inside it was another. And inside that, another still. She unwrapped ten boxes in all, until one very small one lay in the palm of her hand. "I know," she sighed. "It's an Elvis postage stamp, isn't it?"

"Only one way to find out," he replied.

She ripped off the paper and discovered a small black velvet box. But there the game ended. Inside this box, nestled in folds of white satin, lay a gold antique-looking ring with a diamond in its center. She gasped and, wordlessly, turned toward him. Mark had sunk to one knee beside the sofa. He took her hand, and his brown eyes stared directly into hers. "Marry me, April. I love you, and more than anything in the world, I want you to be my wife."

She began to cry.

"I was hoping for a different reaction," he said, looking crestfallen.

A million emotions tumbled through her—love, excitement, awe, joy . . . fear. "Mark, I don't know what to say."

" 'Yes' would be nice. I love you, April. I thought you loved me too."

She cupped his face in her hands. "Of course I love you. And, yes, I will marry you."

His face broke into a grin, and his eyes sparkled. He slid the ring on her finger. The diamond caught the lamplight and twinkled brilliantly. "I know the stone's small, but it once belonged to my grandmother. She left it to me in her will because she always believed that somewhere God had picked out one special girl for me. And she was right."

April blinked back tears. "It's perfect. And I'm honored to wear it."

"I wish she could have known you. She would have loved you too."

April couldn't take her eyes from the glittering stone on her hand. *Engaged!* She was engaged to Mark Gianni.

"When can we get married?" he asked.

"I don't know. There's so much to think about . . . so much to do," she said, still fascinated with the diamond. But in the back of her mind, she knew her parents might not be enthusiastic about her acceptance of Mark's proposal. They would say she was young. That she had four years of college ahead of her. She realized she had a brain tumor that might begin growing once more.

Mark smoothed her hair. "Now that I know you'll marry me, I don't want to wait." He kissed her, long and sweet. Her heart hammered, and she clung to him while visions of herself in a long white wedding gown danced through her head.

The dream ended abruptly the next morning when she told her parents about Mark's proposal. Her mother's face went pale, her father's livid. "You can't be serious!" he said.

April had known they would object. Still, she was determined to marry Mark. "I am serious. What's wrong with us getting married?"

"You're not even eighteen," her father railed. "You're still a child."

She rolled her eyes. "Please. Mom was nineteen when you married her."

"That was different."

Her mother jumped in. "April, how can you think about marrying a man like Mark, who may die at any time?" Her voice was quiet, but it cut through April like a knife.

"Anyone can die at any time," she answered coolly.

"His odds are higher than most and you know it."

"My odds aren't the greatest either," she said. "Or have you forgotten?"

"You're in remission," her father insisted. "And you may remain so forever. And what of your other plans? You just enrolled in college."

"I can be married and still go to college."

"How will he provide for you? He works in a print shop, for heaven's sake. And he plays with cars on the side. Do you know how expensive it is to live in New York? Have you any idea—?"

"Stop it!" She put her hands over her ears. "I won't listen to you tear down Mark another minute." She whirled and ran up the stairs. She threw herself on the bed and seethed. This was supposed to be a happy day. Instead, her parents had turned it into a fight. Why couldn't they be happy for her?

She ignored the soft knock on the door, but her mother came into the room anyway. "I should have locked it," she whispered through clenched teeth. "Go away."

Her mother sat on the bed. "I came to talk, not argue." Her voice was soft, and she sounded weary. "April, I know you think we're being unreasonable, but we honestly have your best interests at heart."

"How can you? I love Mark and you hate him."

"That's simply not true. We like Mark. We just think you're too young to make this kind of commitment. In spite of what you see in bride magazines, once the wedding day is over a couple has to live in reality."

"You're arguing. You told me you wouldn't."

Her mother sighed. "Then let me cut to the chase. Marriage is hard enough without any obstacles. You and Mark have considerable obstacles. Cystic fibrosis is a bad disease and its victims need plenty of care."

"I know what Mark needs." April cut her off. "He needs special medications. He needs therapy. I plan to learn how to do his back and chest thumps. I can handle it."

"It isn't some little thing, like brushing your teeth at night or washing your face every morning. It's serious, life-sustaining business. It means that no matter how tired you are, no matter if you've had a fight and the two of you are angry with each other, no matter what, you have to perform this procedure."

"I can handle it," April said stubbornly. But she knew her mother was right. The responsibility was weighty. "Besides, I'm sure his respiratory therapist won't drop out of Mark's life entirely. He'll still be in the picture."

"There are other things about boys with CF—"

"I don't want to hear about it!"

"Maybe you should talk to his mother. I have."

April jumped off the bed. "You *what?* You've gone to Mark's family behind our backs? I don't believe it! How could you?" Suddenly Rosa's attitude toward April after the birthday party made perfect sense. April's mother had gone to see her. Who knew what her mother may have said?

"Because I love you!" her mother replied. "Because I don't want to see you get in over your head."

"Stop treating me like a baby! I'm old enough to get married if I want to."

"Not without our permission, you're not." Her mother was standing too, and they'd squared off, facing each other.

"I'm going to marry Mark," April said in clipped words. "Whether you and Dad approve or not. I love him and he loves me. We'll get by. I'd rather have your blessing, but I'll do it without if I have to. And if we have to run away to do it, we will. That's a promise."

———

"Engaged!" Kelli squealed over the phone. April had called Kelli in Oregon as soon as her mother had left the bedroom. "That's so awesome!"

"Tell that to my parents," April said.

"They're not glad about it?"

"It's like a war zone around here, although there's a temporary truce right now because they hate upsetting me." April made a face. "I think they're giving me time to 'come to my senses.' But I'm not going to change my mind. Which is one reason I'm calling. If we work this out, will you be my maid of honor?"

Kelli squealed again. "You bet!"

Her enthusiasm warmed April's heart. "So, how's college life?"

"The classes are harder than high school. The campus is huge. And it rains every day."

"But you like it?"

"It's okay. Lots of cute guys around."

April felt a pang of longing. *For what?* she asked herself. Her life was different now; her plans a hundred and eighty degrees from what they'd been even six months before. By the same time a year from now, she'd hopefully be married. No, it wasn't what she—or her parents—had once planned for her. But the new direction pleased her.

"They'll come around," Kelli said across the miles, as if reading April's thoughts. "Your parents will do anything for you, so don't get too bent out of shape. I'm telling you, they'll do this for you too."

17

"I'm sorry this is causing problems between you and your parents. I never meant for that to happen," Mark said.

Late-afternoon sun sparkled on the lake in Central Park, where April and Mark had met after her class at NYU. They sat on a bench, watching geese swim through the sunlit water; the air felt crisp and smelled of autumn. The sky was a brilliant shade of icy blue, and the trees were already tinged with gold and red.

"Kelli thinks they'll come around," April said. She held Mark's hand. "I think she's right. I just wish they'd hurry up about it. I bought one of those bridal books, and there's so much to do before the ceremony. The book says you should start up to a year in advance to plan your wedding."

"A year? I don't want to wait a whole year."

"Neither do I. So I skipped those pages. We can do it in six months, but we need to start now."

"Is it that important to you? I mean, that we have a big wedding?"

"I don't know. I—I just wish Mom and I were planning it together. It would be so much easier. And a whole lot more fun." Weeks after April had announced her intention to marry Mark, her parents still hadn't warmed to the idea. It hurt her to have them act indifferent about it. Her mother had gone off on a fall buying tour for the antique store and her father was busy with a rash of new clients. April couldn't have discussed it with them even if she'd wanted to. A gust of cool wind chilled her, and she edged closer to Mark. "How about your family? How do they really feel about it?" His parents had seemed excited about the news, but she didn't know what they might be saying to Mark behind her back.

"Actually, they're okay about it. Ma's already been to talk to the priest, and as long as we get married in the church, there won't be any problems. But then, the groom's family doesn't have much to do anyway. It's the bride's show."

"There's the rehearsal dinner," she reminded him.

"No problem. Ma's already looking for a place to have it, but you'll have to tell her how many people to plan for."

"See, that's what I mean. There are so many details. I can't even come up with a guest list without my mother's help." Out on the lake the geese rose into the sky, honking and flapping gray and black wings. "Did you know my mother went to talk to yours a few weeks back?"

"Ma told me the other day."

"I can't believe her! She makes me so angry."

"She's just concerned about you."

"Why are you taking her side?"

"I'm not. It's just that I understand. I have CF, April. It's a big deal and she has a right to be concerned."

"I'm tired of everybody's concern," she said peevishly. "I can think and act for myself. I have to learn how to take care of you, you know. I have to learn how to do your thumps."

Mark sighed, rested his forearms on his knees, and stared at the ground. "I know. But it scares me."

"Are you afraid I'll be incompetent?"

"No. I'm afraid you'll be grossed out."

Her irritability vanished, and her heart went out to him. She slid her arm around his waist and rested her cheek against his hunched shoulder. "You could never gross me out. I love you."

He straightened and drew her into his arms. In spite of their heavy jackets, she felt the warmth of his body. "Come home with me tonight. After dinner, Ma will show you what you'll need to know."

"I could learn from Randy," she ventured.

"He'll instruct you too. But we'll start with my mother. She's done it all my life, so she'll be the best teacher."

April nodded. She couldn't admit she was scared, but she was. Could she learn to do his thumps correctly? What if she messed up? She pushed aside her fears. Mark needed her. She wasn't going to let him down. She was going to be his wife.

Overhead, the geese circled in V-formation, honking goodbye forlornly.

That night, April watched Mark's mother pound his chest and then his back with cupped hands and a steady rhythm. Mark coughed and gagged and spit up phlegm. April steeled herself, telling herself that this was a way of life for him and once they were married, it would become her responsibility.

"Now you try it," Rosa directed April.

April cupped her hands and slapped Mark's back.

"Harder," Mark said. "You have to hit harder."

Rosa explained, "You can only hurt him if you don't get the phlegm good and loose. It's got to be broken up and expectorated."

By the time the session was over, perspiration poured off April. Her palms stung and her shoulders ached from leaning over Mark. He straightened, breathing hard, his voice raspy. "That's enough." He went into the bathroom, and April heard him brushing his teeth.

"Are you going to be all right?" Rosa asked.

April reddened. "Sure. Don't worry. I'll get the hang of it."

"It was difficult for me at first too. He was two when he was diagnosed and I had to pound him so hard on the back I was afraid I'd hurt him. At first his father had to hold him down. But he soon got with the program. In a few months, he simply lay down on the pillows for me. He doesn't ever remember another way of life, except to get thumped several times a day." Rosa shook her head. "But when you love your child, you'll do anything for him."

"Was it hard for you when Mark moved out on his own?"

"Very hard. I called him every night for weeks to make sure Randy was doing his job. Mark finally got sick of it and told me to stop. It was difficult, but I did it. Children must grow up. Even sick ones."

April averted her gaze. Her parents loved her too, but they hadn't learned how to let go of her yet. "I wish my parents felt that way."

"They'll change their minds. That day your mother came to talk to me, I could see how much she loved you. She knows that your life with Mark won't be easy, and she doesn't want you to get in over your head."

"But it's my head," April insisted. "I'm sorry if she bothered you."

"She didn't. She was only trying to figure out what you were up against if you married my son. I was honest with her. I told her it wasn't going to be easy, but that I thought you had what it took to deal with Mark's illness."

"You did?" Her compliment pleased April.

"Of course. You're bright and mature. And you know what it is to live with medical uncertainty."

Truthfully, April hadn't thought much about her own problem since the day she'd rushed out of Dr. Sorenson's office. As long as her tumor was dormant, she saw no purpose in dwelling on it. And if it did start growing again, well . . . she figured she'd worry about it at that time. "I really love Mark," she told his mother. "I know a lot of people think we shouldn't get married, but I honestly believe we can make a life for ourselves. Just as long as we're together."

Rosa smiled. "I always knew that it would

take a very special girl to love Mark. When Mark was growing up I lit candles in church every Sunday and prayed that God would find such a girl for him."

April returned Rosa's smile. "I don't know if Mark told you, but my parents went through a lot to conceive me. Mom told me that she's always looked forward to having a grandchild to spoil."

Rosa stiffened, and her eyes grew guarded. "Y-You want children?"

Mark's mother looked visibly upset. April couldn't understand her reaction. "Well . . . sure . . . I guess so." Still, Rosa stared at her silently, and April began to feel unsure of herself. "Oh, not right away, of course. I—I mean, we'd wait awhile. Are you afraid we might pass on bad genes to our kids?"

Before Rosa could answer, Mark walked into the room, and both women turned toward him. "What's wrong?" He glanced anxiously from his mother to April.

"April has just told me she might like to have a child," Rosa said, reproach in her voice.

Mark's face flushed crimson.

"What's wrong?" April asked, suddenly

feeling like a person who'd walked into the middle of a play without knowing her lines.

"I . . . ," Mark began, stopped, then said, "We have to talk."

"Yes," his mother said. "You have to talk. And shame on you, son, for waiting until now to talk to April about this."

"Please," April pleaded. "Will someone please tell me what's going on?"

Rosa said, "I'll leave the two of you alone," and quickly left the room.

With her heart pounding, April stepped closer to Mark, waiting for him to say something.

When he looked at her, pain was etched into his face. "I can't give you babies, April. Not ever."

18

"You don't want children?"

"I didn't say I didn't want them. I said I couldn't have them."

April couldn't grasp what he was trying to tell her. "But why?"

Mark's eyes clouded. "It's the CF. Guys who have CF are sterile. We can never father children."

April felt as if she'd been kicked in the stomach. *How could it?* she wondered. "I didn't know."

He held her eyes with his gaze. "Does it make a difference?"

"I'm not sure," April answered slowly. "Having babies isn't something I've thought a lot about. I mean, my friends and I used to talk about it. Once, one of my friends thought she might be pregnant. It turned out that she wasn't, but it really made me stop and think what it would be like to have a baby."

"Well, you'll never have to worry about an unwanted pregnancy with me. That's for sure." Mark sounded bitter. "But please tell me if it's going to make a difference for us. If children are so important that you no longer want to marry me."

April chose her words carefully. "What bothers me *most* is that you didn't tell me."

"When would I have?"

"When you gave me the ring?"

He gave a short humorless laugh. "Sure. That would have made the night memorable: 'Will you marry me, and oh, by the way, I can't ever have kids.' "

"Mark, once I saw all your medicine bottles, the oxygen tank, all that stuff—well, that might have been a perfect time to have had a heart-to-heart about CF. I asked you to let me learn how to do your thumps, and at first you said no. You've had plenty of chances to talk about it."

"I didn't want to lose you."

"Well, if that was going to break up our

relationship, then we didn't have much going for us, did we?" she asked quietly.

He rubbed his eyes with the heel of his palm, and when he looked at her, he looked ashamed. "I underestimated you, April."

"You've done that a lot."

"I'm sorry."

She felt tears sting her eyes. "I'm sorry too, Mark. I'm sorry you didn't trust me enough to be honest."

He squared his shoulders and hooked his thumbs in the pockets of his jeans. "I never wanted anything as much as I wanted you. The odds are pretty good that you'll outlive me, April." He raised a hand to stop her protest. "No, hear me out. It's the truth and we both know it. I'm not afraid of dying, but there's a lot of living I want to do before death catches up with me. *You* are part of that living. I want you. I have from the first time I saw you. But if having children is a dream of yours, I can't give it to you, no matter how much I want to."

In that moment, April saw her life stretching in front of her without Mark. The image was so bleak, she shuddered. Losing him eventually was inevitable. Nothing could stop it from happening. But she couldn't let him go now, not under any circumstances. With a catch in her voice, she said, "The only thing that's important to me is loving you."

He closed the space between them with a long stride and took her in his arms. "I love you, April. I love you more than anything in this world."

When her mother returned from her trip, April decided she would have to discuss the wedding with her, whether her mother wanted to hear it or not. She wanted her mother's help. She *needed* her mother's help.

So one bright October afternoon, April stopped at the antique store. She opened the door. A bell tinkled delicately and the scent of old furniture, lemon oil, and silver polish hung in the air. She loved the store. When she had been a little girl, she used to go to work with her mother and play among the antique furniture. Tapestries hung on walls alongside gilded sconces. There were expensive Oriental carpets, armoires, richly carved chairs, and old-world furniture that turned the floor space into a wonderful maze. Overhead a series of crystal chandeliers, some more than a hundred years old, evoked images of elegant ballrooms and velvet gowns. Tables were draped with fine lace and crisp linen and held ornate silver bowls, fine English porcelain, and cut crystal vases filled with bouquets of freshly cut flowers.

"April! How nice to see you," Caroline, her mother's partner, called out. "How are you?"

April embraced the slender brown-haired woman. "I'm fine. The shop looks wonderful."

"Thanks to your mother. She's found some positively fabulous Shaker-style furniture. She's in the back inventorying it right now. She tells me you're getting married. Congratulations."

April was surprised that Caroline announced the news so happily. "Thanks."

"I'm so pleased for you. You look around the shop and pick out a gift for yourself. Anything you want." Caroline patted her arm.

Caroline's offer stunned April. She hadn't expected her to be so enthusiastic, especially knowing the way her mother felt. "Thank you! I'll bring Mark some afternoon and we'll choose something together."

"April!" Her mother came out of the store's back room.

"Hi, Mom."

Caroline said, "You two visit and I'll go work on the inventory."

Once they were alone, April's mother asked, "What brings you here?"

"I was doing some wedding dress shopping and thought I'd stop by." She hated that her tone sounded challenging, but she couldn't help it.

"Have you found something you like?"

"Actually, I have. Several, in fact. I need another opinion."

"Would you like mine?"

April held her breath, hoping that she and her mother could come to terms. She didn't like being at odds with her parents. "Yes. I'd like yours very much."

Her mother walked to the back of the store and minutes later returned with her trench coat. "I told Caroline I wouldn't be back today."

"Are you sure?"

Their gazes locked. "My only daughter is getting married soon. I can't let any opportu-

nity go by to help with her wedding." Her
mother hugged April, then held her at arm's
length. Her mother's eyes shimmered.

A lump rose in April's throat. She realized
how much it meant to her to have her
mother's support—even a little. "Thanks,
Mom."

"So do you have any particular dress you'd
like to show me first?" Her mother opened
the door, and the bell sounded its silvery
notes.

"There's one in a shop six blocks away."

"Let's go look at it. Shall I grab us a cab?"

April smiled, looped her arm through her
mother's, and said, "It's a beautiful day. Let's
walk."

Together they headed down the crowded
sidewalk, the crisp October afternoon fairly
crackling around them.

Her parents' unexpected support was a
wonderful and welcome surprise. They threw
themselves wholeheartedly into planning her
wedding. "Can we stick to some kind of a
budget?" April's father asked cautiously.

April and her mother looked at each other
and burst out laughing. "A budget!" her

mother exclaimed. "Oh, really, Hugh, you're so funny. I wouldn't dream of sticking to a budget."

He groaned, and April winked at him, as if to say, *It's okay, Daddy. I won't go crazy on you.*

April's and Mark's parents met to discuss plans and sort through details. April and Mark decided to take them to their favorite restaurant early on the afternoon of Mark's final race for the season. "We'll eat, attack the wedding plans, then we'll all go to the track together," Mark declared.

"I know I can get my parents to go to the track," April told him, "but can you persuade your mother?"

"She's already agreed. She's not turning handsprings, mind you, but she wants to make a good impression on your parents. Refusing to go with the rest of us might be interpreted the wrong way."

So they all arrived at the track together. Mark's father was talkative and beaming; his mother looked nervous. April's parents were curious to see firsthand Mark's obsession with fast cars. Once they were settled in the grandstands, April went down on the infield, where

Mark was climbing into his birthday coveralls. "You look just like a pro," she said, checking him over from head to toe.

"Thanks to you. At least the weather's cooled off. These things are hot." He tucked his helmet under his arm.

"I'm glad you're driving in the first heat. I don't think your mother can stand too much of this."

"Well, if I win, everyone still has to stick around for the finals."

"I'll make sure no one bolts."

He leaned forward and kissed the tip of her nose. "You're one in a million."

"Just remember that when you discover I can't cook."

He untied her scarf and retied it around his arm. "For luck."

She smiled. "See you in the winner's circle."

Back in the stands, April had to shout to be heard above the roar of the cars as they looped the track, waiting for the green flag to drop. She felt a surge of pride as Mark's car nosed a path through the staggered string of starters.

The flag dropped and the cars shot forward. April heard her father shout, "Go for it!"

"It's awesome, huh?" she yelled above the roar of the engines as the cars rocketed around the track. "Keep your eye on Mark and watch how he snakes out the other drivers," she yelled in her mother's ear. "He's really good at this."

She watched expectantly as Mark drafted behind the leader, knowing that in a split second he would floor the accelerator and zip past his opponent. She saw him make his move. But suddenly the lead car swerved. Its engine made a popping sound, and smoke billowed from beneath its hood. She heard Mark's father shout, "The guy's blown an engine!"

She leaped up, watching in horror, as Mark's car clipped the other car's back fender. Mark's car spun out of control, slammed into the retaining wall, flipped, and caught fire.

19

April paced the floor of the emergency room like a caged animal. She couldn't sit still or close her eyes because whenever she did, visions of the past few hours flooded her mind.

She saw Mark's car in flames, men scrambling onto the track with fire extinguishers and then prying open the crumpled door of Mark's car, hauling out his limp body, and a fire-rescue truck speeding him away. Mark had been flown in a helicopter to the huge medical complex in the city, where they all now waited for word of his condition.

With a start, April realized that she'd come full circle—back to the very hospital where Mark had first walked into her room months before and announced, "You're the girl I'm going to marry." Silently she begged, *Please, God, please let him be all right*.

April couldn't stand seeing Mark's mother, sitting ramrod straight in a chair, never moving, not even flinching. All her fears had been realized that night in front of her eyes. And nothing her husband could say brought her any peace. Anything Mr. Gianni said was greeted with a stony silence from Mark's mother that was as impenetrable as a wall. It broke April's heart.

At some point, Mark's sisters arrived in a rush of tears and fell into their mother's arms. Her own parents were troupers, going for coffee and sodas, calling friends and family. "I'll get us a room at a nearby hotel," April's father offered.

April insisted that she wasn't going to leave the hospital, so he'd be wasting his money. And just when she didn't think she would be able to bear the suspense one more minute, a doctor appeared and hustled them into a corner of the waiting room.

"How is he?" Mark's father asked, taking his wife's hand.

April braced herself for the worst.

"He's doing remarkably well," the doctor said, and April felt her knees go weak. "He has a broken foot, three cracked ribs, and first- and second-degree burns on the side of his face and on his left hand. It's very fortunate that he was wearing that flame-retardant suit. It saved his life."

Mark's parents turned to her and she read gratitude in their eyes. Mark was alive! "Can we see him?" April asked.

"I'm having him moved upstairs to a room. He's being sedated so he'll rest more comfortably. You can see him there."

"How soon before we can take him home?" Rosa asked.

"That will be up to the endocrinologist, Dr. Bejar. He'll take over your son's case. Just because Mark's injuries weren't severe doesn't mean he won't need careful monitoring. The suit protected him from burns, but it did little to protect his lungs from smoke inhalation. He's not out of the woods yet."

It was well after midnight before Mark was settled into a room and April and both families could see him. The head of his bed had been raised so that he was semi-upright. The side of his face and his hand were wrapped in gauze and his foot, encased in a soft cast, rested on a pillow. His chest had been wrapped in tape to keep his torso rigid, and an oxygen mask was strapped across his mouth.

His mother and sisters broke down crying. "I'm all right," he told them. "Just banged up. Don't cry." He appeared exhausted and his speaking was laborious, but his gaze kept falling on April.

It seemed like forever before she was alone with him. With her parents waiting in the hall, she leaned over him, slid her arms around him, and rested her head on his shoulder. "I thought I'd lost you," she whispered.

"No . . . such . . . luck," he said with difficulty.

She wiped away the tears sliding down her cheeks. "You need to rest. Dad's forcing me to go to a hotel, but I'll be back first thing in the morning."

"Love you."

She kissed him tenderly. "I love you too. Now get some rest."

He was asleep before she left the room.

By the next day, Mark's color had returned. The oxygen mask had been traded for small oxygen tubes clamped to his nostrils, which allowed him to talk more easily. Still, his voice sounded thick and scratchy to April.

"You gave us all a real scare," she told him after a hug and a kiss.

"Please, I've already heard all about it from my mother."

Rosa had left the room to give Mark and April privacy, but April hadn't been surprised to learn that she'd spent the entire night in the chair by her son's bed. "Are you in any pain?"

"My side's killing me, but don't let my mother know. I told her I feel pretty good. Actually I feel like I was dragged behind my car."

"It was so awful, Mark." April shook her head. The memory still haunted her. "I can't get over the picture of your car overturning and going up in flames."

"Don't think about it. I've called the garage to see how much damage was done to the car. And to get estimates on repairs. It's more work than I can do by myself—"

"You're not really going to race that thing again, are you?"

"I sure am. But not until after we're married. I promise not to do anything to threaten our wedding again." He grinned.

Upset, she cried, "It's not our wedding I worry about, Mark. It's your life!"

"I can't fight about this now."

He coughed deeply and harshly. The sound chilled her. She immediately backed away from her argument. "You're right, this isn't the time to go into this. Just put all your energy into getting well."

He took several labored breaths before he asked, "Have you found a dress yet?"

She jumped at the chance to change the subject. "I think so. It's beautiful, Mark. Kind of simple, but with a long train that's decorated with lace and seed pearls. The store's altering it for me." He nodded and smiled, but she could tell he was weak and tired. "Listen, I'm going to run down to the cafeteria, but I'll be back soon."

He didn't protest, and she hurried into the hall, where she discovered Rosa huddled in a discussion with a dark-haired man in a white lab coat. Rosa introduced April to Dr. Bejar as Mark's fiancée, and the doctor greeted her cordially. "It's good to meet you. I'm sorry it has to be under these conditions."

"How's Mark? I mean how is he *really*?"

Dr. Bejar glanced at Rosa, who gave him a silent nod of assent. Dr. Bejar said, "I'm concerned about his CF. The smoke he inhaled is bad enough, but the broken ribs make it extremely difficult to maintain his daily therapy and break up the congestion."

April hadn't even considered that Mark's broken ribs could be a threat to his health. Suddenly frightened, she asked, "What are you going to do?"

"That's what Mrs. Gianni and I were just discussing. I can insert a drainage tube through his chest and into his lung and increase his decongestant and inhalant medications. I want to keep pneumonia at bay, because frankly, it's a serious risk for him."

Pneumonia. April felt afraid. For Mark. For herself. For all their plans and dreams.

"He's a good doctor," Rosa said once Dr. Bejar had gone. "We trust him completely to do what's best for Mark."

"I just want him to get well."

Rosa touched her April's arm. "Me too, April. Me too."

————

The minor surgery to insert the drainage tube was performed without complications, and Mark was moved into intensive care. April stayed with him as much as the hospital rules allowed and was astounded at how many hospital personnel stopped by to see him once word spread that he was there. Rosa explained, "Mark's been a patient here off and on for many years. These people have come to know him and truly care about him."

Once news got around about Mark, he had a steady stream of visitors—nurses, health care professionals, friends he'd made in the hospital during his frequent stays over the years. April realized that to many of them, Mark was a CF patient who'd, so far, beaten the odds. She only hoped he could do it one more time.

April's mother continued with the wedding plans, partly to give April something else to occupy her mind. When she could pry April away from the hospital, they visited stationery stores and flipped through books of sample invitations. They checked out florists, listening to suggestions for flowers and greenery for the June date April and Mark had chosen. They sampled the wares of bakeries and caterers, and April became entranced by photos of elaborate cakes.

April found herself caught between the dreamworld of a fantasy wedding and the harsh reality of the hospital and sickness. Mark always seemed heartened when she told him about the wedding plans, so she kept working on them. But after he had spent a week in the hospital with no obvious improvement, she began to see his enthusiasm fading and his hope crumbling.

He said, "I'm never going to get out of here."

"Don't talk that way. Of course you will. Dr. Bejar said you shouldn't put a time limit on this stay. Your injuries—"

"Aren't getting better," Mark finished. "I don't want to be pushed down the aisle in a wheelchair, April."

"It's only November. We have months until the wedding." She fingered the chain around her neck, the half of a heart he'd given her. "Besides, my father will strangle you if you break off our engagement."

He managed a half smile. "That will never happen. But if you want to—"

"Stop it!" Her voice was sharp. "I won't

listen to you say those things. I plan to marry you in June, so get used to the idea."

His expression turned grave. "April, I once told you I wasn't afraid of dying. That's a lie. I used to not be scared, but that was before I met you and made all these plans for living. No matter what happens, remember, I love you. And this past spring and summer have been the happiest of my life. All because of you."

"Mark, please, don't give up."

"I can't help it. I know how I feel physically. I know that somehow, this time, it's different."

April tried to change the subject and make him laugh. But Mark was right. That night he developed a fever and pneumonia.

20

"He's on the strongest antibiotic available." Dr. Bejar was updating both families about Mark's condition. "I've ordered a morphine infusion pump too. This way, whenever he's in pain, he can administer a small dose himself."

"But he will get better," April blurted out. "I mean, with this antibiotic, he will get over his pneumonia."

Mark's mother added, "You've always been honest with us, Dr. Bejar. Please don't hold anything back now. We want to know the truth."

The doctor looked serious. "Rosa, his lungs have been badly scarred by years of living with

CF. I can't make any predictions at this time. Let's just take it day by day."

April felt sick to her stomach and didn't dare look at Mark's parents. If she did, she was certain she would crumble. She felt weary, like a swimmer treading water. Her life had been put on hold, and she'd become so caught up in Mark's situation that she felt as if her whole existence revolved around the routine of the hospital. She had dropped her classes at NYU, telling her parents, "I can't concentrate on college."

"How are you feeling?" her mother had asked. "Perhaps you should see Dr. Sorenson. All this stress—"

April had glared at her. "This isn't about me. I'm fine and I don't want Mark thinking about anything except getting well. I'm not leaving this hospital until he does."

After Dr. Bejar left them, April found a quiet corner, took her father's cell phone, and with trembling fingers dialed Kelli's dorm room in Oregon. She'd talked to Kelli twice since Mark's accident, but now more than ever, she wanted to hear her friend's voice. With a three-hour time difference, it wasn't always easy to catch her in but, miraculously, Kelli answered on the second ring. April poured out her story through tears. "He's so sick, Kelli. He's really bad."

"Hey, I have faith in medical science. And besides, I want to be your maid of honor."

She knew Kelli was trying to cheer her up by focusing on the wedding, but it wasn't working. "There isn't going to be any wedding if Mark . . ." She couldn't bring herself to finish the sentence.

"Listen," Kelli said, quickly covering the awkwardness. "I bought myself a beeper. That way you can reach me anytime." She gave April her number.

"I miss you, Kelli. I wish you were here."

"Me too, April. I'd be there in an instant, if I could." April heard tears of regret in her friend's voice. There was nothing Kelli could do, nothing any of them could do except wait. April hung up and returned to the ICU.

The hospital kept several guest rooms for family members of patients in the ICU. April and Rosa moved into one, a cubicle with twin cots, a single dresser, and a bathroom. April's parents kept their hotel suite. Mark's father and sisters stayed at the family house. That way they could be near the hospital.

Mark's breathing became so labored that it hurt April physically to hear him struggle to breathe. Forming words, saying sentences was nearly a superhuman feat, and she tried as much as possible to keep him from speaking. But he struggled valiantly to talk to her, to his family. Every time he saw her, he rasped, "Love . . . you."

After four days on antibiotics, he was no better. April longed to make time stand still, but realized that even if she had the power to make it happen, she didn't have the heart to watch Mark continue to suffer. She took his hand, and when he urged her closer, she bent over his bed, placing her ear near his mouth. "I'm sorry . . . I . . . tried . . . but . . . I can't . . . ," he rasped.

Tears blurred her eyes. "What can I do for you?"

"Live . . . for us. I . . . wish I . . . could have seen you . . . as my bride."

Mark's parents came in his room to be with him, and April went to her father. "Daddy, I need your and Mom's help."

"Anything."

"Please, go get my wedding dress. I know it's not ready yet, but I don't care. Just bring it to me."

April heard the serious tone of her own quavering voice. Her father hugged her quickly and left immediately. Her mother asked, "What can I do?"

"Nothing just now," April told her.

April brooded and paced the floor, overcome with a sense of urgency. Rosa found her and said, "I'm calling our priest, April. I want Mark to have last rites."

April felt icy cold and numb with pain. "I understand," she said.

When her parents returned with a huge box, April took her mother into the tiny room she shared with Mark's mother, and there, she tugged on crinolines, slip, and the gorgeous ivory satin gown. Working hurriedly, her mother tucked and pinned, fitting the dress to April's slim body as best she could. "I have no veil," April moaned as she looked in the mirror.

Her mother left but soon returned with a makeshift wreath of baby's breath and a hastily tied-together bouquet. "I swiped these from every floral arrangement I could get my hands

on." She handed April the bouquet and settled the wreath into her mane of thick red
hair, pinning it securely.

April's hands shook, and she bit her lip hard
to keep tears back. "I can't go into that room
crying," she explained.

Her mother fluffed April's long dress and
through her own tears said, "You look beautiful."

April left the small room. Nurses, lab tech-
nicians, and even office personnel had formed
a line down the corridor. She questioned her
father with her eyes and he shrugged, saying,
"I don't know how word spread, but it did."

She walked toward Mark's cubicle, the ex-
quisite train of the gown sweeping the floor
behind her while the onlookers quietly
watched. "You are perfectly beautiful," said
one of Mark's favorite nurses. "And what
you're doing is wonderful."

At the door, April saw the priest leaning
over Mark, his prayer book open. Her knees
almost buckled. She felt her father take her
arm. "I think it's customary for a bride to be
given away by her father," he said.

Together they entered the room. Startled,
the priest and Mark's parents looked up, and

upon seeing April, Rosa's expression passed from grief to gratitude. They stepped aside, and April moved to the bed. Softly she called Mark's name. She was dry-eyed now, and calm.

She saw his eyelids flutter open, his brown eyes widen, and his mouth turn up in a smile. "Beautiful . . ."

She smiled back, laid aside her bouquet, and took his unbandaged hand. " 'Until death do us part,' " she whispered.

"Until . . . paradise," he answered.

"I love you."

But Mark was beyond hearing.

April passed trancelike through the next few days. At the funeral home viewing, her parents stood on either side of her, supporting her while she stood over Mark's satin-lined casket and looked down at his body. *Not Mark,* she told herself. Only a waxen shell. He wore his racing suit, and April realized how much strength it had taken for Rosa to allow it. Rosary beads were wrapped around his hand, and dangling from a chain around his neck was the half heart he'd carried on his key chain since the day he'd given April hers. She unfastened from her neck the chain that held her matching half of the heart and dropped it into the casket.

The day of the funeral was cold, and the sun played hide-and-seek with the clouds, casting dappled shadows over the cemetery. After the mass at Mark's church, April rode with Mark's family in a black limousine to the graveside, telling herself that it would all be over soon. That she only had to make it one more minute, then the next minute, and then the one after that. Exactly how Mark had taught her to live her life.

Afterward she went to Mark's parents' home, where family and friends gathered to eat and reminisce about Mark. She thought about the first time Mark had brought her here to meet his family. And about the last time for his birthday party.

She returned home with her parents and, once in her room, stripped and crept beneath the covers. There, in the quiet darkness, she called Kelli out in Oregon. "It's over," April said.

"I wanted to be with you so bad."

April could hear that Kelli had been crying. "It's okay, Kelli. You'll be home for Christmas and maybe I'll be better company by then."

"I just want you to be all right."

"I don't know how to be 'all right,' Kelli. Mark was *everything* to me. And now he's gone. Now, I'm alone. All alone."

Darkness as heavy as New York's winter snow settled over April. All around her the city dressed up for the holidays. Store windows bloomed with festive Christmas scenes. Lights, glittery trees, and bell-ringing Santas were everywhere. But April found no joy or peace or comfort in any of it. Wherever she went, wherever she looked, she was bombarded with memories of Mark.

When she went for her checkup with Dr. Sorenson, it took every ounce of strength and courage to walk back inside the hospital. He took X rays and told her, "You're holding your own. The tumor's dormant. If you continue to feel good, I'll see you in three months."

The good news didn't mean anything to her. Her head was all right, but her heart was broken. It wasn't fair.

She went to her father one December afternoon and spread out travel brochures on the desk in front of him. "Daddy, remember these?"

"Yes, from when you graduated."

"Well, now I want to go away. I want us to take that trip you promised."

"Where would you like to go?"

She shrugged. "It doesn't matter. Someplace where it isn't winter."

He pondered her request. "It will take a little time for your mother and me to get things organized here."

"That's fine."

"Are you sure you don't have a destination in mind?"

She shook her head. "You and Mom pick. Just make sure it's warm. I miss the summer, Daddy. I'm so tired of being cold."

21

The villa, nestled high above a cove on a hill on the island of St. Croix in the Virgin Islands, faced the ocean. Cool tropical breezes, fragrant with the aromas of exotic flowers and tangy ocean air, stirred through the wide-open doors and windows. April's bedroom faced west, toward the water, so that the first and last things she saw morning and night were the vivid turquoise waters of the Caribbean and a sweep of blue sky. Sunsets painted the sky coral and red, pink and lavender. Sometimes, when she woke in the middle of the night, moonlight cut a path across the dark face of the sea. Under the spell of the water's eternal beauty, April felt the winter cold inside her slowly begin to thaw.

Surrounding the villa were gardens, lush with thick tropical foliage with wondrous names like hibiscus, bougainvillea, oleander. The house was isolated, the only road to it narrow and winding. Weathered wooden stairs led down from the house to the white sandy cove. April went down to the beach every day, and there she read or simply sat staring out at the sea, remembering. Sometimes she cried. More often, she simply marveled at the way the sound and smell of the island eased the tightness in her chest and soothed the pain in her heart. St. Croix had been the perfect choice.

"I've taken the house for six months," her father had told her while they were still in New York. "And I can get an extension."

"That's so long!" April exclaimed. "How can you and Mom take the time?"

"I told Caroline I'd do some island-hopping and exploring," her mother said with a smile. "Who knows what treasures I'll find?"

April's father insisted, "I can keep in touch with my office via fax, phone, and modem. If I have to go back, I can fly out and be in New York in hours."

April was grateful. She loved St. Croix and

decided that when she felt up to it, she'd go scouting. The island had originally been settled by the Danish. It was twenty-three miles long, with the old city of Christiansted on one end and Frederiksted at the other, and a tropical rain forest between them. St. Croix would have been the perfect place for a honeymoon.

One day April awoke and the sea stretched out glassy calm below her window, the sun sparkled brilliantly, and puffy white clouds floated like cotton candy pillows in the sky. She knew the time had come.

She pulled on shorts and hiking boots and started up the green hill behind the house. The going was rough, but she made it to the top and stood, gazing out at the water, which was dotted with an occasional sailboat. She lifted her face skyward and spun in a circle, her arms flung open as if to hug the breeze. Up on this hill, she felt closer to heaven, and closer to Mark. Remembering her mission, she stopped.

She reached into her pocket, brought out a single red balloon, put it to her lips, and began to puff. Slowly it filled and rounded out. She tied it, reached again into her pocket, and removed a long strand of yellow ribbon. She tied it securely to the balloon and waited for a breeze.

When the breeze blew, soft and balmy from the sea, April flung the balloon upward, shielded her eyes from the sun's glare, and held her breath. She watched as the air current caught it and pulled it upward. Inside the balloon she'd placed her breath, her kiss of life, as Mark had done for her. She wondered if he could see it, sailing toward him in heaven. April watched until it became no more than a red dot, rising ever higher, as if to touch the sun.

For Better, for Worse, Forever

To Flo Conner

He will wipe away every tear from their eyes. There will be no more death or mourning or crying or pain, for the old order of things has passed away. —REVELATION 21:4 (NIV)

1

At the top of the hill, a girl, her red hair gleaming in the sun, stood gazing out at the sea. As she lifted her eyes skyward, she turned and spun in a circle, her arms flung out straight and wide.

She stopped spinning, reached into the pocket of her shorts, and took out a red balloon. She put it to her lips and blew, filling it up so that it rounded out. She tied it off, then reached back into her pocket and pulled out a long thin yellow ribbon. She tied one end securely to the balloon's knotted tail.

As a balmy breeze blew from the sea, she unleashed the ribbon and the balloon flew upward. She shielded her eyes from the glare of the sun and watched as the air current caught the balloon and pulled it so that it rose until it became a tiny red dot lost against the endless blue sky.

Brandon Benedict couldn't believe what he was seeing. A girl—a beautiful girl—with hair so fiery red that it glistened in the sun like sparks from a fire stood shielding her eyes as a red balloon sailed upward into the vibrant blue sky high above the island of St. Croix.

He'd gone hiking alone in the green hills. What an odd thing to discover. She hadn't seen him, so he stayed behind some bushes, out of her line of vision. She appeared to be conducting a private ritual.

Brandon decided not to intrude, but when his heel crushed a dry branch, its loud crack made the girl whirl and catch sight of him. He heard her gasp, then shout, "What do you want?" Her fists were clenched and he thought that she might strike him.

"Nothing."

"Why are you spying on me?"

"I wasn't spying." Her angry gaze bore into him, and he felt defensive.

"Why are you up here?"

He felt his anger rise as he replied, "It's a

free country, you know. I was just out hiking. Sorry if I ruined your day."

Now she looked less angry, more embarrassed. "I thought I was alone."

"And now you will be." He turned and started back down the hill.

"Wait!" she called after him. Her voice was gentler now. "I'm sorry. I didn't mean to yell at you. You just surprised me, that's all."

His irritation vanished and he turned back to her. Her blue eyes were heavy with sadness. He felt it like an electric current. He recognized that sadness. Even now, he could feel the darkness of his own pain, but he shook it off as he smiled. "I'm Brandon Benedict. I live on St. Croix. I hike up in these hills a lot. I had no idea anyone was up here. I didn't mean to scare you."

"My parents have rented that house." She pointed and he saw the white barrel tile of a roof below. "I'm April Lancaster."

"You're renting the Steiner place? I've grown up here. I know most every house and its owners on this side of the island," he explained. "The Steiners were regulars at the Buccaneer Golf Course until Mr. Steiner had a heart attack. They moved back to the

States. I work at the Buccaneer. After school
and during summers, I mean. But I guess I'm
telling you more than you probably want to
know."

She offered a tentative smile. It pleased
him immensely. "It's okay. Actually, we've
been here three weeks and I haven't met a
soul."

"You're kidding! You're so pretty. I—I
mean, all you have to do to meet people
around here is show up in Christiansted." He
waved in the general direction of St. Croix's
largest city. "There's nightlife down there."

The veil dropped over her eyes again. "I'm
not into partying."

He itched to know what would make such
a pretty girl so sad and isolated. "Everything
around here is low-key. Even our parties.
Where did you come from, anyway?"

"New York. Long Island, actually."

"How long will you be staying?"

She shrugged. "As long as it takes."

"As long as what takes?"

"Forget it," she answered quickly, then
added, "we don't have a time limit on our
visit. Maybe until the weather turns horrible."

Brandon laughed. "Then you've got a long visit. It's always beautiful here. Summer can get hot, but that'll be months from now." He came closer and saw that her complexion was the color of cream, with the faintest hue of rose across the bridge of her nose and her cheeks. He realized he was gawking and felt self-conscious. "You need to be careful of the sun. It can fry you, even on cloudy days."

"Thanks for the advice."

He was running out of small talk, but he didn't want to walk away from her. "They say too much sun can cause cancer." She gave him an odd, almost amused look he couldn't read. "You're not afraid of cancer?"

"No." Her answer, low and soft, sounded so final that it made him shiver.

"I'm running off at the mouth," he confessed. "I, um, guess I should be going."

"It was nice to meet you," she said politely.

"Look, if you ever want someone to show you the sights—"

"That's all right. I appreciate it, but I'm not looking for company. Nothing personal," she added hastily.

It struck him that she probably had a boy-friend back in New York. A girl as attractive as April *must* have a boyfriend. "If you change your mind, I'm in the phone book under William Benedict. That's my father."

She shook her head. "I won't change my mind."

Feeling awkward, Brandon turned and jogged downward, skidding on the rough terrain but not looking back until he'd come to the bottom of the hill. Stopping to catch his breath, he turned for a look. She stood, small against the blue sky, looking up. He decided she was searching for the balloon, and he too gazed up. All he could see were puffy clouds and a seagull or two. The balloon was gone. He hoped it had gotten to where she'd wanted it to go. It surprised him when the idea of heaven crossed his mind.

April scanned the brilliant blue sky until the brightness made her eyes water. The balloon was gone. It had been swallowed up. She wished she could still see it. It represented her link with Mark. The red balloon had been her tribute to Mark until the boy had come along and interrupted her. Brandon. Brandon's face was so different from Mark's. Brandon had sun-streaked brown hair and blue eyes; he was tan, muscular, and robust-looking. Mark, who'd had curly dark brown hair and intense deep brown eyes, had been tall and thin, a victim of cystic fibrosis. Mark was dead and nothing could change that awful reality.

She shivered from the memories. Her mother was probably worried about her by now, so April started down toward the villa where gardens teeming with exotic flowers slashed color along the white stucco walls. Her parents, at the breakfast table, looked up, and her mother asked, relief flooding her face, "Out for a walk?"

"Yes. It's a nice morning."

Her father lowered the fax he'd been reading from his office in Manhattan. April couldn't get used to him in Bermuda shorts and flowered shirts; she'd rarely seen him in anything but a suit, back home. "Hi, princess." A smile split his face. "Hungry? Mango and papaya?" He gestured toward a platter of cut-up tropical fruit.

"Maybe later. I'll be in my room."

As her parents exchanged glances, her mother said, "You should eat something."

"I'm not hungry."

She wasn't in her room for five minutes before her mother knocked, came in, and eased onto the bed, where April sat staring out the window at the sea. "Honey, we should talk."

"I don't want to talk."

"We're concerned about you. It's been months since Mark—"

"I know how long it's been. I don't need you to remind me."

Her mother sighed. "We thought that coming to St. Croix would help."

April bit back her irritation. It wasn't her parents' fault. In fact, they'd tried everything to help her feel better. "Coming here has helped," she said earnestly. "If I'd had to stay in New York, I'd have gone crazy."

"But to us it doesn't seem to have helped. You barely eat. You keep to yourself day in and day out. You never want to go anywhere with us. It's a wonderful island, April. We thought we'd go into town tonight and eat at a Danish restaurant in Christiansted. Fine food."

"You and Daddy go. I really don't want to." Why couldn't her mother leave her alone?

"April, it's not only your depression that worries us. We're fearful about your health too. You are feeling all right physically, aren't you? I mean, you aren't experiencing headaches and not telling us, are you?"

April hardly ever thought about her health these days. It seemed as if the headaches, dizzy spells, blackouts, and six weeks of radiation treatments that she'd had to endure because of the brain tumor had never happened. Or at least, hadn't happened to her. She'd been so focused on Mark, so consumed with his hospitalization and, in spite of his imminent death, her commitment to having a wedding that she'd shoved her own problems aside. "Dr. Sorenson told us the tumor was dormant, and I've no reason to think it isn't," April answered truthfully.

"I know what he *said*, but what matters is how you *feel*."

"I feel fine," April insisted through gritted

teeth. "I mean as fine as a person can feel who watched her fiancé die."

"Oh, honey . . ." Her mother reached for her.

April turned away. "Don't. Please. I don't think I can stand one more tear."

That evening her parents went into town for dinner and April moped around the sprawling house. Far out to sea, she saw a storm brewing, the clouds on the horizon gray and angry looking. She fell asleep on the sofa and in her dreams relived the terrible night at the racetrack. In slow motion, she saw Mark's car strike the bumper of the car in front of him. She saw his car spin out of control, hit the retaining wall, and catch fire. She tried to run onto the track, but in her dream, her feet had taken root in the grandstand and all she could do was watch helplessly.

A roar like flames split the night and she screamed Mark's name. Then she bolted upright, and rain was pelting her face. Wind had toppled a lamp and it had broken on the tile floor. Gasping, sobbing, she stumbled off the sofa and struggled against the wind to shut the French doors. By the time she'd closed them, she was soaked, and rainwater had puddled on the floor and stained nearby furniture.

The tropical squall had moved like quicksilver, sending shards of lightning from the sky to the ground, furious in its intensity. She leaned against the door, watching trees and bushes whip in the dark, watching delicate flowers rip from branches and smear on the glass. And she felt a kinship with the flowers. She knew what it was like to be torn apart and sacrificed to the winds of cruel fate.

2

Brandon paced about his room like a caged animal. His father was out of town on business. Not that Brandon cared. They didn't have much to say to each other these days. Brandon flopped on his bed, his hands clasped behind his head, and stared up at the ceiling. It had been a lousy week at school. He'd all but slept through his classes, he'd been so bored. And even though he'd taken on extra hours at his job, he wasn't tired enough to fall into bed so totally exhausted that he could check out. And forget.

He thought about calling his best friend, Kenny, but remembered that Kenny was out with Pam, his red-hot romance of the past few months. Mentally Brandon skimmed his list of other friends and rejected the idea of calling any of them. Truth was, he'd been in such a dark mood for the past five months that nobody wanted to be with him. Even Flo, the girl he'd dated since the previous summer, had dumped him.

"You've got to get over it," she'd said with a toss of her blond head. "Life goes on, Brandon. You can't crawl in the grave with your mother, you know." She'd told him she was sorry, but that she wanted to have fun her senior year, not be tied down to a guy who was so moody.

Brandon sat upright and wandered out of his bedroom and into the kitchen. The place was spotless. His father saw to that. Not at all like the mess his mother had barely main-tained when she was alive. He searched through the refrigerator, now well stocked by the housekeeper who came every day, but nothing appealed to him. He slammed the door and hurried out of the room and into the den, where his father kept a bar.

He pawed through the array of bottles. He could have anything he wanted and there was nobody there to police him. He could get stinking drunk. And pass out. Except that was the course his mother had chosen, and look where it had gotten her. He felt like jumping out of his skin. The house was so quiet. So lonely. He missed his mother. Despite the depression that had ruled her life for the previous three years, he missed her and wanted her back. *People don't come back from the dead.*

Brandon knew he had to get out. Go somewhere. Maybe getting lost in a crowd would help. Maybe it wouldn't. All he knew was that he couldn't hang around this house with its ghosts and memories. He grabbed his car keys and bolted out the side door.

The sound of the doorbell startled April. Her parents were out for the evening and they had no friends in St. Croix that she knew of who would drop by. Maybe it was someone up to no good. It occurred to her that she had opened up the house after the storm. Cool tropical air stirred through the French doors, which led to the garden. Anyone could walk in. No need to ring the bell. In New York doors were locked and bolted, and their house in Long Island had an elaborate security system.

The bell chimed again and she went to the door, flipped on the light switch, and saw Brandon Benedict through the clear glass panes of the front door. He waved and smiled. "Remember me?"

"Yes. What do you want?"

He leaned against the doorjamb. "Company."

The way he stood came across as loneliness. His smile was more bravado than happiness. "Um—my parents—" She stopped. Should she admit that she was alone? Yet, if he'd meant to harm her, he could have done so when they were on the hill. Deciding against sending him away, she unlocked the door and opened it. "My parents are out to dinner, but they'll be back soon. You can come in."

"Thanks." He stepped over the threshold, his hands jammed in his pockets. "I know I shouldn't have just popped in on you. You made it clear that you weren't interested in seeing me again, but I was hoping you might change your mind."

She gestured to the sofa in the living room. The two of them sat, and she curled her legs up under her and turned to him. "I didn't mean to be rude. I just haven't been in the mood to meet new people."

"Being nice can be a pain when you'd rather be alone."

"Sounds like the voice of experience speaking. Don't you have friends? I mean from school?"

"My best friend's got a girl who eats up his free time. No time for hanging anymore."

"My best friend, Kelli, is in college out in Oregon. It's a long way off and I miss her. No girl in your life?"

"We broke up. You out of school?"

"I graduated from high school last June; went to New York University for a couple of months, but had to drop out."

Brandon saw shadows in her eyes again. It looked like the raw pain he knew. Something had happened, but he knew better than to ask. He hated it when people prodded him for explanations of his own moodiness. If she wanted to discuss it with him, she would. "I'll graduate this June," he said. It was now mid-February. "Four more months of utter boredom."

"And then?"

He shrugged. "No plans yet."

She was surprised. He reminded her of guys from her high school, and they'd all been planning on college. The guy she'd dated before Mark had even gotten a soccer scholarship. Brandon looked athletic and she told him so.

"I used to play basketball but don't anymore," he said, and she realized there would be no further explanation.

"I guess it is hard to get motivated in a place like St. Croix," she offered. "It's so beautiful all the time. I can't get very enthusiastic about the future myself." She saw no reason to mention Mark and all her reasons for feeling at such loose ends.

"Even though St. Croix is part of the U.S. Virgin Islands, it doesn't feel much like the mainland down here," Brandon said. "We used to visit Miami, but it wasn't much different there than it is down here. Where you're from, there's winter and snow."

"There's snow, all right." Facing the winter after Mark's death had been unbearable. The night breeze brought the perfumed scent of flowers through the open doors, and from far away, she heard the sound of a ship's horn. "The ocean is awesome and I never

grow tired of sitting and watching it. Did you
know this house has stairs leading down to a
cove and its own private beach?"

"I didn't know." Brandon enjoyed looking at April. She was certainly one of the
most strikingly pretty girls he'd ever seen. In
the lamp's light, her abundant red hair
gleamed in a halo around the top of her head.
"Have you gone snorkeling yet?"

"Why, no."

He saw interest in her eyes and seized on
it. "Then you're missing some of the best
that the Caribbean has to offer. Under the
sea there's a whole other world. Because the
sand bottom's so white, the sun shines down
to great depths, where there are coral reefs
big as a jungle, and fish the colors of rain-
bows."

"I've seen pictures taken under the sea in
brochures."

"I, um, I could take you sometime. If
you'd like to go, that is. I mean, there are
plenty of tourist guides that can do the same
thing, but because I've grown up here I
know underwater areas they've never
dreamed about." He paused, seeing the battle wage in her expression between wanting

to have such an adventure and keeping to herself. "If you want to."

Her eyes sparkled expectantly for a moment; then the light went out and she dropped her gaze. "Thanks. But I don't think so."

Her standoffishness was maddening, making Brandon itch—all the more determined to know what made her tick. "Well, the offer's open anytime."

She glanced toward the open French doors, looked distracted, then turned back toward him. "You know, maybe it would be better if you weren't here when my folks get home. It will mean hours of explanation if they find you here, and I'm just not up to it."

He stood. "Sure. I know what you mean. But thanks for letting me stop by and talk. It helped."

She puckered her brow. Could just a few friendly words have made a difference for him? Yet he did appear calmer, less agitated than when he'd arrived. "I'm glad. I enjoyed talking to you too."

She followed him to the front door, where he paused. "Remember, on Saturdays I work at the Buccaneer, which is a pretty cool place in itself. If you ever want to drop by for a tour of the place, ask for me at the pro shop.''

She agreed, although she believed she never would, and told him good night.

Once Brandon was gone, April couldn't concentrate on the book she'd been reading before his arrival. There was something about him . . . something lonely and full of longing that she couldn't get out of her thoughts. She'd seen it in his eyes. She'd been made aware of such things through her association with Mark. His CF had isolated him and set him apart from his peers all his life. She remembered his telling her about being ostracized and longing to be a part of "regular" life. Her own illness had set her apart too. Except for Kelli, her friends couldn't relate to a girl with a brain tumor. Not that anyone could see it! It was just that once they knew, everything was different. Guys hadn't been able to handle it either. Not that it had mattered in the long run, because it had opened the door for her relationship with Mark. Still, she knew firsthand what loneliness felt like.

Brandon's visit had brought her own loneliness into sharp focus. Only a few months before, she'd been planning her wedding and looking forward to spending the rest of her life with Mark. She hugged the book to her chest, suddenly missing Mark with an intense yearning. Tears gathered in her eyes. She fought against them, but in the end, they won the battle. *Mark! Mark!* She missed him so much.

April went to bed early and pretended to be sleeping when her parents returned. She kept her eyes closed when her mother peeked inside her room, knowing that she was too old to be tucked in, and her mother too involved with her only daughter not to do so.

The next morning, she went out to breakfast, sat down at the table awash in warm tropical sunlight, and said, "Dad, you told me you'd rent me a car so that I could drive around the island when I felt like it. Is your offer still open?"

Her parents exchanged glances. "Of course. But why not let your mother and me drive you around? We wouldn't mind, and besides, driving these roads can be confusing. In the Virgin Islands they drive on the left-hand side of the road."

"I'd rather be by myself," April said. "I'd like to explore, and don't worry, I can drive on the left-hand side just as easily as I can on the right."

"But—" her mother started.

"It's all right, Janice." Hugh Lancaster interrupted his wife's protest. "If that's what April wants, then that's what she'll have. What would you like to rent?"

"How about a Jeep?"

He nodded. "A Jeep it will be."

3

April downshifted and the Jeep wound its way along the coastal highway. Her father had taken her the very next morning into the city of Christiansted, where she'd chosen a black Jeep with a canvas top and zippered sides, all of which she'd removed before driving away. Armed with maps and cautions from her parents, she'd headed east, repeating to herself her mother's anxious warning, "Remember, stay left. Stay left."

Wind whipped through her hair as she bounced along the curving highway, rounding bends in the road to glimpse the jewel-blue Caribbean, an occasional rocky cliff, and lush green distant hills. The sun beat down on her arms and shoulders, and the intoxicating smell of salt air mingled with the sweet aroma of flowers. The roads were few on the island and now, in the height of tourist season, not heavy with traffic. She gripped the wheel and stepped on the accelerator as she remembered when Dr. Sorenson had said that despite weeks of radiation treatments, the tumor entrenched in her cerebellum and brain stem had not responded by shrinking as hoped. He was so, so sorry. There was little else medical science could do for her.

Understanding her anguish at the time, Mark had taken her out to a deserted airstrip and told her to drive as fast and as hard as she wanted. And she had forced his fine old car to its optimum speed and experienced the dangerous but exhilarating balance between control and oblivion. It had been a gift that only Mark could have given her, because he was the only one who understood what it was like to live one's life with the ever-present specter of death.

Mark would have loved St. Croix. He would have sped along the back roads and climbed trails where only four-wheel-drive vehicles ventured. They would have had such a good time together. A mist of tears clouded her eyes and she slowed down the Jeep.

She glanced to one side and saw a large sign: THE BUCCANEER. On impulse, she spun the wheel of the car and drove through the gateway and down a sloping road across acres of rolling green land. The edges of a golf course lay on her right, and far back, on a bluff overlooking the sea, stood a sprawling clubhouse and hotel. She parked in the lot and walked out on a terrace set with tables and chairs. A hostess asked, "Do you have a lunch reservation?"

April cleared her throat and smiled nervously. She had no business being there. "Actually, I was looking for your pro shop."

The hostess directed her there, and April hurried out onto the splendid grounds of the luxury resort, down a tiled path, to the shop. Once inside, she asked for Brandon, then busied herself among the clutter of golf paraphernalia. She chided herself, saying that what she was doing was stupid. She had no real reason to see Brandon. She hoped he wasn't there, that this was a Saturday he didn't work. The door opened and she turned to face him across a rack of golf shirts. His face, damp with sweat, broke into a large grin. "I don't believe it! You came to see me!"

She had to laugh at his genuine astonishment. "I was just driving by and saw the sign. I didn't even know if you'd be here."

"I've been here since six A.M. We open early because golfers like to start before it gets hot. I'm about to take a lunch break. Want to eat with me?"

She wasn't hungry, but since she'd come this far and knew she couldn't leave easily, she answered, "Maybe a salad."

He took her back to the terrace restaurant, ordered and had the food packed in Styrofoam containers, then led her down a winding walkway to a sandy beach area. Hotel guests were sunning themselves and playing in the calm waters. He pulled a small table and two chairs around an alcove of rocks to an isolated strip of sand no larger than a good-sized back porch. "Since the tide's out, we can sit here," he said, planting the chair firmly in the wet sand. "It's private."

She removed her sandals, allowing warm

water to lap over her feet. He sat across from her so that he was framed in blue sky and bright turquoise ocean. His tanned face glowed and his hair looked golden, streaked by the sun. "I'm starving," he said, flipping open his container and lifting out a mammoth hamburger.

Watching Brandon wolf down his meal reminded her of all the times she'd eaten with Mark. But, of course, Mark had had to take pills before every meal because of his CF. She thought of "their" special restaurant and of "their" table tucked in the corner.

"What's funny?" he asked. "You were smiling just then. Have I got mustard smeared on my face?"

Self-conscious, she looked down at her salad. "I was just remembering something, that's all. Nothing important."

"I'll be honest," he said between bites. "I never thought I'd see you again."

"Me neither."

"I'm glad you changed your mind. Why *did* you change your mind?"

"I didn't know I needed a reason."

"My charming personality?" he offered with an infectious grin.

"Certainly that was part of it." She returned his smile. A gull swooped low over the water behind him. "I was knocking around the island."

"And you thought, 'Wonder what old Brandon's up to? Maybe I should go see the geek.'" His joking tone reminded her of Mark's.

"Actually, I was . . . lonely." She kept her gaze on the gull, unable to meet Brandon's. She hadn't meant to tell him that.

He leaned back in his chair and searched her face thoughtfully. "I figured something was up with you. I've seen you twice and you looked sad both times." She didn't respond, so he continued. "I've been lonely myself, so I know how it feels."

"Everybody's been lonely."

"But you don't have to be," he said. "April, St. Croix is a small place. Everybody knows everybody else, especially those of us who grew up here. Tourists come through all the time, and sometimes the locals hit it off with some of them. We know that the person is going to leave. That's a given. But we still have a good time together while

we can, as long as the person is on the island . . ."

She understood what he was trying to tell
her—that he would take her under his wing
with no strings attached. "Like a baby-
sitter?"

"You're no baby," he declared, appraising
her in a way that made her pulse flutter. "No.
As a friend. This wouldn't be only for you.
You see, I could use a friend myself."

"There are plenty of tourists who would
jump at the chance to be your friend, Brandon."

"But I don't want just anybody. I'd like it
to be you."

The way he kept looking at her made her
feel even more self-conscious. An inner voice
asked, *"What are you doing?"* Suddenly she
saw that she was acting flirty, and she was
instantly ashamed. She struggled to stand,
but the wet sand had sucked around the legs
of the chair so that she couldn't move it. "It's
really getting late. I've got to go and you've
got work."

"Don't go yet." Instantly Brandon was beside her, taking her arm so that she wouldn't

fall backward. His touch felt warm, and she pulled away as if it had burned her.

"I have to," she insisted.

"I'd like to see you again. Can I call you? Make a date? I have classes until two, but I'm free evenings. I could show you around St. Croix. Maybe take you over to St. Thomas or St. John."

"I—I don't think so." Despite being in a wide-open space, April felt hemmed in and claustrophobic. "I really have to go now." She grabbed her sandals and backed away. "Thanks."

"Call me here if you change your mind," he said to her as she ducked around the edge of the rocks and fled up the beach toward the parking lot where her Jeep was parked. With her heart hammering, April turned on the engine and shot up the road to the highway, where she forgot the rule about staying in the left-hand lane and almost had a head-on collision.

Jerking the car back into its proper lane, April sped toward the hills and the safety of the villa. She never should have stopped to see Brandon. Not because she wasn't attracted to him, but because she was. And because she kept thinking about another guy who'd wanted to date her but whom she'd rejected at first—Mark. Until he'd won her over with his winsome smiles and caring love and swept her heart away. But now Mark was gone and she couldn't bring him back, and she couldn't start with someone else.

She floored the accelerator and raced toward home, memories chasing her like the wind.

"Did you have a good time exploring?"

Her mother's question cut through April's semiconscious state. She'd hurried home, put on her bathing suit, and gone down to the private beach for a swim. The surf felt warm as bathwater, the white sand bottom soft as velvet. She'd swum and floated to exhaustion, and had finally gone to the beach chair, where she'd slathered herself with sun cream, stretched out, and dozed, hoping to shut off her thoughts. Her mother had come down, bringing a pitcher of cool lemonade. "It was all right," April answered.

Her mother dragged another chair closer. "Tell me about it."

"Nothing to tell. I drove around, that's all."

She heard her mother sigh. "April, I can't stand this noncommunication between us. I know you're hurting, but we used to talk all the time. Now you hardly speak to me. Can't you tell how this is upsetting me? Don't you even care?"

Guilt mixed with irritation, yet April knew her mother was right. Her parents had done plenty for her and she'd shut them out. Just months before, she and her mother had been knee-deep in wedding plans; they'd discussed everything. April struggled to sit upright. "I'm sorry."

"You don't have to be sorry. Just *talk* to me. I love you. I want to help."

"Nothing can help. I can't get on top of this, Mom. I start to feel better and then, *pow,* it hits me like a wall. I miss Mark so much." She took a deep breath. "And every time some guy so much as looks at me, I want to run in the other direction."

Her mother poured April a glass of lemonade, and gulls swooped over the sea, flinging their lonely cries against the sunset-colored sky. "St. Croix is a paradise. It's romantic and makes you want to be with somebody you care about. I understand that."

"But how can I? I feel so guilty to even be thinking about such things."

"I know," her mother said. "I can see it on your face. You feel guilty because you're alive and Mark isn't. And because you want to go on living, as you should."

4

April realized that her mother was absolutely correct. It would be pointless to deny it. She *did* feel guilty because she was alive and wanted to remain so. Yet she also felt disloyal to Mark. "What am I going to do?"

Her mother put her arm around April's slumped shoulders. "Let me tell you a story."

April nodded, still feeling as if she were betraying Mark.

"You know all that your father and I went through to have you. Years of trying to get pregnant and disappointment after disappointment, fertility drugs, and finally going to Europe for in vitro fertilization. Which is why you're an only child. I couldn't do all that again. You're all we ever wanted. You're perfect."

"And then I got a brain tumor when I was five. So much for perfection."

Her mother squeezed her affectionately. "But the tumor was arrested, at least for a time. But what I want to tell you about concerns all those years I tried to get pregnant . . . and about my friend Betsy."

"Who's she?" April thought she knew all of her parents' friends. She'd not only never met this Betsy, she'd never heard of her either.

"She was my best friend for more than eleven years. We did everything together— work, lunch, shop—sort of like you and Kelli, except we were older, mid-twenties to thirties. And we were both trying to have a baby. It helped going through all the frustration and disappointment with another woman. Men can't really grasp the trauma a woman experiences when she wants to get pregnant but can't."

Her mother plucked up a seashell and cradled it in the palm of her hand. "Anyway, at one point Betsy stopped talking to me. She just pulled away and I couldn't figure out why. I begged her to tell me what was wrong. Had I done something to offend her? It was sheer torment for me. Then one day I heard from a mutual friend that Betsy was pregnant. I rushed to her and asked if it was true. It was. And I asked why she hadn't told me. And she said because she hadn't wanted to hurt me. She felt guilty, April, because she had something she knew I desperately wanted."

April heard the emotion in her mother's voice and realized that even now, years later, the event still affected her. "So what happened?"

"I told her I was happy for her, and I was. But I felt so betrayed because she hadn't confided in me. It did irreparable harm to our friendship. She couldn't believe that I could rejoice with her, that I wouldn't be jealous and depressed about it." Her mother paused. "So why am I telling you this? Because you're going through much the same thing. You're alive and Mark isn't. You think he would somehow be disappointed in you if you allow yourself to have fun or date another boy. But from what I know about

Mark, that simply isn't true. No more than my being petty and angry about Betsy's pregnancy would have been true all those years ago.

"Mark understood. He knew what the odds of his dying before you were, even if the wreck had never occurred."

Her mother was right again; Mark had told April as much before their engagement. He had not expected to outlive her. "What are you saying to me?"

"I'm saying it's all right for you to be happy again. Give yourself permission to enjoy your life. To date if you want. To have a good time. It's what Mark would have wanted. And if you'll search your heart, you'll see that I'm telling you the truth. Mark loved you. Now you must honor his love by living, not merely existing."

"But I—"

Her mother interrupted. "Nobody knows how much time she has to live, April. You could have just as easily died before Mark. In an accident . . . anything."

April noted that her mother hadn't said "a relapse." But of course, that was such a real possibility that perhaps there was no need to

state it. April shuddered. She didn't want to
die. The realization almost took her breath
away. But if that feeling didn't make her disloyal, what did it make her?

"Don't you think Mark would have missed
you if something had taken you away from
him?" her mother continued.

"Sure he would have missed me."

"Wouldn't you have wanted him to feel
happy again?"

"You know I would."

"Then stop feeling guilty and start enjoying every day you have to live."

Long after her mother had gone up to the
house, April sat staring out at the sea, now
calm and flat. The sky was deepening to
shades of mauve. Far out against the horizon,
a sailboat looked dead in the water. She iden-
tified with the boat. She felt limp. She longed
for a new breeze, a fresh wind to come into
her life and blow away the clouds of despair.
She hungered to feel as alive as she had when
she'd been with Mark. Was her mother right?
While she couldn't have Mark again, was it
possible to have something to give her life
new meaning?

April decided to give herself permission to get out more and spend more time with her family. When her parents went to restaurants and museums, she accompanied them. They flew to St. Thomas for a day of shopping and antique hunting. She took long drives in her Jeep up into the rain forests of St. Croix and onto the far side of the island to the city of Frederiksted, passing abandoned sugar mills from the island's early history.

She passed the Buccaneer many times, but she never went in to see Brandon. She honestly believed she didn't need the complication of him in her life. She was strolling past shops in downtown Christiansted one afternoon, looking for a gift for Kelli's upcoming birthday, when she heard someone call her name. She turned to see Brandon hurrying toward her. Against her will, her heart gave a little leap. She pasted a smile on her face and braced for the encounter.

"I thought that was you," he said, jogging up. "I mean that red hair of yours is like a stoplight. How've you been? I haven't seen you in a while."

She heard the admonishment in his tone. "I've been around," she told him. "Busy." Even to her ears it sounded lame.

But his grin was quick, forgiving. "Well, now that we meet again, could I buy you an ice-cream cone? That shop across the street has tons of flavors."

The air felt humid and sticky. Ice cream would taste good. "All right," she said, offering him a smile.

Inside the pink-and-white ice-cream parlor, the air was cool and smelled of peppermint and chocolate. They chose different flavors and settled in at a small round table next to the picture window where sun beamed through the glass. "So what's kept you busy?" he asked.

"My parents."

He made a face. "It doesn't sound very exciting."

"I have cool parents. How about you?"

Immediately he stiffened. "My dad and I don't get on too well."

She licked the ice cream, savoring the sweetness. "And your mom?"

"She's dead."

His statement sounded so stark that she gasped. "I'm sorry."

He licked his cone in silence, offering no other explanation.

April cast about for something else to say, something to change the subject. The clock on the wall gave her the opening. "I thought you said you had school on weekdays until two."

"I didn't feel like going today. I skipped."

"Do you have to work?"

"Yeah, but not until three." He leaned back in his chair and stretched out his long legs. "I wanted to come see you but I didn't think you'd open the door for me."

"Look, Brandon—"

"It's okay," he interrupted. "But I want to explain something." She nodded politely, and he continued. "I got to thinking about it and I realized that you've finished high school and I haven't. I figure you don't want to be seen with some local high-school jerk. I'm really eighteen and I should have graduated last June, same as you, but don't go thinking I'm some kind of dumb dork. You see, I had a rough year and I ended up missing too many days, so the administration said I had to repeat most of my senior year. I could have taken a test and gone straight into college. But I, um, I decided to hang back and graduate a year late."

His story surprised her. She suspected there was plenty he wasn't telling her. She wasn't about to dig it out of him either. The less she knew, the easier it would be not to become involved with him. "I didn't have much use for high school by the time graduation rolled around," she told him. "But I was glad I finished. You did what was right for you. And, by the way, I've never thought of you as some high-school jerk."

By now they were both through with their ice cream. "Look, would you like to take a walk on the beach with me? We can go over to the resort, and then I'll be close to my job." He stood and held out his hand. "Please."

She couldn't say no—didn't really want to—so she followed him outside, where they got into their separate cars and drove to the Buccaneer. Once there, they parked and he took her out onto the grounds. The tropical sun beat down and sprinklers arced over the golf course, tossing jewel-like drops of water over the grass. He led her into a forest garden where huge multicolored hibiscus and bright-orange bird-of-paradise flowers grew in well-tended beds. Inside the garden the air felt cooler, and sun-dappled leaves shaded the winding pathways. "I'll never get over how pretty everything is in St. Croix," she said.

Brandon stopped, peered down at her, and, touching the ends of her hair, said, "Yes. I agree. Things *are* more beautiful here."

Her heartbeat accelerated as she caught his message in his eyes. "So where does this path lead?"

"Come. I'll show you."

She followed, and minutes later the path led out of the garden and onto a sunny lawn. There she saw a latticed gazebo, painted white and trimmed with satin ribbons and cascades of white flowers. "How beautiful," she exclaimed.

"We must have just missed the party," Brandon said. He stooped and picked up grains of rice and wild birdseed and tossed them playfully into the air.

"What is this place?"

"It's the wedding chapel. People come from all over the world to be married here."

5

Her heart thudded, and reality crashed in on her. "Can we go somewhere else?"

Brandon looked surprised. "There's no-place prettier than here."

"But I don't want to be here." April spun and hurried back up the path into the garden. The flowers, which only minutes before had been breathlessly beautiful to her, now seemed waxen and surreal.

"Wait!" she heard Brandon call. He ran up behind her and caught her arm. "Don't run off. What's wrong? What's happened? I thought you'd like the place. You said St. Croix was perfect and this is one of the prettiest spots on the island."

He must think she was crazy. Her hands trembled, and her knees felt rubbery. The sight of the wedding chapel had opened a wound on her heart that left her reeling and grief-stricken. "Which way to the beach?" she asked, struggling to hold back tears.

"This way." He took her quickly out of the garden, across rolling manicured grass, and down to the shoreline, where the gentle waves rolled onto the sand.

There she stopped and breathed in great gulps of sea air, calming her racing heart. She kicked off her sandals and began to walk along the shore. The water washed over her footprints, blurring them. Brandon walked beside her, not speaking, allowing her the time she needed to gather her composure. She owed him an explanation but wasn't sure how to begin. "I'm sorry, Brandon. I didn't know that was going to happen. I was caught off guard."

"Exactly what *did* happen?"

"Memories," she whispered. "Just when I think they'll never come back, they do."

Again he kept silent.

She said, "My parents brought me to St. Croix to help me get over something. You see, back home, I knew this guy . . . we were very close."

"I knew it!" Brandon stopped walking. "I knew you were too good-looking to not have a boyfriend."

She turned to face him as the waves washed sand out from under her bare feet. "He was more than my boyfriend. Mark was my fiancé."

A somber look crossed Brandon's face. "Oh."

"But he's dead."

He looked jolted and his face went pale. "How . . . ?"

"Have you ever heard of cystic fibrosis?" She told him slowly, haltingly, about Mark and his disease, his love of racing cars, his accident. "He would have made it—the crash wasn't that bad—if it hadn't been for the CF. In the end, it won."

Brandon listened intently. She couldn't read what he was thinking, but she knew her story had affected him because it showed on his face. "Life stinks!"

"But we can't change how life turns out," she said. "Mark didn't deserve to have CF and he didn't deserve to die so young. After he was gone, I hated being in New York without him."

"So you came here."

"Winter up there is awful . . . the sky all gray and cold. Bare trees." She shivered. "Everywhere I went reminded me of him. Last June, when I graduated, my father wanted us all to go on a family vacation, but at the time I was involved with Mark and I didn't want to leave. Once he was gone . . ." She shrugged, leaving the sentence unfinished. "I love it here . . . the ocean and all."

"What were you doing that day I first saw you up on the hill? It had something to do with Mark, didn't it?"

"CF robs a person of his breath, so blowing up a balloon was a pretty big deal for Mark. He used to blow up balloons for me as a present. Sometimes he'd tuck little notes inside. This time, *I* blew up a balloon for him, and I sent it up into the sky on the chance that he was up there, looking down. I wanted him to know I was thinking about him. And that I loved him."

"Mark was a very lucky guy to have had you."

"No, I was the lucky one." Tears brimmed in her eyes. "We were right in the middle of planning the wedding when Mark died. Seeing that wedding chapel . . . well, it brought everything back."

"I'm sorry."

"You had no way of knowing." She turned to face him, smiling tentatively. "But you're right, it is beautiful."

Brandon shifted from foot to foot. "Now that I know about you and Mark, it explains some things to me. I understand that you might not want some guy pressuring you and coming on to you. But let me be honest. I still would like to see more of you. Nothing heavy," he added quickly. "But I do know every inch of this island and most of the surrounding water. If you'll let me, I'd like to be your friend. I'd like to take you around and show you my island."

His request was eloquent and simple and it touched her. She recognized that Brandon wasn't some kid with a hidden agenda. Like her, he was lonely. He also had something buried deep inside his psyche that was painful. She guessed it had to do with the loss of his mother. She wouldn't probe. If he wanted to talk about it, he would.

"I would like that very much," she said.

She gazed out to the open sea. A sailboat leaned into the wind against the horizon. "You know, I've watched those boats from the first day I arrived, and I'd love to go sailing on one. Do you think we could do that sometime?"

A dark expression crossed his face, prompting her to ask, "You do sail, don't you?"

"We have a boat. A nice one, but it's in dry dock."

"Repairs? Painting?"

He shook his head. The gloom in his eyes passed and he gave a quick grin. "We'll rent a little boat, big enough for two. I'll teach you how to sail it. How to tack and swing the sail about without knocking yourself into the water."

"I'd like to learn."

A beeping sound interrupted them, and Brandon glanced down at his watch. "My cue to go to work," he said, flipping off the miniature alarm. "I'd like to call you."

She'd enjoyed the afternoon and realized she wanted to see him again. "Sure."

He offered to walk her to her car, but she told him, "You go on. I'm going to walk on the beach awhile longer."

"Talk to you soon," he called, and jogged off toward the golf course.

She watched him, gave a deep sigh, and whispered, "I hope this is okay with you, Mark."

By the time Brandon pulled into his driveway, night had fallen. The lights were on inside the sprawling house, which meant that his father was home, returned from one of his many business trips. Brandon couldn't say he was glad. The less he had to do with his father the better. He went into the kitchen through the garage and saw his father sitting at the breakfast bar, nursing a drink over a half-eaten sandwich.

"Where have you been?"

"Working." Brandon crossed to the refrigerator, every nerve in his body tingling.

"I called the Buccaneer at five and they told me you were gone."

"Well, your source was wrong. At the last minute Doug decided the grounds crew needed to mulch the garden near the sixteenth hole. So that's what I did."

"What about your schoolwork? Or are you

going to take yet another pass at your senior year?"

Low blow, Brandon thought, but he ignored the barb. "I didn't have any homework." No need to mention that he'd skipped school that day.

"When I come home after a week away on the job, I expect to see you. I wanted us to have dinner together."

"It was never important to you before," Brandon shot back. "Mom and I ate by ourselves half my life."

"You watch your mouth. I was trying to earn a living."

Brandon glared at his father. "Well, now you have all the time in the world."

Rage crossed his father's face, and Brandon knew he'd stepped over the line. He didn't care. Why should he spare his father's feelings? "You think I chose to leave the two of you alone so much? You think you know so much about taking care of a family? About making sure they have the things they want? Well, I've got news for you, Brandon, you don't know a thing!"

Brandon fished in his pocket and pulled out his car keys. "I know I'm out of here."

His father stood, tipping over the kitchen stool. "You do not have my permission to leave."

"I didn't ask for it."

"You can't leave until I say so."

His father took a step forward, but Brandon met his challenge. "Watch me."

"Your car—"

"Is mine. It belonged to my mother and she left it to me. And I pay for the gas and insurance."

His father raised his hand as if to slap Brandon. Brandon didn't flinch. His father sagged against the counter and buried his face in his hands. "I—I don't want to fight with you, son."

"Too late," Brandon said. He slammed the kitchen door, got into the car, and screeched out of the garage. But he stopped at the end of the driveway. It was after ten and he really didn't have anyplace to go. Why did it have to be this way between him and his father? Why did they always end up in a yelling match?

Brandon bowed his forehead until it touched the steering wheel gripped between his hands. His heart pounded crazily and his body shook. Of course, the questions were pointless. He knew *why*. There was just nothing he could do about it. He turned his roiling thoughts to April and immediately felt calmer. She understood what it was like to lose somebody you loved. But she didn't understand what it was like to lose somebody the way he had lost his mother.

Brandon turned off the car's engine and leaned back against the seat. Exhaustion overwhelmed him. Tropical night air blew through the lowered car windows, tantalizing him with the familiar scent of gardenia. His mother had worn that same fragrance. He waited at the end of the driveway until all the lights went off inside the house. Until the night sounds from the surrounding jungle had blotted out the sounds of neighborhood dogs, TVs, and moving cars. Until he was positive his father was asleep and he could steal inside, alone and unnoticed.

6

The next morning April told her parents about meeting Brandon. Not about their very first meeting, atop the hill, or about the second one, when he came to the house, but about the third. She embellished, saying that she'd gotten lost and he'd come to her rescue at the Buccaneer. "He seems nice, and I think you'll like him. He wants to show me around St. Croix."

Her father poured coffee for the three of them. "I can't say I blame him. You are the prettiest girl on the island."

April rolled her eyes.

"Do you want to see him?" her mother asked.

Their gazes met, and April thought back to

their conversation that one afternoon on the beach. "Yes, I'd like to see him. I'd like to have him show me the island."

"We can show you the island," her father declared.

"Don't be a wet blanket, Hugh," her mother said. "We're just parents. April needs to be with someone her own age. Besides, now that you're commuting back and forth to New York, you'll only be here on the weekends. What's she supposed to do during the weekdays?"

"I only go every other week," he corrected her, then leaned toward April. "You sure you don't want to go to New York with me?"

April shook her head. "I like it here."

"We'll both go with you on one of the trips," her mother offered. "In the meantime, I've been thinking of spending a few days in the British Virgin Islands."

The British counterpart wasn't far away, but to go would mean spending several days there. "Maybe later this summer," April hedged. "Of course, you can go if you want. I'll be fine by myself."

She caught their reluctance to go off and

leave her to fend for herself in their glances at each other. It bothered her that they were so overprotective, but she wasn't in any mood to start an argument about it. Fortunately, the phone rang just then, and her father answered and handed it over to her. "I'll bet it's that Brandon."

It was. She quickly made plans, and later that afternoon when he came, she made sure her parents met him. Once in his car, she said, "Sorry about that," referring to the numerous questions her father had asked.

He laughed. "Do I still have arms and legs? I thought your father was going to bite them off."

"They can't help it. It came with their parenting lease." She remembered apologizing to Mark for her family's possessiveness of her, but he had known about her health problems and made allowances. Brandon did not know.

"They care," Brandon said. "It's no big deal. Forget it."

"So where are we going?"

"Have you driven up into the rain forest?"

"Once. But I was on my way someplace else."

"Then that's where we're headed."

He drove into the hills, where tangled undergrowth and thick tree trunks lined the sides of the road. Brandon slowed, pulled off to one side, took April's hand, and led her into the dense foliage. The air felt damp and heavy. Her hair stuck to the back of her neck. She heard a breeze rustle through the tree branches high above but couldn't feel it. The trees absorbed it, like sponges sucking up water. "It's so quiet," she said. "I feel as if we should be whispering."

"It's not so quiet," he said. "Listen."

She heard a faint clacking sound.

"That's the seedpods of Tibet trees. They're called 'mother's tongue.' "

She giggled. "Yes, I recognize the voice."

Next he took her to an artesian village where wood-carvers were busy shaping everything from small animals to large pieces of furniture from pieces of mahogany. April pronounced it "major cool."

Brandon bought her several hand-carved combs, which she immediately used to sweep up her hair and secure it off her neck. He also bought her a hand-carved necklace.

"You shouldn't buy me so much."

"You're fun to buy for," he said, remembering the many small gifts he'd bought for his mother in an effort to lift her spirits when dark depression overtook her. "Here, let me fasten it for you."

He stepped behind her and slipped the necklace around her neck. He was struggling with the clasp when he noticed the line of blue dots at the base of her neck. "Who's been drawing on you?"

She stiffened. "What do you mean?"

"There's this pattern of little blue specks on your skin. Sort of like blue freckles."

She jerked the combs from her hair and let it tumble down around her shoulders. She knew what he'd seen—the tiny tattoos the radiologist had made when she'd begun her radiation treatments the year before. But she couldn't tell him; she couldn't. "Birthmarks," she fibbed. "Someone in the family was a blueblood."

He eyed her, uncertain as to his response. The dots were too orderly, too mathematical and precise to be a random pattern from birth. Yet her message in her attempt to make a joke about them was plain enough: Don't ask. "Gee, I thought for a minute you'd been abducted by aliens."

"I was, but I escaped," she said, glad he didn't press her for a serious answer.

"Now that I've seen your funny blue freckles, you may as well put your hair back up," he told her. "It's hot."

She complied, lifting her hair and fastening it with the wooden combs, careful to face him as she worked. "Now where?" she asked, pretending the previous conversation had never happened.

"I know where there's a waterfall, but we'll have to hike to it. You want to go?"

She did.

She followed him along a partially hidden trail, the sound of falling water growing in intensity. "It's not much farther," Brandon said.

Just when she was certain they'd never get there, Brandon moved aside overhanging brush and she saw a clearing. Beyond it she saw the waterfall tumbling from a height of rocks and into a stone-littered pool where the water was so clear that she could see all the way to the bottom. Where the falls hit, water boiled up white and frothy, like a milk shake. The air felt cool and moist with water droplets.

"Look," April cried, pointing. "I see a rainbow." Ribbons of color arched over the tumbling water.

"It's the way light hits water droplets," Brandon said.

"Is not. It's fairy dust."

He laughed. "Come on. Take off your shoes, we'll sit on that rock."

She followed him out onto a jutting rock shelf where water lapped against the cool stone. She dangled her feet and sucked in her breath. "It's cold."

"It's right out of a spring. Nice, huh?"

"Very nice. Thanks for bringing me."

"I discovered it one day when I was hiking. I've never brought anybody here to see it with me."

April realized that in his way, he was telling her that she was special to him. She wasn't sure how she felt about his veiled compliment, so she changed the subject. "You hike a lot, don't you?"

"The whole island is only twenty-three miles long, and when you've lived here as long as I have, you get to know it pretty well."

"How long have you lived here? And why?"

"I've been here since I was seven. My father's in importing and exporting. He travels a lot, and this is a good jumping-off place to South America and the rest of the Caribbean."

"So you and your mom spent a lot of time by yourselves?"

At the mention of his mother, April saw him draw away. "Yeah. We did. But she never liked it as much as I did. She was Danish and because the Danish settled this place you'd have thought she'd like it, but she missed her family back in Europe. And Dad was gone so much."

April was on the verge of asking him what had happened to his mother when a wild bird, brilliant with red and yellow plumage, swooped down from one of the trees with a raucous cry. One of its red tail feathers fluttered into the pool, where it floated and bobbed.

"Look! It's beautiful."

"Do you want it?"

"Can you reach it?" It seemed out of his reach and was headed toward the frothy swirl at the foot of the falls. Once there, it would be sucked under and lost.

Brandon grinned and stood. "If you want it, it's yours." He dove headfirst into the pool.

"You'll freeze," she shouted with a laugh.

He surfaced, swam confidently, and captured the feather. He ceremoniously placed it between his teeth and swam back to her, then pulled himself up onto the rock and, dripping wet, bowed with a flourish, presenting her with the feather prize.

She stood and clapped. "You look like a pirate."

His grin dazzled her. "The feather's magic. Make a wish and whatever you want is yours."

She took it, her mind spinning. There was too much to wish for. "I wish . . . I could fly just like the bird that lost this feather."

Mischief danced in his eyes. "You can. Have you ever been parasailing?"

"Are you sure I can do this?" April stood on the back of a speedboat, nibbling nervously on her bottom lip and watching Brandon and two men from the Buccaneer. One was a driver for the boat, and the other was strapping her into a harness that was attached to a huge parachute. It lay in the sea like a flattened orange jellyfish, lines and ropes slack.

"It's a no-brainer," Brandon assured her. "You're going to love this." He'd picked her up the next afternoon and driven her to the resort, where he'd paid the two men on duty to take her parasailing.

"It's not my brains I'm worried about," she muttered. "It's my body being smashed into the ocean and turning into shark bait."

The parasailing instructor laughed heartily. "You'll do just fine, little lady. I haven't lost a client yet." She listened as he instructed her, feeling both apprehensive and excited. "Just hang on and let the boat do the work. You'll have about fifteen minutes in the air, and then I'll reel you in like a big fish." He gestured to a mammoth reel mounted on the back of the boat that held a rope from her harness. The parachute, in turn, was tied to the metal frame of the harness. "Ready?" he asked.

She lied, telling him, "Yes." The driver

pushed the throttle forward. As the boat gathered speed, she saw the parachute begin to fill and rise and felt her body lift gently off the deck. A thrill shot through her as she rose higher and higher, like a human kite adrift on the wind. Below, the boat looked toylike, the vivid blue ocean bright as sapphire. The noise of the boat's engine faded too, and the sound of the wind filling the nylon parachute reminded her of a sheet flapping in a stiff breeze.

She could see for miles and miles, islands surrounded by sugar-sand beaches, green rolling hills, and more ocean, vast and blue and stretching into infinity. *So this is how an eagle feels,* she thought. *This is what flying with wings would be like.* Joy bubbled up inside her, all fear and apprehension gone, blown away by the wind and melted by the warmth of the sun. The vastness of creation, the beauty of sea and sky overwhelmed her. She was flying, anchored to earth only by a long tether of nylon rope.

"Hello, Mark," she said against the wind. "Are you watching?"

7

Brandon became April's constant companion. Whenever he wasn't attending classes or working, he either went to her house or took her to do something. His father was working almost round the clock, taking trips that stretched for days at a time, which Brandon decided was the best thing for both of them. It kept them from fighting. Besides, Brandon liked being with April. He liked her parents too. They catered to her, but she seemed unaffected by their lavish indulgences. The contrast between Brandon's home life and hers was startling to him. Even when his mother had been alive his home life had never been like April's. And even though his father made plenty of money, his home had never had the warmth and togetherness of the one her parents rented on St. Croix.

He made good on his promise to take her sailing one Sunday afternoon toward the end of May. He borrowed a two-person sailboat from a friend and, hitching it to a trailer, drove with April to the far west end of the island, where powder-white beaches surrounded a boat launch. Once they were out on the water, he gave her the tiller.

"What am I supposed to do?" she squealed, gripping the lever that was attached to the rudder that steered the boat.

"Just keep her headed into the wind. If the sail starts to flap or go slack, move the tiller and chase the wind."

Chase the wind. April had never experienced such sheer exhilaration as she did in the sailboat. Even parasailing didn't compare. She was intoxicated by the rise and fall of the bow as it sliced through the water, the sound of the sail filling with wind, and the salty spray of the water wetting her face. She wondered if Mark would have loved it too. He'd been fascinated with fast cars, but she'd never cared much for the smell of exhaust and the noise of roaring engines. The scent of the sea and the sound of the breeze were much more to her liking.

She watched Brandon covertly. His sun-streaked brown hair was windblown and his skin glowed with a golden tan. He wore a bright red tank top and swimming trunks that showed off his muscular arms and legs. She realized with a start that she was attracted to him and that she cared for him. After Mark, she'd never thought she would care for another guy. And, she reminded herself, with her medical history, she shouldn't be thinking about such things. It wasn't fair to Brandon.

"Bring her about!" Brandon shouted, snapping April back to the present.

April turned the tiller until the sail went slack. The boat floundered.

"Watch out for the boom when it comes around."

The bottom arm of the mainsail slowly swung around as the sail filled again, and as the sail changed directions, so did the boat.

"You're very good at this," Brandon said, moving to sit beside her near the tiller. "You sure you've never sailed before?"

She shook her head. "But you can bet I'll

do it again. Tell me about your boat—the one in dry dock."

"It's a thirty-two-footer with beautiful teak decks. It can sleep four and has a galley—that's a kitchen—and it was built in Denmark."

"Who taught you how to sail?"

A faraway look crept into his blue eyes. "It was my mother's boat, really. She's the one who taught me how to sail."

He told her nothing else, but she sensed his sadness at being reminded of his mother. She was sorry she'd brought it up. "Well, thanks for bringing me today and for taking the time to teach me. It's wonderful fun."

"Maybe your father could get you a small boat. There's got to be water up where you live."

Now it was April's turn to back away emotionally. She knew that her time on St. Croix was limited. That sooner or later she'd have to go home. And at home, she'd have to figure out what to do with the rest of her life. "The water around Long Island can sometimes get cold," she said. "It's not the same as St. Croix."

When Brandon dropped her off late in the

afternoon, he asked, "How about dressing up and going to dinner with me tonight? I'll take you to the Buccaneer. They have a band that plays on Saturday nights. A rock group, not one of those snooze bands."

She hadn't dressed up in a long time and thought it might be fun. In the house, she found a note from her mother that she'd gone grocery shopping and that Kelli had called from Oregon. April looked at her watch, realized that it was not yet noon in Oregon, and hurried to the phone. The sound of her friend's voice brought a lump to her throat.

"I miss you and wanted to hear your voice," Kelli said. "The term's over in three weeks."

Kelli had a whole year of college behind her. April felt a pang of regret that she couldn't say the same for herself. "So will you go home for the summer?"

"Not right away." Kelli sighed. "My folks aren't going to make it, April. Dad was in Seattle last week on business and he came to see me. He said he and Mom were calling it quits."

"Gee, I'm sorry." But April wasn't surprised. She'd known that Kelli's parents had struggled for years to keep their marriage together. "What are you going to do?"

"I'm staying here for the summer term. And I've got a job waiting tables at a coffeehouse in town. I figure I'll take some extra hours and save up spending money. My parents are selling the house. Mom's going to stay in New York, but Dad's relocating to Denver. And you're all the way in St. Croix. I feel like a homeless person."

April heard a catch in Kelli's voice, and her heart went out to her friend. "You could come here," she suggested.

"I can't. I have to go to New York after the summer term to see Mom. I hate missing St. Croix, but right now I don't see it happening any other way. When will you go home?"

"I'm supposed to go for another checkup and battery of CAT scans in August, so I guess that's when we'll leave here for good."

"How are you feeling?"

"Sometimes I get light-headed, but no headaches." The debilitating headaches the year before had been her warning that her

childhood brain tumor had resumed growing.

"Maybe you should get your checkup
sooner."

"I'm sick of doctors. I don't want to see
another one ever again."

"Yes, but—"

"But nothing. Don't worry about me. I'm
doing fine and I'm having a good time. I go
to the beach every day."

"Do you think you'll go back to NYU in
the fall?" April had been attending New York
University when she and Mark had decided
to get married.

"Probably . . . maybe . . . I don't know,
Kelli, I just don't know what I want to do."

"How about the rest of you? Are you feeling better about Mark?"

"I'll always miss Mark. But I've met someone here, Brandon Benedict. He's been
pretty nice to me and it's helped me sort out
what happened to Mark and me."

"Why, that's awesome!" Kelli's delight
crackled through the phone line. "Now I
really feel bad about not coming. What's he
like?"

April told Kelli as much as she could about Brandon. "I know he's got some family problems, but I understand how it feels to lose someone you love. I mean, to have his mother die when he was a high-school senior was hard for him."

"Sounds as if you're good for each other."

"I don't know about that, but I do know I like being with him."

"April, I have to go. I have an exam in a half hour. Just promise me you'll get home in August, same as me. I really want to see you."

"It's a deal." The lump rose again in her throat. "I miss you, Kelli."

"I miss you too."

April hung up and stared out to sea. New York and her other life seemed far away and almost dreamlike. Sometimes she could hardly recall what her house looked like. Or the faces of her old friends. Or even Mark. Quickly she went to her dresser and seized the framed photo of him. She studied Mark's face, memorizing every detail until her heart stopped thudding. *I won't forget you. I won't!* She hugged the photo to herself until the cool glass warmed from the heat of her body.

———

"Wow. You look beautiful." Admiration danced in Brandon's eyes. He sat across from her at a small table on the restaurant's veranda, out under the stars.

She smiled her thanks. Brandon looked good to her too. He wore a suit, the first she'd ever seen him in, and she liked the effect. "Nice place," she told him.

"Nice company," he returned, giving her a look that made her heartbeat quicken. "We had a senior dance here last year. I didn't go."

She didn't ask why, and he didn't volunteer. She asked, "Isn't the school year about over?"

"I'm taking exams now."

"What will you do this summer?"

"Work until it's time to go off to school."

"Have you picked a college yet?" She remembered his telling her about being accepted into several colleges in the States.

"No. But that's not what I want to talk about. I want to know how much longer you plan to be on the island."

"Maybe until August."

"Perfect," he said, leaning forward. "Then

we can leave together—you to go home, me to go off to college."

It didn't seem like a bad idea to her. It would be fun to spend the summer with Brandon, and after so many months of unhappiness, she felt in the mood to have some fun. She was sure her parents wouldn't object—

"Hello, son."

The man who stood next to their table interrupted April's train of thought. She saw Brandon stiffen and his expression harden. "Hi, Dad." Brandon squirmed uncomfortably.

"Aren't you going to introduce us?" Brandon's father stared down at April.

She saw Brandon's likeness in his face, but his coloring was darker. Saving Brandon the chore, she said, "Hi. I'm April Lancaster."

Brandon's father smiled. "I suspected there was someone special taking up Brandon's spare time. Since you're having dinner, would you care to join us?" He gestured toward a table across the room, and a deeply tanned, pretty, dark-haired woman dressed in white waved. "If I'd known you were coming here—"

"No thanks." Brandon cut off his father. "We were just leaving." He stood, and his napkin flopped onto the floor.

April questioned him with her eyes. They hadn't even ordered. What was so terrible about joining his father for dinner?

"Come on, April." Brandon held out his hand, and she took it hesitantly and stood.

She saw color in his father's cheeks and realized he'd been stung by Brandon's rudeness. "Um—nice to meet you," she called as Brandon hustled her out of the dining room.

Outside, in the humid tropical night, he skidded to a stop and took a couple of deep breaths. She saw that he was trembling. "What's going on?"

"I didn't expect my father to pop in on us."

"He just said hello," she said, defending him. "Was it seeing him with another woman? I mean, if your mother's been dead for more than a year—"

"And it's his fault!" Brandon blurted out hotly. "She's dead and it's all his fault."

8

Shocked by Brandon's accusation, April gasped. "What are you talking about?" He'd never openly discussed his mother's death with her, nor had she asked him for details.

"Let's walk," Brandon said. "Would you mind?"

"I don't mind."

He led her through well-lit paths to the garden area, where the accent lighting was noticeably dimmer and stars peeked through palm branches. He found an empty bench and sat, his forearms resting on his thighs, his head bowed. "I'm sorry," Brandon said, sounding subdued. "I didn't mean to sound off back there."

Sitting beside him, she asked, "Well, now that you have, tell me what you meant. How is your father responsible for your mother's death?"

"I've never told you how my mother died."

"No, you haven't." She imagined a car wreck with Brandon's father driving.

"My mother committed suicide."

Just the sound of the word made her stomach lurch. *Suicide*. It sounded violent, irrevocable. And she couldn't imagine anyone choosing to die. "How?"

"She took the sailboat out one afternoon. She wrote a note to us, swallowed some pills, and died. The coast guard found the boat drifting and went on board and found her. She loved that boat. She turned it into her coffin."

And April knew that Brandon had loved the boat too. He'd learned to sail on it, and now it held bad memories. "Is that why it's in dry dock?"

"Yeah. Dad hauled it out of the water after Mom's funeral and it hasn't been wet since."

"Would you want to be on it again?"

"Yes." His answer was so soft, she had to lean forward to hear it. "It was the only place I remember her being happy. We spent a lot of time on it together when I was a kid. We sailed for hours and . . . and . . . I miss it."

"Maybe if you talk to your father—"

"Forget it. He didn't care when Mom was alive. He doesn't care now."

"Are you sure?" She remembered when she'd thought her parents were against her union with Mark and how she had attempted to plan her wedding on her own. She'd needed her mother, but believed that her mother was ignoring her by staying uninvolved. It hadn't been true, but the rift between them had turned into a gulf in no time. "I mean, how do you know?"

"I know because he's never home. His business"—he fairly spat the word—"is much more important to him than we ever were. She was so lonely. And it got worse and worse as I grew up."

"Maybe you just noticed it more and more."

He snapped his head up to glare at her. "I know how things were at the house. My mother didn't have any friends except for my father, and he ignored her. She started drinking just to get his attention, she told me. But that didn't work either. Suicide became her only way to get noticed." Brandon shook his head. "It was his fault, all right. He could have stopped her if he'd only paid attention to her. If he'd only seen how much she was hurting."

April didn't agree with his reasoning. "But don't you think she had a choice, Brandon? Don't you think she could have gotten help if she'd really wanted it?"

"My mom wasn't like that. She didn't want the whole world to know her problems. No, my father should have been more sensitive to her."

"*You* were sensitive to her, and that didn't stop her," April said before she realized how her words would hurt him.

He pulled back in horror. "Don't you think I tried? I wanted to help; I skipped school some days when she was really low just to keep her company. But other days I got caught up in the things I wanted to do—seeing my friends, dating, having fun. In the end, I let her down too."

"But you were a kid. You *should* have been busy with those things."

He grunted his disapproval at her willingness to let him off the hook.

April's heart went out to him. He was tortured by thoughts and feelings that didn't seem valid to her. She'd talked to Mark enough to know that some things people can change and some things they can never change, and that it did no good to beat yourself up over the things you couldn't control. "It's like hating yourself because you have blue eyes," he'd told her during one of their discussions about their illnesses. "I was hurt by the way people treated me because I had CF, but while I couldn't control their feelings, I could control mine. I learned to live with it and to be friends with the kids who did overlook my disease."

She knew illness wasn't an easy burden to carry. She hadn't wanted to be pitied or to be made to feel like a freak by kids she knew, but when the truth had come out about her tumor, her real friends stuck by her. Others, like her onetime boyfriend Chris Albright, had dropped her. *His loss.* She said, "Brandon, don't blame yourself. And don't blame your father."

He jumped to his feet. "I didn't expect you to take his side."

"I'm not taking anybody's side," she insisted, grabbing hold of his hand. "Except for you, I never knew anybody in your family. How can I take sides? I'm just wondering if either you or your father could have stopped your mother no matter what you did. She made the choice to die, Brandon. She took the pills all by herself."

"He should have figured out what she planned to do," he insisted stubbornly. "He was *married* to her."

"Being married can't stop something bad from happening to a person, no matter how hard you try."

"How can you understand? I'm sorry I told you. Just forget it."

April could have told him plenty. She could have told him she was no stranger to the pain of feeling helpless and powerless. She could have told him about her brain tumor. But he didn't need the added shock right now, and she didn't need to become too embroiled in a relationship with him. She wanted to be around him as long as they could be friends and have fun. At the end of the summer, they would go their separate ways. "You're right," she told him quietly. "I don't understand, but please don't be sorry we talked about it. I'm not. It helps me to understand you better. And you're the one I care about. I'll never bring it up again, if that's what you want."

He stared at her. "I—I didn't mean to yell at you. I know you were just trying to help." He dropped beside her on the bench and took her shoulders in his hands. "I've never met anybody like you, April. It's like you can sometimes see inside me, and that makes me scared because I'm afraid you'll see all this bad stuff and hate me."

"We all have bad stuff inside us. I could never hate you, Brandon."

"I'm not used to talking about . . . about what happened to my mother. I miss her."

"I miss Mark."

His eyes, only inches from her face, looked moist. "He was very lucky to have you to love him." She felt her heart thudding and heard her pulse roaring in her ears. "I know I could never take his place, and I'm not trying to, but April, I really like you. I . . . would . . . like . . . to kiss you."

Her mouth went dry and she wanted to tell him, *"No, don't,"* but couldn't force her lips to say the words. She had kissed no one except Mark in more than a year, but suddenly, with all her heart, she wanted to kiss Brandon. She raised her chin in acceptance. He pulled her closer and tenderly kissed her parted lips.

So, this is what it feels like to fall in love, Brandon thought as he sat on the sofa in the great room of his house, mindlessly flipping through TV channels with a remote control. His best friend, Kenny, had tried to describe the emotion when Kenny had fallen for his latest girl. "It's a rocket ride, man. You feel like Superman and you want to walk on the clouds."

Well, Brandon agreed. Ever since the night before with April, he'd wanted to fly. She was everything he'd ever dreamed about having in a girlfriend—beauty, brains, sensitivity. He loved her, but he was afraid to tell her. She was still entangled with the memory of her dead fiancé, and Brandon wasn't certain how to untie her from her past love and get her to see him as a new one. His attraction, his attachment to her, had been happening for months, but it had all come to a head when he'd opened his heart concerning his mother. A pang shot through him as he realized the two of them would never meet.

His father's bedroom door opened, and his dad wandered sleepily down the hall. He stopped when he saw Brandon. "I didn't know if you'd be home."

Brandon flipped off the TV and looked at his father. "I have exams next week."

"You, um, doing okay with them?"

"If you're asking if I'm going to pass this year, the answer's yes."

His father went into the kitchen area that adjoined the great room. "You want some coffee?"

"I've had some, but there's more in the pot."

His father sat down at the breakfast bar that separated the two rooms and sipped his coffee. "It's good. Thanks for making it."

Brandon shrugged. Suddenly a thought

occurred to him as he remembered the pretty woman having dinner with his father last night. He stiffened and glanced down the hall toward his father's bedroom. "You are alone, aren't you?"

"I'm alone. Elaine's a nice woman and I'm sorry you and your girl didn't join us for dinner. Can you tell me a little about April?"

Brandon told his father about their meeting, her family, the plans the two of them had made for the summer. "I want to show her a great time before she leaves in August."

His father set down his cup. "She's a beautiful girl, son. And you looked as if you were having a good time with her. That's good. You should be having a good time. Maybe I could take the two of you to lunch sometime."

The offer surprised Brandon because the two of them rarely did things together, mostly because Brandon hadn't wanted to be around his father. "Maybe," he said.

"No one can show April a better time than you. You know this island like the back of your hand." His father sounded downright buoyant.

"I took her sailing. She liked that."

A heartbeat of silence; then his father said, "Sailing's a lot of fun, and you're a good sailor."

But not fun for us, Brandon thought. He stood. "Well, maybe I'd better go cram for today's test. Graduation ceremony is next Saturday," he added. "In case you want to come."

"Of course I want to come. You're my son and graduation is a big day. We'll do something afterward—lunch at the club. Oh, and be thinking about what you want as a gift. If there's anything special. If not, you'll have to take potluck."

I want my mother back. "I'll let you know." Brandon left the room without saying another word.

9

Brandon invited April and her parents to his graduation ceremony, and his father extended an invitation to all of them for dinner at the yacht club. Although the graduating class was small, the ceremony in the school's auditorium was well attended. Brandon ripped off his cap and gown as soon as his father finished taking pictures outside in front of the school seal. "This thing is suffocating me," he grumbled.

"I hated mine too," April assured him. "My friend Kelli said we looked as if we were wearing waffles on our heads."

She looked gorgeous to him, dressed in a summery cotton dress. Her long coppery hair caught the sun and shimmered. He saw her take several pills at the water fountain and asked, "You all right?"

"Fine. Just a slight headache. It'll pass."

At the yacht club, Brandon's father had reserved a table overlooking the sparkling blue waters of the ocean, where sailboats glided in a stiff westerly breeze. Brandon's father and April's parents seemed to have plenty to talk about, which gave Brandon the opportunity to concentrate on April. He told her, "I know my summer work schedule at the golf course—mornings from six until noon. I cut back on my hours—no weekends. That way I'll have every afternoon and evening free. I want to spend as much time as I can with you."

She rubbed her temples. "You didn't have to do that."

"Why not? You do want to do stuff together, don't you? You haven't changed your mind?"

"What about your other friends? Don't you want to be with them? I shouldn't hog all your free time."

"I was sort of a loner this year, April, and so I don't fit in too good anymore. Most of my friends are going away, and my friend

Kenny is stuck on his girlfriend still, so I wouldn't see much of him anyway."

"This might be your last chance to be with your friends. Once high school is over, everyone goes their separate ways."

"I should care? Until I leave for the States in August, I want to spend all my time with you." Suddenly embarrassed, he added, "I mean, that is, if you want to spend the time with me."

A slow smile lit her face. "Of course I do. It'll be a super summer. But it's okay if you change your mind at any time and want to include others in your life."

He nodded but knew that she was the only person in the world he wanted to be with. There was no one else. And perhaps there never would be anyone as special as April in his life again.

The room was spinning. April lay on her bed clutching the sheets, feeling as if she were caught in a whirlwind. *Stop! Stop!* Her vertigo had come on gradually over the past few weeks, sometimes making her feel as if she were aboard the pitching hull of a sailboat, sometimes as if she were being sucked into a whirlpool. She knew better than to try and stand; she'd fall over and the thud would bring her mother running, and the questions would start: "How long have you been having dizzy spells?" "Do you have headaches too?" "Why didn't you tell us?" "We're calling your doctor." "We're going back to New York immediately!"

April knew what would happen if they found out she was experiencing problems, and she didn't want to leave. She loved it here. She was happy. She didn't want to break her promises to Brandon. The loss of his mother had been devastating. How could she add to his unhappiness? The two of them were supposed to go sailing today. Brandon had told her, "I'll pack a picnic lunch and take you to a special little island where we can snorkel. You'll love it."

Her forehead broke into a sweat, and she felt nauseated. She swallowed a couple of pills, took deep breaths, and prayed for the vertigo to pass. She didn't want to think about what might be causing it. Perhaps it was only the start of an inner-ear infection. Or maybe she was anemic again. Iron deficiency was common in girls her age. She'd been treated for it while she was still in high school. It couldn't be something horrible . . . like the tumor . . . it couldn't be. She wanted more time.

Slowly the room stopped spinning, and she sat up shakily. As soon as she ate breakfast, she'd feel better. She wobbled to her private bathroom, where she showered and changed into a bathing suit. By the time she got to the breakfast table, she felt better. Her father was off playing golf, and her mother was reading the morning mail.

"A letter from Caroline," her mother said as April poured herself a glass of orange juice. "She says the things I shipped last month have really sold well in the store. She wants me to send more."

"Can you?"

"Brandon's father told me about an auction next week at one of the old sugar plantations on the west end of the island. I think I'll go. Why don't you come with me?"

April had often attended auctions with her mother and found them exciting, with people bidding against one another for estate furniture—the once-prized belongings of generations past. And driving from one end of the island to the other took little time. But April didn't want to commit to such a long day. What if she started feeling sick? "I've promised Brandon we'd do some things together."

"It's only one day. And you spend most of your free time with him as it is."

"Mom—please don't pressure me."

"I'm not pressuring you." Her mother set down Caroline's letter. "Honey, I'm glad you've got a friend like Brandon; he's a nice young man. I just think it would be nice for us to do something special together."

"I'll think about it," April hedged.

"Pity about his mother." April had told her parents about Mrs. Benedict's suicide.

"He doesn't talk about it much. I think he feels as if there was something he should have done to stop her."

"I knew a woman once whose mother committed suicide, and she really had a hard time getting over it. If a person ever really does get over such a thing. That's one of the things that's so pitiful about it. The victim's family often feels somehow responsible, although psychiatrists say that's not true."

"That's what I told him. But he's mad at his father, as if *he* might have somehow stopped her."

"My friend was angry for a long time too. Truth was, she was angry at her mother for killing herself, but she couldn't tell her how she felt. She couldn't do anything except suffer mentally."

April understood. She saw how much Brandon was suffering over his mother's death. Even she felt angry at Brandon's mother for making him hurt so badly. She hoped he would be able to find some path out of his pain and make peace with his father. There was nothing she could do to help him. Worst of all, she was only going to go away from him too.

Brandon set sail with April to a tiny, isolated island called a cay, several nautical miles from St. Croix. "These cays are all over the place," he told her. "They're made up of sand and coral rock, and I'll bet I've explored every one of them. Mom and I used to anchor off-shore and swim in to search for shells." He'd borrowed a bigger boat than the first one he'd taught April to sail. She took the tiller under his direction, turning the mainsail into the stiff breeze, tacking and coming about until the boat approached the white-sand cay he'd chosen for their picnic.

He jumped off into waist-high water and guided the boat ashore, then jammed the keel, the part of the boat that balanced it underwater, into the soft sand bottom. The sun seared through the shallow depths. She could see every ripple in the sand below. A crab scurried out of the way.

April helped Brandon carry their gear ashore. He pitched a small dome-shaped tent to shield them from the brutal heat of the sun. They spread out large towels and set down a cooler and a picnic basket. Brandon raised side flaps to catch the tropical breeze. "This is great," she told him, stretching out on her stomach so that she could gaze at the water lapping the shoreline and the boat.

"Well, don't get comfortable yet. We're going snorkeling." From a mesh bag he dragged out two sets of flippers, two face masks, and two bright orange snorkel tubes.

She held up the flippers. "You must be kidding. I'll look like a giant frog."

"With red hair," he joked. "Don't scare the fish." He pulled out a large bottle of sunscreen.

"I've already put some on me."

"You'll need more."

She turned her back and lifted her mass of hair, quickly twisting it into a knot and fastening it with a scrunchie. He drizzled the cool lotion on her warm skin, making her shiver involuntarily. His big hands smoothed it along her back and down her arms. He didn't hurry.

"Now what?" she asked, not meeting his gaze, her flesh tingling from his touch.

"Now we hit the water."

She followed him to the water's edge, where she put on the flippers and the mask. After a few minutes of instruction, he led her out deeper and helped her to float facedown. Below the surface, she clearly saw the white-sand bottom and Brandon's flippered feet. He towed her farther out to a coral reef shelf, and the undersea world changed dramatically. Fish, in shades of yellow, green, and even purple and silver, darted through a forest of living vivid-red coral. Starfish clustered around coral branches, their arms hugging the surfaces for dear life.

Once she got the hang of it, April easily sucked air through her snorkeling tube. Brandon never let go of her hand, and together they floated like voyagers from another planet. He tapped her shoulder and pointed to their left. She stared, awed, as a giant manta ray swam past, flapping its wings like a quiet bird of prey, its undersides flashing white in the blue water. Shafts of sunlight streamed downward, lighting beds of coral like spotlights that faded as the coral shelf dropped off and the ocean grew deeper, darker.

A curious parrot fish swam up to her mask, its bright blue lips making silent statements no human could understand. Startled, she flapped an arm, and the fish zipped away to the safety of the reef below. Brandon tapped her shoulder again, and she turned in time to spot a sea turtle, large as a rock but as buoyant in the water as Styrofoam, swimming downward. The world beneath the sea captivated April, and when Brandon pointed toward the shore, she didn't want to go.

"I loved it!" she squealed once they were back under the tent. "I had no idea it was so beautiful down there."

"Scuba diving's even more fun. But you need a tank and some lessons first," he said with a laugh. Bringing her pleasure, seeing her happy, made his heart swell. The girls who'd grown up on St. Croix were unimpressed by such sights, but showing it to April was like seeing it for the first time himself.

"Will you take me scuba diving?"

He laughed at her childlike enthusiasm. "I told you, this is your summer to do anything you want—" He stopped in midsentence. Suddenly April had lain back on the towel, her eyes squeezed shut, her face pale and pinched. Beads of sweat popped out on her forehead. The towel was wadded in her fists, as if she were trying to hold herself in place on the ground. "April! What's wrong? What's happening to you?"

10

Fear ripped through Brandon.

"Dizzy . . . ," April mumbled. "Very dizzy."

He tore the lid off the cooler, grabbed a handful of ice, and pressed it to her temples and throat. "Sit up. Maybe you're hyperventilating."

He helped her sit, but a wave of nausea made her groan.

"Take deep breaths," he said, pressing more ice against the back of her neck.

Nothing was helping. April couldn't stop the world from spinning. She sagged, folded against him, clung for dear life. He stroked her hair, held her in his lap, soothed her skin with a damp towel. "Breathing through your mouth for so long probably made you dizzy," he said, trying to comfort both of them.

With all her heart, she wanted to believe him, but she knew it wasn't so. She was sick and experiencing vertigo and there was only one explanation. "It'll pass," she said weakly, all the while praying, *Please make it go away. Don't let me be sick in front of him.*

"I'm really sorry, April. I wanted today to be fun."

She should have known her medical problem would catch up with her sooner or later. Why, *why* couldn't it have done so later? Tears squeezed from behind her closed eyelids. "It isn't your fault." She knew she should tell him the truth about herself, but all she remembered in the darkness behind her closed eyes was the expression on his face when he'd told her about his mother's suicide. How could she wound him again? Wouldn't it be better to simply let him think she was sick from some other cause? Anything—except the truth? "I—I think I ate some bad fish at supper last night. I wasn't feeling all that great when I got up this morning, but I wanted to come so badly that

I made myself feel better. I guess it's finally caught up with me. So much for the power of positive thinking."

"Let me pack up and get you home," he said. "Lying out here in the heat isn't helping you any."

She agreed, but she didn't want to go. She wanted to stay on this sandy strip of island and be with him. She wanted to feel the warmth of the sun. She wanted to hear the gentle sloshing of the sea against the shoreline. She wanted to remain in paradise. A headache crept up the back of her neck and settled around her head like a vise. The pain turned her skin clammy.

She heard him moving around and concentrated on the sounds he made, trying not to think about the mounting pain of the headache. He took the tent down last, after gently carrying her to the boat. The swaying of the boat caused her to totally lose her equilibrium. She felt like a matchstick tossed on a sea of waves, unable to get her bearings.

"I wish this thing had a motor," he grumbled. "Our boat has a motor. But my father won't take our boat out of dry dock."

Brandon was talking to no one but the

wind. Every time he looked down at the pale, motionless April, his heart lurched. She'd got sick so quickly. He'd been taken completely by surprise. His mother's moods had been mercurial—one minute she was happy, the next depressed—but eventually depression had won her over to its dark ways. That was his only experience with sickness, and even though her sickness had been in her mind, it had affected her physically.

He recalled days when she couldn't pull herself out of bed. He recalled nights when she drank and walked the floors, crying inconsolably. He'd felt helpless. And he felt helpless now. April's skin looked pale as paste, and she'd put a damp towel over her eyes. He didn't want anything to happen to her. He loved her. Of course, he couldn't tell her because he doubted she would believe him. And she loved the mysterious Mark. How did a guy compete with a dead person?

Fortunately, a stiff breeze allowed Brandon to make good time, and as soon as he arrived at the Buccaneer, he tossed his friend Billy the lines and shouted that he'd be back later for the gear. He got April into his car and drove as fast as he dared to her house.

He screeched into her driveway, leaped out, and ran to the front door. When her mother opened the door, he told her that April was sick.

Janice's eyes went wide, and the color left her face. "Help me get her into her room."

Again, Brandon carried her. Janice had thrown back the covers, and he laid April on the bed and stepped aside while her mother hovered over her. "Should you call a doctor?" Brandon asked. "You could call the one my mother—we use." He corrected himself.

"I'll call her doctor back home," Janice said, grabbing the phone.

"All the way in New York? We have doctors here."

"It's all right. He knows April."

"Whatever." He surveyed the room, April's room, filled with signs of April's life. Perfume bottles on the dresser. Bathing suits, a whole collection, piled in a heap near the closet door. A framed photo on her bedside table of a grinning guy in an auto racing uniform. *Mark*. He knew it instinctively. A knot formed in his stomach, seeing the image of his dead rival. So this was the guy she'd planned to marry. Brandon had wondered about him, about why she'd fallen in love with someone with cystic fibrosis. Why would she consider devoting herself to caring for a sick person? What magic power had Mark held over her?

Brandon heard April's mother talking softly into the phone, using words he didn't understand and phrases he couldn't quite catch.

She turned toward him. "Brandon, will you do me a favor? My husband is playing golf at the country club today. Would you go find him and tell him what's happened?"

"Sure." Brandon was glad to have something to do. "She will be all right, won't she? I mean, maybe you should take her to the emergency room. Maybe it's more than eating bad fish. Maybe it's food poisoning."

"Bad fish? Is that what she told you?"

"Yes."

Janice nodded. "As soon as her father gets here, we'll check it out."

"I'm on my way." Brandon strode to the door.

"Thank you," April's mother called. "Thank you for taking care of her."

He glanced back to see that her face was

still pale but her expression was calm, almost serene. And incredibly sad. It startled him, but he didn't have time to think about it. Brandon jumped into his car and drove like a madman toward the country club golf course.

"Why didn't you say something, April? Why didn't you tell us what was going on?" The tremor in her father's voice betrayed his attempt to be stern with her.

"I didn't say anything because I knew how you'd panic." She felt fuzzy, still floating from the effects of the shot of morphine the doctor at the hospital had given her. The headache had subsided for now.

"Panic?" her mother said. "You pass out from pain and you think we might panic? Over such a small, ordinary thing like that?"

"Don't be sarcastic, Mom. I'm sorry I didn't say something to you, but I just didn't want everything to end. I knew what was happening, but I didn't want to admit it."

Her father stroked her arm. "We don't know for sure what's happening. We have an appointment to see Dr. Sorenson in New York the day after tomorrow."

"I don't want to go home."

"He wants to run tests."

"I'm sick of tests. We all know what the tests are going to tell him. They're going to say that the tumor's growing again. And he's going to say the same thing he told us last year. There's nothing else medical science can do for me!" Her voice had risen, and in spite of the calming effects of the morphine, she began to cry.

Her mother scooped her into her arms, rocked her, and cooed, "Oh, baby. Oh, my sweet little girl."

"I'm not giving up," her father insisted. "You're our daughter, April. You mean everything to us. I won't let them tell us there's nothing else that they can do. I don't believe it."

April wept silently into her mother's shoulder, missing Mark, then Brandon. Life was being sucked away from her, snatched like a purse stolen by a thief. She'd known her prognosis all along. No one had ever hidden the truth from her. Maybe it would have been better if they had hidden it. The knowledge was overwhelming. *Goodbye to paradise.*

"I'm going to make arrangements now,"

her father said. "We'll pack what we need. And what we don't take we can get at home. We have a house full of stuff on Long Island."

"Will we come back?" April's voice sounded dull and thick.

"Probably not."

She winced as if he'd struck her.

Her mother smoothed her hair. "Do you want to call Brandon? Would you like me to call and talk to him?"

"No. I'll call him from New York."

"Are you sure?"

April pictured his face. He would pity her. Or worse, he'd withdraw the way her old boyfriend Chris had when she'd told him about her tumor. Better to go away and call Brandon and tell him over the phone. The miles between them would act as a cushion to soften his reaction. "I'm sure," she said finally. "When he calls later"—as she knew he would—"just tell him I'm resting and that I'll talk to him when I'm able."

"If that's what you want," her mother said in a tone that told April she didn't agree with her plan.

"That's what I want."

The island of St. Croix slipped away under a blanket of clouds below the airplane's window. The water turned into a rippled piece of blue taffeta, and April could scarcely bear to look down at it. Like spoils from an old corsage, a few hand-picked hibiscuses lay on her lap, the red and pink petals' edges wilting, the yellow pollen clinging to her fingers. She felt terrible. The pills the doctor had prescribed made her feel groggy and out of sync, but at least there was no headache. She imagined Brandon coming to the house, knocking on the door, seeing the note. Hastily she'd scribbled: WE HAD TO LEAVE. FAMILY PROBLEMS BACK HOME. I'LL CALL YOU IN A FEW DAYS. Of course, it was all lies. She hoped she'd have the courage to talk to him soon. Tears wet her face as the plane climbed higher and the sea slipped away under more clouds. She closed her eyes and allowed the medication to lull her into a drugged sleep.

Brandon stared at the note, incredulous. April was gone. Just like that. Not even a word of goodbye. She could have called. She could have told him personally or even over the phone. He turned the piece of paper over, hoping for more of an explanation on the back. It was blank.

She could have said, *"See you soon."* Or *"I'll miss you."* But she hadn't. She and her family had sneaked away, leaving him with a hundred unanswered questions. The hibiscus bush next to the porch had been picked clean, all the flowers gone, the leaves shining green in the sun. He knew she'd taken them with her. But he also realized that she'd taken much more than the rich red and pink flowers. She'd also taken his heart.

11

July in New York was just as hot, humid, and sticky as April remembered. In the past, during the sweltering days, her family had taken vacations into the mountains or to Europe. Except for last year, when she'd been with Mark and hadn't wanted to go anywhere he didn't go. The city felt oppressive to her now, teeming with people in a hurry—a shock to her system after the easygoing atmosphere of St. Croix. Even her childhood home seemed uninviting. Her parents had called ahead to have it opened and aired, but musty odors from having been shut up for months still lingered. Her room had been cleaned and fresh linen put on her bed, but she missed looking out at the sea, missed the aroma of tropical flowers and salt-tinged air, and as much as she hated to admit it, she missed Brandon too. In short, she didn't want to be back home.

On Wednesday morning the three of them headed into the city for the hospital and the rounds of testing she didn't want to face. Two days later, as they sat in Dr. Sorenson's office, April felt drained and, like a child in a cruel mazelike game, right back at square one—the place she'd started from more than eighteen months before.

Dr. Sorenson was as pleasant as ever, exactly as she remembered him, but he looked preoccupied, more reserved than in past visits. He placed the MRI films on the light board and drew a circle around the now-familiar dense glob pressing against her cerebellum. "It's growing again," he said matter-of-factly, his voice tinged with sadness.

Deep down, it was nothing she hadn't known, but seeing it on the film, hearing him state the obvious, made her suck in her breath. His actual words gave finality to her situation. It closed doors.

"So where do we go from here?" her father asked sharply, after a moment of silence.

Of course, they'd been all through her options before she'd ever left for St. Croix: She had none. The tumor was too aggressive for treatments, too large for gamma knife surgery.

"I wish I had better news for you," Dr. Sorenson said now, picking his words carefully.

"Then this is it, isn't it?" April asked boldly, suddenly wanting to get everything settled once and for all. "There's really nothing else you can do for me, is there?" Tears stung her eyes, but she refused to let them out.

"You've had two rounds of radiation—the maximum—and chemotherapy won't touch this type of tumor. I'm sorry, April."

"Her mother and I won't accept that." Her father struck his fist on the edge of the doctor's desk. "I have money. There are other doctors. Other hospitals."

"Your daughter's prognosis won't change. You can spend thousands, hundreds of thousands; it won't make a difference."

"Experimental drugs," her father shouted. *"Something."*

April recoiled. She didn't want to be somebody's lab experiment.

"If there was anything on the medical horizon to help your daughter, I would have suggested it. Certainly there are quacks in the world, Mr. Lancaster. There are many people who promise cures but can't deliver them. Many charlatans who'll take your money, make April suffer, but not cure her."

"So you're saying we just have to abandon hope? We won't, sir. We can't."

"Oh, Hugh . . . ," April's mother cried. "Do something. Please."

April stood. The last time the doctor had tried to close the door on her hope she'd shouted at him too, and then had run from his office, refusing to listen to any more grim news. And she'd gone on to have a few wonderful months with Mark, followed by spring and most of the summer in St. Croix. This time, she was resigned. "Please stop shouting." Her knees trembled, but she stood her ground and stared at her distraught parents. Unbelievably, a calm settled on her. "It won't help, Daddy. It won't change things. The doctor's out of miracles."

She sat on her mother's lap like a child and nestled her head against her shoulder, reached for her father's hand, and pulled him closer into the circle.

"Oh, baby," her mother wept.

"Tell us, Dr. Sorenson. Tell us what to expect." April was dry-eyed now.

The doctor cleared his throat. "I'll be increasing your steroid medication to keep down the swelling of your brain as the tumor advances."

She winced. Even though the pills had helped the headaches in the past, she'd hated the side effects: weight gain, a puffy moon-shaped face, and swollen hands and feet. The treatment had deepened her voice and made hair grow in usually hairless places on her body. "And then? Please tell me everything."

"You'll have memory lapses, equilibrium problems, trouble with speech and probably sight and hearing. Eventually you'll be bed-ridden. You'll slip into a coma. Your lungs will fill with fluid, and you'll stop breathing."

The progression sounded logical to her. Her body would slowly shut down as the tumor choked out her life. "Will I have to be in the hospital?"

"No, not if you don't want to be. Hospice

is a wonderful group that helps families keep their loved ones at home . . . until the end. You can have a nurse, a hospice member, anyone you want with you."

"I'd like that. I'd like to die at home."

"Except for headaches, which will pass in time, you won't be in pain. That's a unique feature of the brain. It has no nerve endings. That's why we can perform complicated surgeries on it with nothing more than a local anesthetic. Patients can be wide awake through several types of brain surgery, even talk to the surgeon and give reports on what they are feeling."

Cold comfort, April thought. She said, "So, I'll just go to sleep and not wake up?"

"Yes, that's pretty much how it will be."

It was impossible for her to imagine nonexistence, to think of herself not of this world. She hugged her mother tightly and squeezed her father's hand. "I want you with me the whole time."

"We'll be with you, baby," her mother whispered. "You know we will."

April closed her eyes, shutting out all but the sound of her own breathing.

———

Later, April told them she didn't want to talk about it. She wanted to concentrate on what was happening in the here and now, not in the future. But when she was alone, she steeped her senses in touching, tasting, seeing. She walked in the yard, fingered flower petals, sniffed the roses, all the while mourning the loss of them. Once, she held her breath for as long as she could, but gave up and gasped for air just as she started to feel light-headed. Would she do the same thing when she was in a coma? She wished she'd spent more time talking to Mark about dying, about giving up and letting go.

And she thought about Brandon too. She wondered if he hated her for running off without a word. She thought about calling him but wondered what she would say to him. It was as if she were two people: the girl in New York who was dying, and the girl in St. Croix who was carefree and happy and having a wonderful time. How could she merge the two? How could she expect Brandon to understand? She'd been unfair.

She wondered too how his mother could have tossed away her life. The pain her suicide had caused Brandon was immeasurable.

Hadn't she considered what it might do to him? April knew that if she could do anything to hold on to her life, she would. It made no sense to her that someone would throw away what she so desperately wanted.

The hospice people came out to the house to visit, to talk. They were kind people, understanding, with their own losses behind them. But April realized they were more for her parents' benefit than hers. Her parents would be the ones left behind while she would go . . . where? She'd always believed in heaven, had been taught about it in Sunday school. She tried to remember what she'd been told but could only recall that heaven was a place of great beauty where there would be no more sadness or sorrow.

But thoughts of eternal peace and perfect happiness brought her little comfort. There were still so many things she wanted on this side of heaven. She had wanted a career and to get married, maybe to have children. Until now, she'd given no thought to growing old, but suddenly it didn't seem like such a bad thing to do. What would she have looked like? Would her hair color have faded? Would her complexion have wrinkled?

"The trouble," she told herself one morning as she studied her face in the mirror, "is
that you have too much time to think." She
needed to talk to someone, be with someone
other than her parents. Kelli wouldn't be
home for another few weeks. April needed
someone now. Which was how she ended up
calling Mark's mother and making plans to
visit her. Yet as she climbed up the steps of
the old brownstone on a hot, muggy morning, she felt it might have been a mistake.
The pain of the happy memories she'd shared
with Mark at his parents' home engulfed
her. She almost turned and skittered away,
but the door was flung open and Mark's
mother, Rosa, threw her arms around April
and dragged her into the cool quiet of the
foyer.

"Praise be!" Rosa said. "How good to see
you, April. When did you get home? How
was your trip? You look wonderful! So tan
and beautiful." She held April at arm's
length, stroking her with her gaze.

To April, Rosa was ever pretty, with lively
eyes and black hair sprinkled with gray. She
looked so much like Mark, it brought a lump
to April's throat. April gave a brief account-

ing of her time, leaving out her reason for
returning to New York.

Rosa herded her into the kitchen, where a
giant pot of simmering soup filled the room
with its tomato aroma. Rosa sat April down
at the table and proceeded to ladle up a bowl
of soup. Never mind that April wasn't hungry. "Tell me everything," Rosa insisted, sitting with her at the table. "Did I say that
we've missed you? Thank you for the post-
cards . . . such a beautiful place."

April talked glowingly about St. Croix, not
mentioning Brandon, of course, and finished
by asking, "How have you all been?"

"Mark's father is well. Still working too
hard, but such is a detective's life—there's so
much crime out there. And it's good for him
to have a job he loves. Marnie and Jill still
aren't married, but Marnie's met a nice Italian boy and we have hopes for her."

April smiled, recalling Mark's pretty sisters
and their parents' desire to see them married
and settled. It didn't seem to matter that
both were competent, professional women.
To Rosa, marriage and children were the only
real-life choice for a woman. "You tell them
hello for me."

"Why me? You tell them yourself. Now that you're back, you and your parents can come for dinner."

"We can do that." April felt her mouth getting dry and knew she was having an attack of nerves. There was so much she had to tell Rosa, but how should she begin? "I miss Mark," she confessed. "In St. Croix, I thought about him every day. He would have really liked it there."

Rosa's smile turned wistful. "Not a day goes by that I don't think of him too. I . . . we . . . miss him very much. But I want you to know how much happiness you brought him the last year of his life. I will always love you for that."

"I still have the wedding dress. It's packed away in a huge box in the back of my closet."

"You were beautiful in it. Maybe you can wear it for another."

April dropped her gaze. "I was wondering if you would do me a favor."

"Ask me for anything."

"Come with me to the cemetery. I want to visit Mark's grave."

12

The cemetery stretched green and quiet in the hot sun. Manicured lawns were broken by aboveground mausoleums, statues of saints, and carved stonework and bronze markers with vases. April watched sprinklers spew sprays of water over sections of grass as Rosa drove slowly along the internal roadway toward Mark's grave. The cemetery was more beautiful than April remembered from the day of Mark's burial, but she'd been so numb at the time she'd hardly noticed anything.

"It's over there," Rosa said, stopping the car.

They got out and wound their way through a field of markers until Rosa halted near a weeping willow tree. April stooped down. A marker held Mark's name, his birth and death dates, and the inscription BELOVED SON. AT PEACE FOREVER. Rising over the marker stood a statue of the Virgin Mary, her arms open. A bronze vase held fresh flowers. "I wanted him to always have flowers," Rosa explained. "The groundskeepers put them out once a week for him."

"Do you come often?"

"Maybe once a month. It hasn't been that long, you know."

He had died in the fall. April stared down at the marker, imagining her name etched in the metal. She took a quivering breath. "I'm dying, Rosa." It was the first time she'd ever called Mark's mother by her first name. Always before, she'd addressed her as Mrs. Gianni.

"What?" The woman stepped backward as if she'd been struck.

"The tumor's growing again. There's nothing the doctors can do."

"Oh, April, no. It can't be true."

April looked at her, saw tears swimming in her eyes, and swallowed against the lump of

emotion wedged in her own throat. "It's one
of the reasons we came home from St. Croix.
I started having problems again. We had to
get them checked out."

"This isn't right. You don't deserve this."

Mark's family had always known about her
brain tumor, but Mark's problems were so
overwhelming, Apirl's had taken a backseat.
"Mark didn't deserve CF either. We knew
that this was a possibility when he and I first
met. For a long time, it scared me so much I
didn't even want to date him. But he was a
hard one to say no to." April smiled, remembering his long pursuit of her and the way he
had worn down her resistance. "We loved
each other, but sometimes I forgot about the
illnesses. I didn't believe either of us would
actually . . . you know . . . really die."

"There must be something the doctors can
do for you."

"They introduced us to the people at hospice. I don't want to die in the hospital." The
memory of Mark's last days haunted her.
There had been nothing friendly, nothing
comforting about the cool technology of the
hospital's machines and antiseptic smells. She

wanted her departure from the planet to be different.

Rosa crossed herself. "You mustn't give up."

"I'm not giving up. I'm being realistic. It's better to face the truth than to pretend it isn't happening."

"Is there anything you want me to do for you? Just ask."

"My parents . . . it's hard on them. If you could be here for them . . . you know . . . afterward."

"Absolutely. If they ever want to talk, tell them to call."

Mark's parents knew what it was to lose a child. Funny, April hadn't thought of herself as a child in many years, but she felt like one now. She felt small and frightened. She wanted the bad things to go away. She didn't want to go through what lay ahead.

"And I was thinking . . . do you think I could be buried here? By Mark?" She wasn't Catholic, but all at once it was important to her to think about having a place to belong to, a place for her parents to come and visit.

"I'll talk to my priest. You were planning

on marrying in the church. What can it matter if you want to rest beside your fiancé forever?"

April knelt and ran the palm of her hand across Mark's name. The bronze felt smooth and warm from the sun. Shadows from the willow tree danced across the grass beside her. She too would soon become a shadow, shifting in and out of the sunlight. Her body might be placed below the ground, but her spirit— "You believe Mark's in heaven, don't you?"

"Yes. I believe Mark's with God. The only thing that makes losing him easier is knowing that, and that he isn't in any more pain. The pain he suffered was always the hardest part for me . . . although he rarely complained." She sighed. "Long ago, I resigned myself to knowing that I would never hold a grandchild of his."

Because boys with cystic fibrosis are sterile, April reminded herself. She remembered the night he'd told her he'd never be able to father children. He'd been so afraid she'd leave him. As it was turning out, she'd never give her parents a grandchild either. Her parents' genes, her family tree, ended with her. "Do you think God will tell me why, if I ask him?"

"Why?"

"Why Mark and I had to die. Why we were ever born in the first place."

"I certainly plan to ask him," Rosa said with a shrug. "My priest says God has a reason for everything, but that he doesn't owe us any explanations."

April wondered if once she was dead, she'd understand God's purposes. The meaning of life and God's purposes were too vast a subject to think about now.

She said, "I'm ready to leave now."

"Of course." Rosa began walking to the car.

April followed. In the distance a sprinkler sent water skyward, and in a quirk of the light, a rainbow formed. She watched it shimmer and thought of childhood stories of pots of gold at the rainbow's end. Somehow it seemed fitting, and also a kind of foreshadowing. At the end of the rainbow of her life, the ground would swallow her. And she would lie beside Mark in death, as she had been unable to lie beside him in life.

———

After hugs and promises to keep in touch, April returned home. Her father insisted on taking April and her mother to a restaurant overlooking Long Island Sound for dinner. They sat in a quiet corner booth with lit candles, watching the sky turn from orange to red to purple with the waning light of the sun.

April stared out at the water, a deep navy blue, so different in color from the intense turquoise of the Caribbean. Lately all things seemed different to her. Music sounded more beautiful, colors appeared more vibrant. Did knowing that she would soon have to leave this world make her time in it more precious? She wasn't sure. She only knew that she felt balanced on the brink between dread and expectation. "I visited Mark's grave today," she told her parents.

They looked startled. "Was that wise?" her father asked.

"I miss him. I wanted to be near him again."

Her mother's lips pressed together. April could tell she didn't approve. "I hope you aren't dwelling on dark thoughts. You should be putting your energy into positive ones.

Doctors don't know everything. Miracles happen."

"Is that what you think will happen for me? A miracle?"

Her mother's face flushed. "I just don't think it's smart to abandon hope."

"I'm not. But I have to know what to hope for. A cure doesn't seem likely. So I have to hope for other things."

"Such as?"

She shrugged. "Courage. The next few months aren't going to be easy. Not for any of us." Her parents said nothing. "Mark's mother said that you should call her. That she knows what you're going through and that she'll be there for you."

April's mother turned her head and jabbed furiously at the napkin in her lap. "I know she means well, but she can't possibly know what I'm feeling. She can't begin to understand how angry I am." Her voice cracked. "You are my only child. Rosa has others."

April blinked, incredulous. Would knowing you had other children make it easier to lose one? "That doesn't make sense."

"And your dying does?"

April's father put out his hand, and April's

mother took it. April watched as their grip on each other tightened and wished she could hang on too. After she was gone, they would still have each other. She was glad of that. "Mom, I don't want to die. I don't want to leave either of you, but I can't help it. Please, don't make me feel as if there's something I should be doing to stop it." Tears welled in her eyes.

"Is that what you think?" Her mother looked stricken. "Do you think I'm holding you responsible because you're dying?"

Her father said, "We know you can't help it, baby. We know it's not your fault."

The incredible sadness of the moment was breaking April's heart. A part of her wished she could save them all from the horrible process that lay ahead for them. But a part of her desperately needed them with her to help make the leaving easier. She felt torn between wanting to spare them and needing them to shield her.

"I'm sorry," her mother whispered. "I had no right to dump my frustrations on you. There's nothing you can do to stop this from happening. There's nothing we can do either. But I feel helpless and powerless. And so very angry. We have all this money, and it counts for nothing when it comes to stopping what's happening. When we wanted a baby, we turned to medicine and it helped us. Now the medical community has abandoned us."

By the time their food arrived, none of them had an appetite. April toyed with her fork, feeling absolutely strung out. She didn't want her last months—maybe only weeks—to be like this, with each of them sad, angry, and locked in a prison of pain. If she allowed it, death would have a double victory over her. And *that* she could not stand. It was hard enough to lose her life. She would not also lose her spirit, her capacity to feel joy and show love. Mark had shown her love up until the very end of his life. His last breath had gone into forming the words "I love you." She couldn't—wouldn't—allow hers to say less. This, then, was her season of goodbye, her farewell to a good life. She vowed to make each and every minute that was left to her count for something.

13

The arrival of April's friend Kelli in mid-August was like a fresh breeze blowing through the stagnant air of April's life. April flung open the front door and they threw themselves into each other's arms. Kelli squealed, "How are you? I've missed you so much!" She dropped her duffel bag on the floor, for they'd already planned that she would spend the night.

"Same here!" April cried. She held Kelli at arm's length. "Wow! You look fabulous! When did you cut your hair?"

"Ages ago. Do you like it?" Kelli spun, showing off her short dark cap of curls. "But look at you! You're absolutely golden brown.

And your hair. I'll bet it's three shades lighter."

"All that sun in St. Croix."

Kelli peered closely at her. "Have you put on weight?"

"Um—I'm back on that headache medicine for a while. You remember how it makes me puff up like a blowfish."

"But why—"

April grabbed Kelli's arm and dragged her up the stairs to her room. "We'll talk about me later. First I want to hear all about you. And college. And your summer job." She scrambled onto the bed and hugged her knees. "So, start talking."

"School's awesome," Kelli said, plopping down across from April, Indian style. "It was scary at first, being so far from home and all, but now I love it. My roommate, Cheryl, is a real athlete—she's on a basketball scholarship—and she lives down in San Francisco, so that's where I crash over major holidays when the school shuts down. She's dragged me hiking and rock climbing and blading—" Kelli ticked off on her fingers. "I've never had so much exercise in my life."

"And classes? You do go to classes, don't you?"

"I only sleep through the morning ones. Actually, I like classes. Much better than high school. Can you believe I'll be a sophomore in September?"

April didn't need reminding. She too would have been a second-year college student if only cancer hadn't happened to her. "And your job? Are you the boss yet?"

"Work is work. But waiting tables at a coffeehouse all summer was kind of fun. I honestly didn't want to quit and come home, but I had to . . . Mom was pressuring me. She hasn't seen me since Christmas break, so I had to make an appearance."

"How is your mom?"

Kelli shrugged, and her bright smile faded. "She's adjusting to being divorced. She's living in the city now that the house has been sold, and she's got a job in a florist shop. She's doing good, but I think she misses her old friends."

"And your dad?"

"He's into his second childhood out in Denver. He's dating a girl who's only eight years older than me. Can you believe it?"

Kelli didn't wait for a response. "What do I care? He's paying my college tuition."

But April could tell that Kelli cared very much. "Any cool guy in your life?" she asked, changing the subject.

"There's Jonathan." Kelli's expression softened. "He's a junior and going for a degree in restaurant management. We worked at the coffeehouse together. He's perfectly wonderful."

"Kelli! Are you *serious* about him?"

"Define *serious*. He makes my knees weak when he looks at me, and when he kisses me the earth moves. Just a crush, I'd say."

April squealed and swatted her friend with a pillow. "You're in love! I know the signs."

"Well . . . maybe just a little. Not as serious as you and Mark were, of course, but I really like him." Kelli's eyes sparkled. "Which leads me to ask about Brandon."

Now it was April's turn to look serious. "I don't think I'm on Brandon's favorite-person list. I, um, sort of ran out on him."

"What do you mean?"

"We left St. Croix in a hurry. I didn't tell him goodbye."

"But why? That's not like you."

"Oh—you know, we waited until the last minute to pack up and then the next thing I knew we were on the plane and on our way."

"You haven't written him? Or called him?"

"I will," April said dismissively. Once again, she wasn't up to confessing the whole truth to Kelli. As long as they could just talk about this and that, she could pretend that she was normal. She could make believe that everything was perfect, and she wouldn't have to tell her best friend that she was dying.

They went for ice cream, and as April drove through the familiar streets she recalled their days of growing up together. Every street corner, every neighborhood, blossomed with memories. The dance studio where they'd taken ballet classes in the third and fourth grades was open and conducting classes, and a group of little girls could be seen doing exercises at the barre through the plate glass window.

Kelli licked her ice-cream cone, not paying much attention to April's meandering tour. "I can't wait to get back to Oregon," she said. "I'd forgotten how muggy summer is around here."

"You're right. It's even cooler in St. Croix than it is here."

"I'm sorry I never got down there to visit you. I would have loved it. Will you go back?"

"Probably not." April regretted not returning. Not merely because she missed the beauty of the island, but also because she would never see Brandon again. All that lay ahead for her now was a downward spiral into sickness. She shifted gears. "How'd you like to run by school?"

"Whatever."

Their former high school, a large redbrick building, had been closed for the summer, but a few of the teachers had returned to prepare for the fall term, so the doors were open. April and Kelli strolled down the empty halls, their footfalls echoing in the quiet. The scent of chalk and white paste sent a wave of nostalgia through April. She'd never thought she would miss the place, but suddenly she did miss it. She'd been an excellent student and had received high honors. Once she'd even dreamed of becoming a TV journalist.

"I wish you could see my campus," Kelli

said, seemingly oblivious to the spell of the building. "It's majorly cool, while this place is so rinky-dink." They'd stopped in front of the trophy case. "Look, there's your name." Kelli pointed to a tall silver award won by the debate team in April's junior year. April's name was etched in the metal.

"That was fun," April said with a wistful smile.

"Immortalized for all time," Kelli said brightly.

April figured that once she was gone, the trophy and photos in the yearbook would be all that remained of her. "I think you should go to the twenty-fifth reunion," she told Kelli.

"Sure. We'll go together." April didn't answer, but headed for the parking lot and the car. "Hey, wait for me," Kelli called, jogging after her. "What's the rush?"

"No hurry. Just thought of somewhere else I'd like to go." April drove slowly and turned down a side street. "Have you been by your old house?"

"Not yet."

"Would you like to?"

"I guess," Kelli said halfheartedly.

The quiet tree-lined street was just as April

remembered it. "The last time I drove down this street was that day last year when you left for college."

"I think I knew then that I wouldn't be back to live here. My folks were barely speaking."

April pulled up to the curb and shut off the engine. The old brick house looked well kept. The shutters and front door had been painted blue, and a stranger's car was in the circular driveway. "I missed you from the second you rolled out of the driveway."

"You were making plans to marry Mark."

"I wish I could have had more time with him."

Kelli stared out at the house for a long time before sighing. "It seems like a million years ago that I lived here."

April heard the emotion in her friend's voice. "I know what you mean. When I got back home, everything seemed out of sync. It was as if I didn't belong here anymore."

"I really *don't* belong here. And I guess my parents' split is for the best. They've been unhappy together for so long. I think they just stayed together because of me. Still, it's weird."

"What's weird?"

"Seeing the house, knowing that someone else lives in it. Knowing I don't have a home anymore—just a college dorm room halfway across the country."

"I didn't mean to make you sad," April said softly.

"I'll get over it. I mean, you were ready to start a new home with Mark last summer. Isn't that the way things are supposed to be? You grow up, move out, get married, and make your own life."

Yes, for some people, April thought. She switched on the engine. "Let's get out of here. It's almost time for supper, and Mom will be miffed if you don't eat with us."

"Has her cooking improved?"

"Not much."

Both girls broke out laughing, and April sped back toward her house, anxious to dispel the gloom that had fallen over them both.

Dinner would have been subdued if not for Kelli's animated chattering. April's father asked questions about college, and Kelli told about her campus, her classes, her aspirations.

"I have to declare a major by the time I'm a junior, and right now I'm leaning toward a degree in public relations. I like working with people, and I'm getting good grades in a couple of advertising classes."

"You'd be good at PR," Hugh told her.

"Maybe April and I can go into business together someday."

April's mother caught April's gaze with a questioning look that asked, *"Haven't you told her?"* and April flashed her a look that said, *"Not yet."*

But once dinner was over and April and Kelli climbed the stairs to April's bedroom, Kelli shut the door firmly behind her and turned to face April. She said, "All right—it's time you told me everything."

"Everything? What do you mean?" April's mouth went dry, and her heart thumped nervously.

"We've talked about everything but you. We've gone a lot of places today and tripped down Memory Lane. I've known you for most of my life, and I know when something is bothering you. Your parents look totally depressed, and I haven't asked you about

your health because I figured out real fast
that you didn't want to talk about it earlier
today. But now I want to know. Please, don't
keep me in the dark any longer. Tell me,
April, what's going on?"

14

April stood in the middle of the room, looked Kelli straight in the face, and told her. She'd thought she would be able to get through the whole story without crying, but as she quietly delivered the news about her impending death, as she watched Kelli's eyes widen and her hand clamp across her mouth to stifle sobs, and saw tears trickle down Kelli's cheeks, April wept with her.

"No! No!" Kelli kept shaking her head.

April closed the distance between them and took her friend in her arms, trying to comfort her. "Don't cry. I hate to see you cry." It struck April as odd that she, the one who was dying, should be comforting the one who was not, but it seemed the right thing to do. Kelli was devastated, and April wanted to help ease her pain. It was as if she were removed from the situation. As if it weren't her they were talking about, but some other person, some mutual friend.

Between sobs, Kelli managed to say, "I knew it was going to be bad news. I knew by the way you were driving around today, visiting all the places where we grew up, that you had something heavy to tell me. Oh, April, I'd give anything if it wasn't this kind of news."

"I wish it was something else too."

"Your doctor . . . he's positive? There isn't any mistake?"

"No mistake." April fumbled for tissue from a box on her vanity and handed a wad to Kelli. "It's been hard to even think about it. Some mornings I wake up and I feel real mellow, and then it hits me: I'm going to die. It sort of spoils the whole day."

Kelli blew her nose and attempted a smile at April's dark humor. "It isn't fair."

"What *is* fair?"

"Well, not *this*!" Kelli sank onto the bed and grabbed April's hand. "That settles it. As long as you're here, I'm not going to leave you. I'm quitting school and moving back home."

"Kelli, you can't drop out of school. I won't let you."

"And I won't let you die without me." Kelli dissolved into fresh tears.

April settled beside her on the bed. "Everybody has to die sometime or another, Kelli. You have to go on with your life."

"I'm putting my life on hold and you can't stop me."

"Look, I don't even know when this might happen to me. You can't sit around in some kind of deathwatch." She made a face. "It's unnatural."

"Says who?"

"Says me. You've planned to go back to Oregon in two weeks, and that's exactly what I want you to do. I—I don't want you to hover over me, waiting for me to keel over."

"That's not what I'll do."

"You won't mean to, but it'll happen. I remember what it was like to watch Mark die. I didn't believe it was happening. I felt helpless because I couldn't stop it. It was a nightmare, and you shouldn't have to go through it."

"And so what am I supposed to do? Sit in Oregon and wait for my phone to ring? Wait for your mother to call and drop the bomb on me?"

"Yes."

Kelli shook her head furiously. "I won't. I won't be three thousand miles away while you . . . while you . . ." She couldn't finish her sentence.

"Everything you've told me about has been about Oregon. It's where your life is. It's where all the people you care about live. It's your home. And it's where you should be."

Kelli stared down at the soggy tissue in her hands. "I care about you too."

"Then go back to school. Go do all those things I can't do."

"What about these next two weeks?" Kelli switched tacks.

"We'll have a good time. Just like we used to have together."

Kelli eyed April skeptically. "Right. We'll have a great time thinking that this is the last time we'll ever be together."

"I don't like it either," April said sharply. "But I can't make it go away. It's hard enough watching my parents going crazy over it. I don't need to see you suffering too. I—I need to have fun, Kelli. I need to concentrate on something besides what's happening to me."

This was the argument that persuaded Kelli. April saw acquiescence on her friend's face. "We'll go into the city. We'll spend a few days at my mother's. Her place is small, but it's in SoHo and there's a million things to do, lots of places to go."

"We'll be like Siamese twins," April said. "Joined at the hip."

Kelli gave her a bittersweet look. "Until we're surgically separated," she said. "Or whatever it is doctors do with twins who share one heart."

Kelli's mother welcomed them, hurrying off to her job in the mornings and letting the girls sleep in. They roused themselves by midmorning, then set out with an agenda to do only the things they felt like doing. They spent two full days browsing department stores and boutiques, trying on the choicest clothing, the most fashionable wardrobes. On another day they ate lunch in Central

Park on a blanket under a tree, rode the subway from one end of one route to the other, and spent the rest of the rainy day in a giant bookstore in Times Square.

They spent a day at a trendy beauty salon, where Kelli had her dark hair streaked with bright fuchsia and April considered cutting hers but chickened out at the last minute. She opted instead for a rainbow manicure, having every fingernail painted a different color. They pierced their ears in three more places and bought diamond studs at Tiffany's for every new hole. They had tattoos put on their ankles. Kelli chose a dolphin and April a hibiscus. "It reminds me of the islands," she said.

One night Kelli's mother brought home a gorgeous arrangement of tropical flowers—orange-hued bird-of-paradise, red and yellow hibiscus, pale pink and lavender orchids, and snow-white gardenias. April sat it on the kitchen table and stared at it all evening. The scent was heavenly, and when she closed her eyes she could almost see the turquoise ocean and smell the salt-tinged air. And she could see Brandon's face, sun-browned, his hair bleached blond, his eyes as blue as the sky.

April told Kelli about her love of sailing, describing the sound the wind makes as it billows out the sails, the sharp snap the nylon makes when the boat comes about. "That settles it," Kelli said. "Whenever I get married, I'm going to demand a honeymoon in St. Croix."

"Lots of people do." April told her about the wedding gazebo she'd seen with Brandon.

"Sounds like heaven."

"Just like heaven." Afterward, April grew quiet, and that night she went to bed early, choosing not to stay up and watch the video she and Kelli had rented that afternoon.

As their two weeks together passed, April began to experience more frequent episodes of vertigo. One day she couldn't even get out of bed. Kelli sat by her bedside, and they played cards and board games. April kept losing her concentration and had to give it up when she started having double vision. Kelli asked if she should call April's parents, but April refused adamantly. The following day April seemed fine.

Two days before Kelli was scheduled to return to college, they stayed at April's for one final sleepover. "I'm going to miss you," April told Kelli in the privacy of April's bedroom after dinner with her parents.

"I can cancel my ticket. Just say the word."

"You've seen how it's going to be for me. Once I start getting worse, I won't even know you're in the same room. Believe me, it's better that you remember the fun we've had. Not the bad stuff."

Kelli turned her head, and April knew her friend didn't want her to see any tears. April got up from where they were sitting on the floor and went to her closet. "There's something I want you to have," she said. She disappeared into the walk-in closet and emerged dragging an enormous box.

Kelli's eyes widened. "Big box."

April plopped it in front of her. "Open it."

Kelli lifted the lid, pushed aside layers of tissue, and gasped. "It's your wedding dress."

"It's yours now."

"But I can't—"

"Yes you can. We're the same size. At least we were until I started this stupid medication. I know it'll fit you. Try it on." April stood and lifted the ivory-colored gown, wrapped in tissue, from the box. "Please, Kelli."

Mutely Kelli stood, slipped off her nightshirt, and slid on the undergarments that April offered her one by one from her dresser drawer. When Kelli was sheathed in silk, April helped her into the magnificent dress. Seed pearls, sequins and lace, and layers of satin caught the lamp's light and gleamed. April fluffed the skirt, pulled the train so that it flowed behind Kelli on the carpet, and stepped aside. "Look," she said, nodding toward the full-length mirror on her wall.

Kelli stared at her reflection. The cut of the dress made her waist look tiny. Her trembling hands smoothed the bodice. "It's the most beautiful . . ." Her voice broke as words failed her.

April watched her friend and felt a lump rise in her throat as she remembered the day she had worn it for Mark. "Till death do us part," she had whispered to him. And death had parted them quickly.

"I don't even have a fiancé," Kelli said, her gaze never leaving the mirror.

"You will someday. It would make me very

happy to know that you wore this dress on your wedding day. I'll make sure Mom knows you're to get it. She'll put it into special storage until you're ready for it." April paused. "It's important to me, Kelli. I want you to have it."

Tears slid down Kelli's cheeks. "It will be an honor to wear this dress in your memory."

April stepped behind her and gazed at both their images in the glass—Kelli dark-eyed, dark-haired; April with a mane of red hair and light blue eyes. Their reflection reminded her of a superimposed pair of photographs, of two images slightly misaligned: Kelli alive and vibrant, April pale and otherworldly. Like a ghost staring over the shoulder of her friend.

She did not go to the airport to see Kelli off, but once Kelli had flown away, April felt desolate and friendless. And she kept experiencing dizzy spells, nausea, and more slurring of her speech. A woman from hospice who'd lost a son to cancer came for a visit, and April's parents made arrangements to convert the dining room into a sickroom. And finally one morning she sat upright in bed as her words to Kelli about sitting around in some kind of deathwatch came back to her. She had bid goodbye to everything and everyone who had meant anything to her in New York. She padded downstairs into the breakfast room, where her parents sat. They glanced up, startled by her sudden appearance.

"Honey, are you all right?" her mother asked, springing up to take her hand.

"I want to go back to St. Croix," April said. "That's where I want it to happen. Please, Daddy, please, take me back there right away."

15

Brandon had taken up the habit of driving into the hills whenever he got off work. He couldn't explain why he often took a route that caused him to pass in front of the house April and her family had once rented, but he did. The real estate agent had come and lowered the storm awnings over all the windows and arranged for a gardener to keep the bushes and hedges trimmed. The place looked deserted and forlorn, empty of life and activity. Some days Brandon sat in his parked car staring at the house. And brooding.

He never understood why April had left without a single word of goodbye. Neither, in the weeks that she'd been gone, did he understand why she'd never once attempted to call or write to him. He had misjudged her. He'd fooled himself into thinking she'd cared more about him than she really had. At first he'd been angry, but his anger had faded. Now he felt only disappointment and the keen edge of loneliness. It cut through him like a knife. Everyplace he went held some memory of her. He wished he could eradicate every trace of her from his mind and heart, but he couldn't. He had loved her, and she'd hurt him—without reason or provocation.

He reviewed their days together a hundred times in his thoughts, but he could think of nothing he might have said or done to make her shun him so completely. He'd saved her note, expecting some explanation of her "family problems," but when none came, the cold truth dawned on him. She didn't care about him. She never really had.

He felt that his life was unraveling, just as it had when his mother killed herself. Losing a girl was not the same as losing his mother, but the end result was the same. He was alone with no explanations, no understanding. His inner turmoil made him decide to wait until the winter term before heading off to college. He knew he couldn't handle the pressure right now. For once, his father was in agreement with him. After Brandon's announcement, his father told him, "You're only eighteen. Hang around. Work. Go away in January."

One afternoon in the middle of September, Brandon drove past the house and saw a workman on a ladder raising the awnings. He stopped his car and got out. "What's up?" he called.

"The place is rented," the man answered in his lilting island dialect.

"Do you know who's taking it?"

"No, man. The office did not tell me. They just sent to have the house opened and aired."

It pained Brandon that someone besides April would live there. In his mind it would always be her place.

Days later, unable to stem his curiosity, he again drove past the house. This time it looked occupied, although he couldn't see any of the occupants. After work on Saturday, he went hiking up in the hills near the house. By the time he'd reached a hill's summit, clouds had cluttered the sky and hidden the sun. He looked down at the house and saw into the cove, saw the wooden stairs leading to the beach, saw someone lying on a beach chair. He'd brought binoculars and aimed them at the person in the chair. The sun peeked out from behind a cloud bank, and light caught and glinted off a girl's red hair. His heart leaped into his throat.

It was April. She had returned and not told him. Sudden, blinding anger welled up inside him. She wasn't going to get away with it! She wasn't going to sneak in and out of his island, his life, at will, with no regard for his feelings. Determined to confront her, he half-jogged, half-slid down the long trail, through the underbrush, to the top of the stairs, and down the stairs to the sandy beach.

April must have heard him coming because she sat up and watched him approach along the final few yards between the stairs and her chair. Her hair was tied back and held with a scrunchie; her eyes were calm and clear, not at all surprised by his appearance. His heart thudded as he stood over her chair, panting with the exertion of the run, his shirt sticking to his back, sweat running down his face.

"Hello, Brandon," she said quietly. "I've been expecting you."

Her greeting startled and silenced him. He regained his composure quickly and, in a voice dripping with sarcasm, said, "Well, I wasn't expecting you."

"I know you're mad at me."

"No joke."

"You're mad because I left without ever telling you goodbye. I know it wasn't very nice of me, but I had good reasons for leaving."

"Such as?"

"I was sick."

"And now you're all better?" He kept the sarcasm in his tone. She didn't look sick.

April stood, somewhat unsteadily. "Can we walk down the beach while we talk?"

He studied her more closely and saw that she looked puffy and a little dazed. For the first time, his anger wavered. "After you."

"Could I hold on to your arm?"

He let her take hold of him and was surprised by how clumsily she moved. Yet her hand felt warm and familiar. The scent of her skin and hair reminded him of their summer afternoons together, filling him with the old longing to hold her in his arms. "All right, so I believe you. You've been sick." He remembered the day they'd gone on the picnic. "Has it got something to do with that day we went sailing?"

"Yes."

By now his anger had evaporated. Dread arrived to take its place. "So what was wrong?"

"The same thing that was wrong when I first came to St. Croix." Her gait was awkward, but still she walked along the edge of the water, her delicate painted toes washed by small lapping waves.

"You never said anything to me about your being sick," he said suspiciously. "We were together plenty, so it's not like you couldn't have said something before now."

"No, I never told you."

He stopped walking and looked down at the top of her bowed head. Except for that one day they'd gone snorkeling, she had seemed happy and healthy to him all the time they'd been together. "And so that's why you left? Because you got sick? St. Croix has doctors, you know."

"I went back to New York to see my doctor. I've been under his care for a time, and he knew my case very well."

"So what did he tell you?"

"He repeated some tests."

"He did?" Brandon knew he wasn't asking the most obvious question of all—*"What's wrong with you?"*—because he couldn't bring himself to say the words. He knew in his gut something bad was wrong, and he really didn't want to hear it. It had been easier when he'd thought she'd gone away without a word because she hadn't truly cared about him. Then he could be angry at her, dislike her, think of her as inconsiderate and selfish. But now he was discovering she wasn't any of those things. Now she was telling him that she'd had a terrible reason for going.

"Yes. After the tests, he told me . . . us, my parents and me . . . that I still had an inoperable brain tumor. That the tumor was growing once again. That I probably only had about two to three months to live." Her voice never quavered. She said the words quietly and without emotion.

For Brandon, time stood still. The world stopped spinning, the waves stopped rolling, the sun stopped shining. Only once before in his life had such a phenomenon happened to him.

Brandon rushed into the kitchen, books in hand, ready to seize an apple and head out again. He skidded to a stop because his father was standing at the counter, his face pale as paste. "What's wrong?" Brandon asked.

"Your mother took the boat out this morning."

Brandon's heart froze. "Has something happened to her?"

"She killed herself, son."

"Liar!" He lunged at his father.

His father held up a piece of paper. "It's true. She left us a note."

Brandon grabbed the paper. He felt the world stop turning as he read her words of farewell.

Now, to April, he said, "You have a *brain tumor*? I thought Mark was the one who was sick."

Her gaze found his. Her eyes were incredibly clear, their expression absolutely serious. "Mark and I met in the hospital. We were both patients. He saw me through my radiation treatments. My doctors had hoped that the tumor would shrink, that they could do gamma knife surgery on it. It didn't. They couldn't. But at that time it had stopped growing. And so Mark and I planned to be married, to get on with our lives. Except he had the car crash and died."

Although she had told Brandon about Mark already, hearing it in the context of her own illness made it especially heart-wrenching. "Why didn't you tell me sooner? You should have said something before now."

She gazed out at the sea. He watched her face and realized she was having trouble concentrating. He knew he shouldn't press her, but he couldn't help it. He had to know. With effort, she said, "I didn't know how to tell you. You were so hurt about your mother, I didn't want to hurt you any more." She paused, then turned back to face him. "But it was for selfish reasons too. I wanted so much to be all right. You were so nice to me. I wanted you to remember me as someone you had fun with . . . someone you passed one very special summer with. I didn't want to be sick. I didn't want to be pitied. I wanted exactly what you gave me—a wonderful time. Thank you."

"Why did you come back now to St. Croix?" His heart pounded and his stomach tightened because he already knew the answer.

"It's a beautiful place to die. It's where I want to die."

Her speech had slowed, slurred. Emotion clogged his throat, tightening around it like a noose. His arms shot around her, and he held her close against his chest. He stroked her hair, pulling off the band, letting the red-gold mass fall and catch the breeze. He kissed the crown of her head and lifted her, carrying her to the stairs. He heard footsteps and looked up to see her mother clattering down toward them, anxiously asking, "Is she all right?"

April wound her arms around Brandon's neck and lifted her head so that she could see her mother. "I'm . . . all right," she managed.

But Brandon knew it was a lie. She wasn't all right. And she never would be again.

Once April was settled in her room, Brandon sat on the sofa with Janice. A storm had come up, and rain pelted the French doors, smashing leaves and flower petals into the glass. He thought back to that first night when he'd stopped by to see April . . . the girl from the hilltop, spinning in the sunlight, sending a balloon skyward to celebrate the memory of a dead love.

"I'm glad you understand why she left without a word," Janice was telling him. "She never meant to hurt you."

"I know that now," Brandon answered. "What's going to happen to her?"

"She'll steadily decline. Coma, then death."

"How long?"

"As long as it takes."

He felt sick to his stomach. "It's hard to believe."

"We've hired a nurse who'll come by every day, see to her medical needs. There won't be many."

"There's a good hospital in Christiansted."

Janice shook her head. "That's not what April wants. And it wouldn't make any difference anyway. Her father and I want her to have things exactly her way."

A clap of thunder startled them both.

Brandon turned. "Can I . . . do you mind if I sort of hang around with her?"

Janice studied him. "Why?"

"Because I care about her. Because I want to say goodbye." He thought about his mother. He'd never been able to tell her goodbye. "I know I'm not family. But I won't get in your way, and it will mean everything to me if I can be with her until . . . well, you know."

"Will your father mind?"

"I think he'll understand." Watching April's mother, seeing her sadness, her helplessness, helped Brandon realize that his mother had abandoned both him and his father. April had told him his father hadn't been to blame, but he'd fought with her about it. Brandon swept his fingers through his hair. "Please, let me be with her."

"Her dying won't be easy to watch."

"Believe me, I know."

"Yes . . . I suppose you do."

They said nothing more, only sat and watched the storm hurl its fury at the garden outside.

16

Later that night, when Brandon told his father about April, Bill Benedict stared in disbelief. "Are you serious? Why, that's terrible. Terrible! She's so young and pretty and with her whole life in front of her. How can this be?"

Brandon had figured that the news would affect his father but was surprised by the intensity of his reaction. "I didn't believe it at first, but I talked to her mother and there's nothing more the doctors can do."

"I know this girl is special to you, son. I'm sorry for your sake too."

A surge of emotion clogged Brandon's throat. He cleared it away. "Yes . . . she's pretty special to me."

His father began to pace the floor. "Her poor parents. They must be devastated. I liked the whole family. The way they came to your graduation and all—well, that was really nice of them. Hugh and I talked business for more than an hour. Listen, if there's anything they need or want, you let me know. I'd like to help out."

"You would?"

He stopped his restless pacing. "Of course I would. They're strangers here. They have no one to support them."

Until then, Brandon hadn't thought about April's parents' position. He'd been concentrating on April, and on his own feelings. But his father was correct; the Lancasters didn't have anyone in St. Croix to call on. "I'll tell them you'd like to help."

"I might have thought that April would have wanted to be in her home back in the States. Why did she want her last days to be in St. Croix?"

"She's always loved it here," Brandon said. "I don't know. Maybe it's because choosing your place to die might be the only thing a person has control over. Sort of like Mom did, I guess." The comment had simply spilled out of Brandon. He hadn't meant anything mean or cruel by it. He was really discussing April, not his mother.

His father measured him carefully with a look. "She did pick her time to die, all right."

"I didn't mean—"

His father waved him off. "Forget it. No matter what you think, Brandon, I couldn't have stopped your mother from doing what she did. She'd been clinically depressed for years, but she wouldn't go get help for it."

Clinically depressed? It was the first time he'd heard the term used in conjunction with his mother. "She was?"

"Surely you noticed that she was different, that she wasn't like your friends' mothers." His father's tone sounded acidic.

It was true. Sometimes she'd slept away entire days, then stayed up, wandering around the house all night. And of course, there'd been her drinking. "I—I always knew she wasn't happy."

"And you figured it was my fault, or perhaps even your fault."

Brandon felt his face color but didn't comment.

"It was *her* fault, son. She drank booze and popped pills to escape from real life. I couldn't stop her. Don't you think I tried?"

His father's words echoed what Brandon had said to April when they'd talked about his mother's suicide—that Brandon had tried to help her but couldn't. "You were gone most of the time," Brandon said stubbornly, feeling as if he needed to somehow defend his mother's actions. "She was always alone. That depressed her."

"We've been over that before." His father's voice grew cool. "She was the same whether I was around or not."

Brandon sighed. He didn't want to rehash the past or any of its old arguments. Tonight shouldn't be about his mother's death. Or his and his father's problems. Tonight should be about April, the girl he loved, who was dying. "Look, Dad, I don't want to argue with you. Right now, it means a lot to me that you want to help April and her parents through this bad time. I appreciate it, and they will too."

His father offered a tentative smile. "Good. I don't want to argue with you either. But I really meant what I said earlier.

Have her family call me if they want anything. I know plenty of people in the islands, and they'd be happy to pitch in."

"I don't think I'd spread around too much information about them. I mean, they're private people and they wouldn't like a lot of attention. At least, not for April's sake."

"I know what you're saying. Don't worry, I'll be discreet. Nobody wants a bunch of strangers in their faces no matter how well-intentioned their motives."

In his father's statement, Brandon recognized the man's own philosophy—after the suicide, he'd shut everybody out, even Brandon. "I may want to quit my job to be with April," Brandon said. "Not right away, but as she gets worse. So that means that I won't be saving as much money for college and all as I told you I would."

"It doesn't matter. The job, the money— they were for your sake, not mine. I always found work to be therapeutic. I'd hoped you might find it to be the same."

Brandon's father escaped into work to distract himself, but Brandon knew that he couldn't do things that way. He wanted to saturate himself in April's presence, hold on to her for as long as he could. He told his father good night and went to his room, walking down the long hall that led past what had once been his parents' bedroom, where he paused. He resisted the urge to open the door and look inside. Throughout his life, he'd come home many an afternoon to find his mother holed up inside that bedroom. She would be lying on the bed, the room darkened, the pillows propped to elevate her head and shoulders. The TV would be on at low volume in the corner, a glass and a bottle of whiskey on the nightstand. She might wave him inside, she might not. If he came in, she would cling to him, her breath smelling of whiskey, and she would cry and dump her misery on him.

Yet right now, despite all her shortcomings, Brandon longed to see his mother, tell her about April and hear words of sympathy. He inched past the room, then walked rapidly around the corner and into his own room, the ghost of his mother's memory following along behind.

Over the following weeks, Brandon grew respectful of his father for the things he did to help April's parents. He often had dinner sent up for them from the best restaurants in Christiansted. A ring of the doorbell and a delivery-truck driver would be on the front steps with packages of hot food. "How kind and thoughtful," Janice always told Brandon.

His father insisted that April's father go golfing with him. "You're a phone call away on our cell phones," Bill would reason. "The golf course is less than twenty minutes from the house. Plus, Brandon's here. He can handle any emergency until we get back."

It pleased Brandon that his father considered him capable of handling any emergency, even though he hoped he wouldn't have to handle one. He loved April and respected her parents immensely; he didn't want to ever let them down.

On her good days, Brandon helped April down to the beach, where she'd lie in the beach chair, facing the sea, holding his hand and drifting in and out of sleep. She slept a lot. But sometimes she'd have better days, when she was more alert, not nauseated, and able to concentrate. He waited patiently for those days, praying for them, enjoying them when they came to her.

One afternoon while they were together on the patio under a canopy, out of the heat of the sun, April in a lounge chair, Brandon beside her in another, she awoke, stretched, and asked, "Are you still here?"

"Where else would I be?"

"Sailing? Out having fun?"

"I want to be here. With you."

"This is very kind of you, Brandon."

"I don't do it to be kind. I'm not into good deeds, and you're not a charity case."

"Still, you don't have to spend all your free time with me."

"Says who?" He pulled his sunglasses down the bridge of his nose and peered over them at her. "You getting tired of me? You trying to let me down easy? Get rid of me?"

She giggled, and the sound pleased him immensely. "You're silly. I'd never want to get rid of you."

"Same here," he told her softly.

She turned her face away. "You never told me why you didn't go away to school the way you were planning to."

He repositioned his sunglasses to cover his eyes. "I'm not sure myself. There was just so much to think about—packing up most everything I owned, trading living in my house for a dorm room. I just wasn't ready. I'll go in January." *After you're gone,* he told himself.

"Where will you go? Did you pick a place where it snows?"

He shook his head. "No snow. I've decided on Texas A&M. Maybe I'll major in landscape architecture. I like working outside. And I like to make plants grow."

She reached over and squeezed his hand. "You'll be good at it. But for right now, I'm glad you're here, and so is my mom. I think she really likes having you around."

"Seriously? I don't want to be in the way."

"You aren't in anybody's way."

"Your mom's a great mom," he said. "She talks to me like I'm a person, not some dopey kid."

"Is that the way your mom talked to you? Like you were dumb?"

He shook his head sadly. "We'd talk sometimes, but mostly she cried."

"So does mine. I hear her at night sometimes."

"Your mom has a reason to cry. Mine just

cried." Remembering was painful because it made him feel so helpless. "Some days I'd come home from school and she'd be locked in her room. Some days I'd come home and she'd almost pounce on me and ask a million questions. It wasn't so much that she was interested in my life, but that her life was so horrible that mine seemed great by comparison. It's like she got her excitement through me. What's that called?"

"Vicariousness," April supplied.

"Except for when we all went sailing. She really loved that."

"I love sailing too."

He thought about his mother's choice of a place to die. If only she hadn't chosen their boat. If only she hadn't done it at all. "Is it as much fun as car racing?"

"It's quieter."

He smiled. Now she was careful not to mention Mark around him. Not that he would have minded anymore. Brandon was certain that she had feelings only for him. He knew he loved her and always would. He would go on living, and every day of his life he would remember her.

He reached over and laced his fingers through hers. "If you were strong enough to go sailing, I'd take you."

She shook her head. "I'd like to go, but I know I'd get sick."

"Do you hurt?"

"Not really." She repeated what Dr. Sorenson had told her about the brain and its inability to feel pain. "It's not much comfort, really. The dizzy spells make my stomach queasy, sort of like a permanent case of seasickness. That's why I stay in one position so much—to keep the dizziness away. I've been told that throwing up on a guy isn't very romantic."

He laughed out loud, amazed at her ability to make jokes. "Probably not."

She drifted off to sleep, and Brandon raised their joined hands and pressed his lips to her fingers. *I love you, April,* he said silently. *I love you so much.*

17

April hated the days when she could barely keep her eyes open. Sometimes she felt tangled in a thick clinging fog that clogged her memory and sapped her strength. It worried her that the stupor of perpetual drowsiness would push her into oblivion. She wasn't ready for oblivion yet. Some nights she set her alarm clock and put it under her pillow just so that she could hear it and struggle to the surface of sleep. As long as she could hear it ringing, turn it off, and listen to its ticking, she knew she hadn't passed into timelessness, into eternity.

She was rarely alone anymore. Her parents took turns sitting beside her bed. Her mother read, her father arranged a makeshift desk and did paperwork. Their presence brought her comfort. She'd wake and sense that one of them was there. The flutter of papers meant her father. The occasional turning of a book's page meant her mother. When April was unable to come to the table for meals, they brought their meals into her room. She didn't eat much—no appetite. At some point, the nurse (whom she recognized by her quick, efficient movements) inserted an IV into April's arm.

"For hydration," she heard the woman tell her parents.

I'm drinking through a needle, she told herself. *Yummy.*

Brandon often came to be with her too. She liked that. He usually held her hand and watched TV or videotapes, which her father kept in good supply. The drone of the television almost always meant that Brandon was with her. On the days when she felt more alert, she wanted to be taken down to the beach, or at least outside to sit by the pool. She found the sight of sunlight on water very comforting. She didn't know why. And she liked to talk, although her speech was often slurred. Talking connected her with those she loved. She recalled Mark's struggle to talk during his last days, how he had fought to say everything that was in his heart. She felt the same way. If only she could push the contents of her mind into those surrounding her. If only she were telepathic.

One evening, when her parents were with her in the sickroom, she said, "I don't know how much longer I can stay awake."

"Don't try," her father said, easing onto the bed and touching her cheek. "You just sleep. Your mom and I'll be right here."

"That's not what I mean." Her mother and father glanced at each other questioningly. April tried again to express what she wanted to say. "I know I won't be waking up one of these times."

Her father's hand tightened on hers, and her mother shook her head. "Don't say such things. You've got plenty of time."

"No," April said. "No, I don't."

Neither one of them contradicted her.

"I want you to know," April said, every word a struggle, "that you're the best parents in the world. And I'm lucky to have had you for mine."

"And you're the best daughter," her father said, smoothing her thick red hair.

"We've been the lucky ones," her mother added.

"Would you rather have had a son?"

Her father drew back, a look of disdain on his face. "Are you joking? I always wanted a girl. From the time your mother and I were first married, I told her I wanted to be surrounded by beautiful women." He glanced at his wife. "Isn't that right, Janice? Didn't I always tell you I wanted a girl?"

"It's the truth," April's mother said. "Scout's honor."

"That's nice." April didn't know why she'd asked such a dumb question, but she appreciated their answer. "I wanted a boy," she said. "Even though Mark couldn't have children, I still would have wanted a son."

"You've given us all we ever wanted," her mother said. "Just not for long enough."

It was breaking April's heart to see her parents so sad. She asked, "Do you know, some of the best times I ever had were when I was growing up and we'd all go out to eat at those fancy restaurants. I felt so grown up sitting at the table with you both. I had my own wineglass filled with ginger ale. And you let me order peanut butter and jelly. It wasn't ever on the menu, but you made them fix it for me."

"The first time we took you out to dinner, you were two years old." Her father smiled, remembering. "You knocked over a water glass, then crawled beneath the table and played in the puddle."

Her mother shook her head in dismay. "I was embarrassed, but then I got the giggles and couldn't stop laughing. The maître d' looked as if he would have a heart attack. The very idea of our bringing a child into such a fancy place almost made him faint."

Seeing them smile over the shared memory made April feel good. They'd been sad for so long on her account. She didn't want them sad. "I guess we didn't go back there to eat again."

Her father snorted. "They acted as if a child were a parasite instead of a pleasure. No, I would never have taken you back to such a place."

Her mother patted April's arm. "We

waited until you were a bit more mature before we ventured into four-star dining again with you, however."

"I remember my birthday party when I was six. You took me to some restaurant that had a dance floor and one of those balls that spun overhead and sparkled all over us." She looked at her father. "You danced with me." She'd stood on his shoes and he'd twirled her around the dance floor while a band played a song she could still hear inside her head and speckles of light spilled across them.

"Well, I couldn't very well step on your toes," he said. "I would have squished them."

"We'll never dance on my wedding day." Her smile faded. "I didn't mean to say that. I—I don't want you to feel bad."

Her mother turned her head aside. Her father rubbed his thumb across April's knuckles, over and over, as if touching her was something he couldn't get enough of. "If I could take your place now, baby, I would."

"No . . . that's not right. You need to stay with Mother. It's a horrible thing to be left alone." April brightened. "And don't you worry about me. Mark's in heaven waiting for me. Before he died, he told me he'd be waiting and watching for me to come to him. So, you see, I won't be alone. I have you and Mom on this side of life, and Mark on the other side. I'll be fine, Daddy. Really, I'll be fine."

"He'd better take good care of you. If not, he'll answer to me when I get there." Her father's voice was barely a whisper.

April's eyelids felt heavy, and concentrating was becoming more difficult. But she felt good that she had been able to tell her parents some of the things that were in her heart. To her mother, she said, "You remember about the wedding dress, don't you?"

"Yes. It belongs to Kelli."

April closed her eyes. The conversation had exhausted her, and sleepiness was beginning to shut down her ability to think and talk. "When Brandon comes, make sure he has some new movies to watch. He's seen the ones next to the TV set already."

"I'll take care of it," her father said.

His voice sounded as if it were coming through a long tunnel. "I think I'll take a little nap now," she said. She felt her mother kiss her cheek. "Is the moon out tonight?"

"Half a moon," her father said.

"Is it pretty on the water?"

"Beautiful."

April remembered parasailing, the sensation of flying, of looking down and seeing the world from a bird's-eye view. "Will you open my window? If I wake up late tonight, I want to see the moonlight. The moonbeams come into my room late at night, you know. They make a path on the water and on my carpet, and across my bed. Sometimes . . . I feel as if I could . . . get up . . . and walk straight up the path. Into heaven. Mommy, Daddy, I love you."

She felt her mother kiss her cheek as she tumbled into sleep.

18

The times when April was awake and aware were fewer and farther between. Every time she was asleep, Brandon would wonder if this might be the time she'd slip into a coma and not wake up. One afternoon her eyes fluttered open and she looked around the room as if she didn't recognize it. Anxiously Brandon leaned over her. "April? You okay? It's me."

Her gaze slowly locked onto his face. She blinked. "Brandon." Her smile was crooked, as if she couldn't control one side of her face. "How long have you been here?"

"Not long," he lied.

"Did I fall asleep? Sorry . . . rude of me."

"It doesn't matter."

"Is it raining?"

"A storm moved in about ten minutes ago." He moved aside so that she could see through the window facing the sea. Rain splattered the glass, and the sea was a froth of churning foam. "But you know how the weather is in the Caribbean. The sun will be out again in no time."

"That's good. I love the sun."

She didn't say anything else for such a long time that he thought she'd fallen back to sleep, but she finally said, "I want to tell you something."

"Tell me."

She held out her hand, and he took hold of it. Her skin felt cool and dry. "Did you know that I love you?"

His heart skipped.

"It's true. But *shhh* . . . don't tell Mark. It would make him sad." She was talking as if Mark were alive in the room with them. Brandon felt a prickly sensation up his spine. Mark was waiting for her. She would cross over to him and he would have her forever. Would April meet Brandon's mother? Was there a place in heaven for those who had shed life like a piece of clothing? "If you see my mother—"

"I'll tell her you love her. And that you forgive her."

Tears burned and brimmed and stung his eyes. "Yes . . . I forgive her," Brandon said, hardly trusting his voice. "I love you, April."

"Aren't I lucky? I've been twice loved. Don't let anyone tell you that you can't love two people with all your heart." She turned her head so that she could see Mark's photograph on the bedside table. "Mark, this is Brandon. And I love him." She turned her eyes back to Brandon. "Now, you go find someone else to love too. Please."

"I don't want—"

"*Shhh*. We don't always get what we want." She drifted away from him, back into her blanket of fog, to the world of semiconsciousness where he could not follow.

Later he returned to the living room. April's mother was sitting on the sofa, looking out at the sea and the driving rain sweeping past the plate glass window in sheets. The world looked gray and soggy; even the palm fronds battered by the whipping wind were a dull green. She turned when she heard him, and her eyes were as colorless as the rain, as dull as the leaden clouds. She asked, "Is she sleeping?"

"Yes. She fell asleep a while ago. But I didn't want to leave her."

"I know what you mean."

He lowered himself to the love seat that butted up against one arm of the sofa, feeling totally helpless, unable to find words to comfort either April's mother or himself.

"I still can't believe she's dying," April's mother said. "It makes no sense to me. Parents aren't supposed to outlive their children." He winced. She paled. "Oh, Brandon, I'm sorry. That was so insensitive of me."

"But it's true. Even if a parent chooses to die. It's more natural than for the child to die first." He stared out at the driving rain, at the whitecaps skidding across the surface of the sea in the distance. "Did you know that if you dive down deep under the ocean, you can't even tell if there's a storm on the top side? It's quiet in the deep. And cold. When I saw my mother in the casket, I touched her. She was ice-cold. All the warmth had leaked out of her, the way sand oozes through your fingers underwater. I can't stand to think of April that way." His voice grew softer and faded.

"I can't stand it either. When she was five, when they first discovered her tumor, I used to stand beside her hospital bed and hold on to her even while she slept. I guess I thought that as long as I held on, death couldn't come for her. Or that if it did, it would have to bump me out of the way and I could grab it, throttle it, throw it out of her room. But death isn't something that comes from the outside. I think it lives in all of us and it lies in wait, like a lion crouching near its prey. Then, when our guard is down, our body defenseless because of disease or trauma or inconsolable bad feelings like your mother's, death comes out and stakes its claim."

Brandon told himself that if she was correct, nothing could drive death out. It had to leave on its own accord. And when it did leave, it took life with it and left behind body shells, just as sea creatures vacated outgrown shells, leaving the old ones abandoned on the ocean floor. "Do you know that I think April is the prettiest girl I ever saw? I'll never forget the color of her hair. Where'd she get it from? Neither you nor her father has red hair."

Janice smiled. "My great-grandmother came over from England and married a New Yorker. She was renowned for her beauty. And her hair of red gold." Her smile faded. "Corrine—that was her name—lost three babies. One to diphtheria. One to pneumonia. One to measles. Diseases that we banish now with injections and antibiotics. I wonder if they'll ever have an inoculation against cancer? Against death?"

Or against a person wanting to die? he wondered. "It must have been hard to bury so many babies," he said, thinking of April's great-great-grandmother.

"Nothing can be harder than burying your children," Janice said.

"Burying a mother is pretty hard too."

"That's true. My mother died when I was thirty-five, my father when I was forty, and it was difficult to lose them. I'm so sorry you had to go through that so young."

He stood and walked over to the glass door. The storm had stopped, but the sun had not yet emerged and the world looked flat and dull. He shoved his hands deep into the pockets of his shorts and rocked back on his heels. "I still wonder why," he said, barely aware that he'd even spoken. "Her note said life hurt too much . . . as if that's a reason. I see April and I know how much she wants to live. It makes no sense to me that someone like my mother wouldn't want to live. You know?"

"It doesn't make any sense to me either," Janice told him.

He looked down and blinked against moisture that had filled his eyes, embarrassed at having said so much to April's mother concerning his most private feelings. "Sorry. I don't mean to talk so much."

"It's okay, Brandon. Really. I only wish I could answer your questions. The truth is, no one knows how another person truly feels because we can't walk around in each other's skins." She got up from the sofa and stood beside him, gazing out the glass door with him. "But I do know one thing. I know that she had one fine son."

He glanced at Janice, saw that her expression was kind and sincere. He felt his cheeks redden. "That's nice of you to say."

"It's the truth. I would have been proud to have called you my son."

"Thanks."

"I mean it."

"You should have had lots of children. Tons of them."

She laughed. "I always thought so too."

The sun suddenly broke through the bank of billowing gray clouds, hurling breathtaking shafts of light into the sea. The water turned from gray to green where the light penetrated, as if some alien's spaceship were anchored beneath the surface. With the sight came a feeling of hope to Brandon. Here, in this house, standing beside the mother of the girl he loved, he felt a sense of peace and belonging. He couldn't stop time. He couldn't turn it back. All he had was this precious slice of it, and it felt good to be alive.

Early the next morning, as Brandon drove up to the house, he saw an ambulance sitting in the driveway, its red light swirling and casting eerie reflections on the surrounding trees and brush. It punctuated the gray morning light with urgency. All was silent. Brandon cut off his engine, flung open the car door, and raced up to the house. The front door was ajar, and he hurried inside. April's father stood in the living room in his bathrobe and bare feet. He looked up, and his face was haggard and creased by grief. He said, "She's gone."

"Gone?"

"She died in her sleep. The paramedics are with her, but there's nothing they can do. My little girl is gone. Gone."

Brandon's back stiffened and, without comment, he edged out the front door and walked quickly into the surrounding woods, heedless of the wet foliage slapping against his arms and legs as he plowed deeper into the jungle. When he came to a small clearing he stopped, turned his face skyward, and screamed.

19

April Lancaster was going home.

Brandon stood on the tarmac along with his father and April's parents at the St. Croix airport, next to the jet plane that was to take April and her family away. A long black hearse drove through the security gates toward them. The baggage handlers, who'd been busy tossing luggage onto the conveyor belt, ceased their activity as the hearse stopped beside the plane. Pallbearers from the local funeral home got out of the vehicle, opened the back, and slid out a rolling cart that held a long pink casket trimmed in silver and with silver handles. Flecks of metallic paint caught the morning sun and glittered like jewels.

Brandon was grateful that his father had pulled strings to allow the four of them to stand out on the loading area, so close to the casket. As the men rolled the casket toward the conveyor belt, April's mother stepped forward. She touched the hard shell that held her daughter's body, leaned forward, and kissed it. Brandon's throat constricted, and he forced his gaze away. The sadness was as heavy as the humid tropical air that surrounded them.

Because the St. Croix airport was so small, he could hear taxi horns and the voices and laughter of tourists as they prepared to board the flight and return to the States. At the end of the single runway the sea sparkled, and in the other direction hills rose, lush and green. He returned his gaze to the casket and saw the pallbearers lift it onto the conveyor belt. The belt moved forward, and the glittering pink casket slid upward into the dark belly of the plane.

He knew this was April's wish—to return to New York and be buried beside Mark Gianni, the man she had chosen in life to be with forever. At least in death, she could have her final wish. Moisture filled his eyes, and the casket became blurred. He felt April's mother take his hand.

"I guess that's it. I guess it's our turn to get on board now."

He couldn't see her eyes hidden behind the dark glasses but saw the tracks of tears along her cheeks. "I guess so."

April's father put his arm around her shoulders, as if to hold her up, and put out his hand to Brandon's father. "Bill, thanks for everything. You made a lot of things go more smoothly for us and I'm grateful for that. If you're ever in New York . . ."

"Sure. I'll call."

Hugh turned to Brandon and extended his hand. "You're a fine young man, Brandon. I'm glad we had the opportunity to know you. In spite of the circumstances."

Brandon nodded, not trusting his voice.

April's mother hugged him, and he hugged her hard in return. Everything was slipping away from him. He couldn't hold on to anything he loved. "You take care of yourself," she said. "You have a great time in college, and send us an invitation to your graduation, because we'll come. It's a promise."

"Sure," he managed.

The four of them walked back inside the airport, and when the boarding call came, Brandon waved April's parents into the plane. All around them, tourists chattered and dragged bags loaded with souvenirs of the islands. All Brandon wanted to do was get away from them. Didn't they know what was going on? Didn't they realize that April was dead and that he hurt so badly that he could hardly breathe?

Outside, in the bright September sun, he fumbled for his sunglasses. He stood beside his father, and together they watched the large jet back away from the gate, taxi down the runway, rev its engines, and gather speed. The air was split by the roar of jets, saturated by the smell of hot fuel. Slowly the plane lifted, a silver bird headed to another time and place. Brandon watched until it disappeared behind a bank of snow-white cumulus clouds. And out of his life. He felt his father's hand on his shoulder.

"Son," he heard his father say.

"What?" Brandon felt desolate.

"I, um, was wondering if maybe we could have lunch together."

"I'm not hungry. And it's only ten-thirty."

"Well, I was wondering something else too."

Brandon removed his sunglasses and stared straight into his father's face. His father looked nervous, anxious. "What else?"

"A couple of weeks ago—when I knew this day was coming for you—I had the boat taken out of dry dock."

Brandon felt a flush radiate through his body. "You did?"

"It's down at the marina in its regular slip, and I was thinking that if you would like to, we could take it out this afternoon. Just the two of us. It's been a while, but I thought it was something we could do. I mean, that is, if you want."

The boat. Their boat. His mother's boat. Longing filled him. He wanted to feel the wind in his face. He wanted to taste the salt air. He wanted to touch the decks, the galley, the chairs where his mother had last been. In his father's eyes, he saw uncertainty. A tremor flickered along his rigidly held jaw as he waited for Brandon's answer.

His father added, "I was also thinking it

might be good for us to take some time together . . . take the boat around to some of
the cays and islands. You don't head off for
school until January, and I'd like to take
about a month off from work and spend it
sailing. You don't have to decide right now,
but would you think about it?"

Brandon understood that his father was
reaching out to him, wanted to make things
right between them. He wasn't sure what *he*
wanted, but he did know he was tired of feeling angry and resentful. "I'd like to go sailing
today," he said. "I'll think about the other."

His father grinned and nodded profusely.
"Good! Very, very good, son. So let's go
home, change, and head to the marina."

"I'll meet you there," Brandon said. "In a
couple of hours. There's something I have to
do first."

"All right." His father looked at his watch.
"See you at, say . . . one o'clock?"

"I'll be there."

An hour later, Brandon drove his car to the
now vacant house where April had once lived.
He parked, got out, and started up the hill
behind the house. At the crest of the hill he

stood, catching his breath and gazing out at
the bright blue Caribbean sea. A breeze lifted
his hair off his brow. *Good*, he thought. He'd
hoped for a good stiff breeze.

He reached into his back pocket, pulled
out a red balloon, and filled it with air. He
tied it off, reached back into his pocket,
pulled out a yellow ribbon, and tied it onto
the balloon. Then he raised his hands over his
head and let go. The ribbon trailed against
his arm, and he resisted the urge to grab hold
and not release it. By letting it go, he was
letting April go too. He was telling her goodbye. He was giving her to Mark. Forever.

He shielded his eyes and watched as the
balloon drifted higher and higher against the
vast blue sky.